For Millie

THE SHADOW KEEPERS

MARISA NOELLE

love Marisa :)

Magnolia Press

Cover Design by Dionne Abouelela

Edited by Nicole Tone

Digital Edition ISBN: 9780463307434

Print ISBN: 978-1-7331037-0-1

For Mom and Dad,
Thank you for your endless support.

ONE

I REACH a finger to a racing raindrop and follow it down the car window, mirroring the shooting bursts of speed interspersed with lazy meanders, until it disappears. And then I find a new raindrop. Raindrop. Teardrop. Essentially the same. But I hold mine in for now. The tyres come to a crunching halt on the deep gravel. My mother turns off the engine. She shifts in her seat to face me, a hesitant smile plastered on her lips.

"Georgia," she says.

Beyond the window stands an imposing edifice built with grey bricks and grey slate. The air of misery it exudes matches the weather. The building towers up six stories, high and sterile, fluorescent strips shining in most of the windows. Expect for the top floor. The top floor rests in the eaves, and the windows remain dark, unframed by the softening effect of curtains as on the floors below. A large, black crow flies close to the building and straight into a closed window. I imagine the sickening thud as bone meets glass. It falls to the ground, stunned, or more likely dead. I avert my gaze as its expressionless eyes stare towards the sky.

I glance at Bart beside me. But he's face-down in his phone, a flop of walnut hair falling in his eyes. His shirt is wrinkled and stale alcohol seeps from his pores.

"Georgia," Mum says again. "We're here."

I hunch deeper into my seat. "I can see that."

My stepfather rests a hand over my mother's. She inhales one of her deep yoga breaths and holds it. Some old crooner's version of a love song trickles from the speakers at a respectable volume. She snaps off the radio.

"Georgia—"

"Why don't you believe me?" I sit bolt upright in my seat. If Mum, or the damn court, or anyone of my non-existent friends actually tried to believe me . . . they'd know the court- order was bullshit. "I'm not crazy!"

My mother and stepfather exchange a look. It's one I've seen a hundred times in the last few months. They've been here before. We've had this conversation before, but they've made up their minds without taking on board a word I have to say.

"No one is saying that," Mom says softly. "But after the incident . . ."

Bart chucks his phone between us. "Give her a break, Mum. I'm sure she remembers."

I reach for his hand and he squeezes it back.

Another yoga breath for my mother. She sets her face into an emotionless mask; guarded eyes, flat smile. "We know you're not crazy, sweetheart."

"Then what am I doing here?"

"We don't have a choice. It's what the court decid-ed," my stepfather replies. "It's only ninety days."

Three months. A quarter of a year. I'll miss Halloween. Out in time for Christmas, if they think I'm better.

I look at the miserable, grey building again. Brook-wood Hospital. Or Lunacy Asylum for the Insane and Unreachable. It's the place people with money put their loved ones when they don't know what else to do with them.

"I don't belong here." I can hear the edge in my voice, like a caged animal knowing there's no escape.

"Georgia," Mum says with that flat smile again. "This place isn't what it used to be. They don't do elec-tric shock therapy or hose down patients. It's not like that anymore. There's no shame in it. The doctors and nurses here are the best suited to understanding you and helping you."

"We've shown you the website," my stepfather butts in. "You've seen the activities, the art therapy, the group excursions . . . hell, looks like a holiday—"

"Why don't you go then?" I snap.

A stony silence fills the car. I bury my head in my hands and think about the plastic smiles of all the teenagers on the website my mother showed me, her smile just as fake. The psychiatric nurse who will lead group therapy and the psychologists and the psychiatrist who will pump me full of new meds. The girls sat around tables with their heads down, but their eyes dangerous and their limbs inked. I saw through it all. No one wants to be there.

"Why can't you help me?" I stare at the racing raindrops, refusing to look at Mum.

"We've tried, sweetheart. And we haven't been able to. Now it's time to let others in. You heard what the judge said; it's here, or it's the NHS hospital. We no longer have a choice. And to be quite honest, Georgia, there's nothing else I can do for you."

Bart nudges my arm, and his wobbling smile crushes my resolve not to cry.

"Your father never got the help he needed," Mum says. "I don't want that for you. I watched him struggle every day until he died. He joined the army because he felt he had something to prove, that he was tough and could look after all of us. He went off to Afghanistan and he died trying to prove it. You're so like him, Georgia, in many ways. You need to be here. You need to get better."

"Georgia," my stepfather says. His solid fingers grip the steering wheel. He looks at me in the rear-view mirror, which I avoid. "We don't need to rehash everything again. You have . . . issues, and with the smoking and the drinking and the breaking of the mirrors in every shop you go in, you need help. Real help."

"It was one mirror!" One broken mirror and I'm labelled a loon.

My stepfather wilts my complaints with one sharp look. "You've met the doctor and had your assessment. He's going to help you now. There's nothing else we can do. So, let's try and toughen up a bit . . ."

Tears prick my eyes as I tune out his words. I dare a glance at my mother. Her eyes are wet too. Bart's hand still holds mine, squeezing, but I can't bear to look at him. The pity in his eyes would break me. Who am I kidding? I'm broken already.

"Georgia—" Mum starts in again.

I hold up a hand. "Just stop. As you said, we've been through it all before. I'm on my own now."

"Georgia—"

I open the car door and storm into the rain. Pulling my hood over my head, I march up the stone steps to the covered portico.

"Georgia!" Bart runs after me.

I nudge the heavy front door with a wet trainer, testing its strength, hoping it's locked so I can remain in the world of the sane for just a little longer. It remains firmly closed—a small miracle—but I know this is only prolonging the inevitable. The court ordered me here, and here I must stay. I stand there, waiting for my parents, feeling my anger pooling in my stomach, my skin prickling with indignation.

Bart arrives at my side and throws an arm around me. I collapse into his warmth and his familiar vodka smell. My mother and stepfather follow shortly thereafter, my stepfather dragging my suitcase through the puddles. *Gee, thanks Dad.*

They join me in the portico. My stepfather turns the outrageously ornate handle of the heavy door—a lion with a ring through its mouth—and together we go through the wide front doors and drip rainwater onto the wood floor of the yawning entrance foyer. There are two nurses and a doctor there to greet us, standing erect like teeth in a monster's mouth. Their Stepford smiles have me taking a step backward and looking over my shoulder at the Range Rover I've just climbed out of. It's warm and cosy in there and I long to be back on the leather seats, watching the rain drip down the window.

Behind the nurses, positioned in front of a grand staircase is a large stone statue of a bird. It's tall—taller than me. It wears its chip marks and dents with pride, as if to say nothing could ever destroy it, not even time. At some point in its life, it was kept outside; old bird stains mottle its surface. Its stone eyes keep vigil over the foyer with half-erect wings, as if about to take flight. My heart picks up tempo. My mouth goes dry, and my tongue becomes this weird, heavy object that I am sure doesn't really belong in my mouth. The panic attack is coming, building. It will be here soon.

"Georgia Boone?" One of the nurses asks, distracting me from my quickening pulse.

I turn towards the voice. According to her label, she is the head psychiatric nurse, and her name is Marion. She wears a blue nurse's dress and the old-fashioned money belt around her waist is pinched so tightly that I think she might explode out of one end or the other.

She holds a clipboard in her hands and stares at me out of grey-blue wishy-washy eyes. An unflattering bob surrounds her face, and her left cheekbone supports the largest mole I've ever seen. It sprouts five long, brittle, grey hairs that move every time she speaks.

"Yes," Mum answers for me. "Yes, this is Georgia."

"We've been waiting for you," Marion says.

Looking down her bulbous nose at me, she holds a no-nonsense clipboard in her fingers, and her feet are planted in a wide, manly stance. And why do I feel like I'm supposed to say *great*?

I ignore her comment and examine the second nurse. Deputy Psychiatric Nurse Willow is the exact opposite of Marion. Taller and skinny, so skinny that her blue dress hangs off her and could do with a couple of pins to keep it in place. I stifle a giggle as I think the first nurse might be feeding off the second, slowly eating her away until she ceases to exist. Like some b-rate science fiction movie that's only ever aired at midnight on Movies4Men.

But back to Willow. Her long hair trails down the middle of her back, lank and loose, and the roots border on greasy. It's neither brown nor blonde, but some indescribable colour in between. Her eyes are blue, and I detect a flash of some intrinsic warning in them when she looks at me. She shuffles restlessly from one Hush-Puppied foot to the other. Her hands grab at the skirt of her dress, rolling a finger in the extra material and then unrolling, only to do it again. I recognize the signs of a nervous disposition. Maybe she ought to be the patient. I'll gladly swap roles with her.

My heart thuds painfully in my chest again. It picks up speed, as if trying to gallop out of my body completely. I clutch my mother's sleeve.

"I'm Nurse Marion," the one holding the clipboard says. "And this is Nurse Willow." She points to the other.

"Hello, sweetheart," Willow says, with a gentle five-finger wave.

"I'm Paul. I'm a psychologist here," the man says, stepping forth to offer his hand. My stepfather shakes it, and my mother smiles warmly at him. "Don't be alarmed. We'll take good care of Georgia. That's what we're here for after all."

"Yes, of course," Mum replies.

"We need you to sign some paperwork," Marion says to my parents. "Paul will show Georgia and her brother to a pot of tea." She gestures to an office that leads from the foyer.

My parents follow the two nurses into the room and leave Bart and me standing in the large foyer with Paul under the penetrating gaze of an antique grandfather clock. It leans Pisa-like on the thick carpet, its gentle ticking is the only audible noise in the hushed expectancy of the foyer. It strikes the hour, and I jump, grabbing onto Bart's arm.

"This way." Paul leads us around a corner to a small niche with a couple of floral sofas and polished coffee tables. A pot of steaming tea sits on a tray with a couple of cracked mugs and a plate of biscuits.

Paul pours two cups of tea and excuses himself for a moment to take my luggage up to my room. I sip at the tea, but it scalds my throat.

"Easy," Bart says.

I point to the other cup. "You could do with some sobering up."

He gives me his sideways grin.

"Was it a big night?" I ask.

He winks. "It's always a big night."

I sigh as a tremble shoots through my legs. Bart notices and rests a heavy hand on my knee. "I wish I could go with you. I wish you could stay. I wish . . ." I close my eyes against the threatening tears.

Bart brings me in close and hugs me, smoothing the back of my head. "I wish all that too. But we can't get out of it. I've tried."

Bart is a junior lawyer for a swanky outfit in London. During my case, he was allowed to liaise with my defence attorney. But there's nothing to be done. I hurt another individual. The last straw in a string of offences.

I stare into the swirling tea. "I was with you when I first saw them, you know."

Bart pulls away. "Saw what?"

"The shadows."

Bart nods. Everyone knows about the creatures I see in mirrors. We just don't talk about it anymore.

TWO

BART LOOKS LEFT AND RIGHT, as if afraid we might be overheard. I didn't check the dark hallways for people, but I did check for mirrors. None. I'm safe for now.

"When was it?" he asks.

I swing a foot at the carpeted floor, kicking up a whirl of dust. "I was six. The day you took me rowing on the lake behind the house. The day you let me have a sip of beer."

Bart was sixteen, which I guess is pretty normal for starting to experiment with booze, at least in my own experiences. I'm that age now. But I have reasons to drink. I'm trying to blot the shadows out of my life. Alcohol helps. And pot. Anything that takes me out of myself helps me to ignore the insidious whisperings from the mirrors.

"I remember that day. It was just after Dad died," Bart says. "The water was so calm."

I tilt my head. "Too calm. Just like a mirror."

"Oh." Bart frowns. "What . . . what did you see?"

My throat tightens and I glance around the corner at the stone bird statue, but I push the words out. "At first, I thought it was reflected clouds scudding across the surface. And then I realised they came from within the water. Dark shadows that look like birds. They had red eyes and sharp beaks . . ." I shake my head, wishing I could forget the image. "And ever since then, I've seen them everywhere."

Bart lifts my hand to his lips and kisses my knuckles. With his eyes closed, he whispers, "I'm so sorry, Georgia."

"It's not your fault."

It isn't just mirrors. Any reflective surface. Windows at night, metallic cutlery—even the shiny plastic of polished tables. And of course, no one believes me. No one. Except Bart, maybe. I don't want to know whether he's pitying me or believes me. I need to believe someone is on my side. As the anxiety grew and the OCD behaviours began, my mother took me to a line of doctors. Nothing helped: no doctor, no therapist, no medication. My stepfather forced me to stand in front of a mirror until I peed myself. This is my life. The shadows are here all the time, watching me, tilting their bird heads, examining me with their red eyes, waiting.

It's only recently they've started whispering. Nothing I can understand, but I know something bad is going to happen. I feel it in the tingle that creeps up my spine, slow and steady like a shadow of a tower growing in the setting sun.

"They're going to make me look at mirrors here," I say, my voice shaking.

Bart turns my face to him and wipes away my tears with his thumbs. "I'm still working on getting you out of here. I haven't given up. Hell, you can come and live with me in London if I can swing it. But you gotta hang on, ok?" I nod and grip his wrists. "Give me some time. I'm doing everything I can."

"Thanks, Bart," I whisper.

A door opens and my parents and the two nurses spill out of the office. Bart and I stand and go to greet them. We draw level with the ticking grandfather clock. My mother shifts her weight from one foot to the other and repositions her handbag.

"It's best to say your goodbyes now," Nurse Marion says. "If you drag it out, it just makes it all the worse."

My mother wraps her arms around me. For a moment, I lose myself in her smell. The lavender in her perfume, the vanilla scent of her body wash and another smell I can never place, but only belongs to her. A safe and homely smell. The one I craved when I was a child and would climb into her lap and put my nose into her neck just to breathe in her scent. That's when I felt safe enough to ask her about my father, how he was when I was born. She'd tell me how he'd tickle my feet and kiss my nose. I'd make her tell me about it again and again. I barely remember my father. The man in the photographs at home doesn't seem real. I only have an impression of a deep voice and the smell of cigars. Everything else is what I've been told about him. I was so little when he died.

I lean into my mother, savouring the feel of her arms around me. I leak out a few desperate tears, hoping she'll change her mind and take me home with her.

"Please don't leave me here," I whisper into her neck.

Suddenly I am five again and want nothing more than to be swept against my mother's chest where I can be protected from all manner of evils, imaginary or otherwise. I cling to her, like a koala to a eucalyptus tree.

She squeezes me tighter, her heart beating faster to match my own panicked one, but then my stepfather claws at her arm and leads her away. She looks at me, a tear running down her cheek, making a track through her makeup. "I love you, sweetheart," she says.

"As soon as I can," Bart whispers at me and presses something into my hands. A framed photo. Of the two of us at our cousin's wedding last summer. "I know it's a bit cheesy, but I thought it might help."

"Thanks."

The front door closes, and I'm left standing in the middle of the grand entrance foyer with the two nurses.

"Georgia."

My head snaps towards the voice.

"Georgia," Marian says again. She stares at me, her mouth all pinched, like she pities me, like I'm some wounded animal. Maybe I am. I swipe at the tears on my face. "Let's go get you settled in."

Mumbling something inaudible, I trip over the carpet and land in an undignified heap on the floor, humiliated. Nurse Willow squats down beside me. She takes my arm and looks into my eyes.

"It's going to be ok, Georgia." She hoists me to my feet. She is surprisingly strong for a waif. Her icy blue eyes drill into my soul and I look away. When I draw level with the bird statue, I hesitate. I can feel it examining me, feel the weight of its stare, of all those patients who have come before me, pushed into the arms of the nurses and into a life of misery. I can almost hear the heavy bolt of an old iron jail closing behind me. Trapping me here forever.

Towards the front of the building, where the light streams in through the wide lead-lined windows, a door opens and closes. Maybe Bart has come back. My heart stops beating for a moment and then, as if to make up for its brief, ominous absence, comes back with a painful boom and catapults me into a full-scale panic attack.

I collapse on the first step, my hands bearing my weight to the floor. My vision blurs, my head pounds in my too-tight skull, and anxiety's flush heats my skin. A dizzy spell attacks. If I was still standing, I'm sure my jelly-legs would have given way. The panic attack arrives with claws that dig in deep.

I wrap my arms around my knees, bury my face into my jeans and rock myself back and forth. Desperate, lonely tears race down my cheeks. How can they leave me here? Why don't they believe me?

"Georgia? Here." Paul kneels in front of me and offers me a paper bag.

"Thanks." I snatch at the brown bag with trembling fingers, shake it out and position the edges over my mouth.

"That's it." Paul remains in his squat in front of me, watching, waiting.

I suck in a lungful of brown air. Then another. And another. Slowly, very slowly, too slowly, while I blow out the breaths in a measured count, my heart rate begins to slow.

Willow sits beside me and puts one small hand on my shoulder. She gives it a gentle squeeze. "That's it, sweetheart, keep breathing."

I suck in more breaths, finally calming down. All the while, Paul squats there and waits. He watches and waits. All three of them do. This isn't the first panic attack I've endured in public, but it is one of the most embarrassing. Although I know they're all professionals and here to help me with exactly this problem, it's not going to do much to prove I don't belong here. Paul's sympathetic eyes and the warm twist of his mouth have me cursing the anxiety and the cruel judge who didn't even try to listen to me.

The other two are staring at me in a clinical fashion, inspecting me, trying to decipher the extent of my problems, trying to determine just how far gone I really am. *Screw you.*

"Thanks," I say, handing him back the now crumpled paper bag.

"No problem," he replies, getting to his feet.

I nod, blushing again.

Marion and Willow resume the climb up the grand staircase. I follow them, wiping the tear tracks from my cheeks, distracted by the various portraits dotting the walls, the sound of my footsteps lost in the thick carpet.

They are all old, from a time when cameras didn't exist, and people sat for portraits regularly. They seem to watch me as I make my way up the stairs and along the narrow corridor, their eyes darkening as I pass, flashing warnings of danger. I can almost hear them whispering at me as I pass. I can almost feel their delicately folded arms reaching for me, a ghostly, insubstantial grip, trying to protect me from what lays ahead. If I venture any further, I'll come out crazier than when I came in.

The portraits are surrounded by gold-plated frames. In the dim lighting, a black shadow streaks along the length of the polished metal. I gasp and turn my head but come face to face with another portrait. As if the accusing eyes within the portrait aren't bad enough, another dark smudge moves the length of this frame too. An unexpected scream rips out of my throat, and I dip my chin, trying not to look at any of the paintings. But black shapes move in rectangular paths along all the frames.

The shadows are here. They've found me.

THREE

I RUN down the hall and duck under an ornate antique table, covering my head with my arms, hoping if I squeeze my eyes closed the awful creatures will leave me alone. The smell of wood polish rushes up my nose, the exact same fragrance my mother uses. My throat tightens until I can't swallow.

"Georgia?"

I open my eyes. Willow squats down beside me, and her hand floats towards my shoulder. "Are you ok, sweetheart?"

I nod and allow her to help me out from under the table. "Just thought . . . I saw something."

Willow smiles. "It's an old building. Lots of nooks and crannies, lots of noises and shadows."

I flinch at the word. She pats my hand and leads me down the hall. I glance briefly at the golden frames, but they seem undisturbed for now. Marion mutters something about a lot of girls under one roof and hysteria. I scowl at her back.

"Here we are, sweetheart." Willow flings open a door about halfway down the dark corridor.

I take a moment to examine the room that will be my home for the foreseeable future. The walls, painted in an oh-yes-you-will-get-better-here sunflower yellow, are an attempt at banal cheeriness. The curtains framing the one large window contain a bright blue Aztec pattern. I rub the material between my fingers; cheap, ready-made, end of line, store-bought chintz and they hang loosely from the curtain pole. A yellow blackout blind, as equally bold as the walls, blocks daylight from entering the room. But I'm glad for the obstruction because light isn't the only thing that comes through windows.

Three institutional-style beds take up most of the room. Made up with crisp, white, cotton sheets and those hospital blankets that are issued for babies and are full of holes. I know from the first time I spent a night shivering in a hospital bed that these blankets will do nothing to ward off an evening chill once the weather drops, let alone the loneliness. Beside each bed is a small table with a lamp. Personal objects adorn two of the tables. I'll be sharing a room with two other crazy people. Real crazy people.

Willow plucks my suitcase from the ground and slaps it down on the vacant bed with a ceremonial flourish. I step forward when she starts undoing the zips.

"That's my stuff."

Marion presses her lips together in a gesture of strained patience. "We need to go through your belongings and take away anything that may be of harm to yourself or the other patients. Don't worry," she rushes on when she sees my face drop. "It'll be kept in the nurses' station and you'll get it all back when you leave."

Ninety days.

Marion hands me a bundle of clothes which I only just notice she's been carrying. "Please put these on."

I hesitate. I don't want to get changed in front of these two, but I'm not about to go into the bathroom anytime soon. Marion's strained look quashes my silent plea for privacy. My scalp prickles and the twitchy feeling snakes down my neck and through my limbs. I'm still a bit trembly for the panic attack downstairs and now I have to choose between humiliation and monsters.

I put the clothes down on the bed next to my suit-case, noticing my nails are chipped and the polish flaking. Will they let me paint my nails in here? Will the chemicals inside be considered dangerous? Willow opens my suitcase, like an overstretched jaw, and rummages through my stuff.

I remove my mobile phone from my jeans. Marion holds out a brown cardboard box. It already has a sticker with my name on it.

Georgia Boone.

And underneath it: *Brookwood Hospital.*

It's official, then. I am crazy and there is no better place for me than a lunacy asylum. Ok, ok, *ex*-lunacy asylum, but still. The history oozes from the brick and mortar, from the ancient light fittings and the clanking plumbing. If the building could talk, I wonder what secrets it would tell.

"You need to concentrate on your treatment, not Facebooking, Instagramming, Snapchatting, or whatever it is you young people do with your friends," Marion says. She doesn't even offer a smile. Or a light touch on my arm. How I suddenly crave to be held again; encased in a protective shield of arms that will ward off the worst of evil. The lines in her face seem deeper, wider, and are probably reinforced with cement. I will find no comfort here.

With an exaggerated sigh, I drop my phone into the box. "We don't have Wifi here, and the cell reception isn't great anyway." Is that supposed to be conciliatory? It's an abysmal attempt.

I unfold the bundle of clothes she hands me. There's a pair of navy tracksuit bottoms, elasticated around the waist, not drawstring. A navy sweatshirt, no zipper, no cords. Navy socks and a navy t-shirt. A pair of black plimsolls round off the whole affair. No laces.

"You can never be too careful," Willow says when she sees me eyeing the plimsolls. She pulls my selection of bras from my suitcase. "Underwired." They go into the cardboard box.

"Hey!"

"We can issue you with a standard non-wired bra, or we can take the wires out of your own. But you won't get them back in again," Willow says.

"Seriously?" The prickling feeling grows until it swarms over my cheeks and stings the skin behind my ears. "What am I going to do with a bit of wire?"

"Oh, you'd be surprised how inventive some of the patients have been," Marion replies. "Which would you prefer?"

I sigh, blowing my hair out of my face. "I'll take the standard." I have no energy left to argue. The scene with Bart and my mother has sapped the last of my reserves. The inevitability of my situation lends me a general feeling of hopelessness, which I have an inkling is here to stay. And I'm not about to let my bras go to ruin, even if I can't wear them for—a lump forms in my throat, hard and immobile—ninety days. Minimum. And I'm not permitted to speak to my mum for a month; the settling in period. They can't have patients crying on the phone to their mum's; it only leads to constant phone calls from emotional parents that the receptionist isn't equipped to handle.

"It'll be sent up from laundry later."

Tears prick my eyes and run unabashedly down my face. I slump onto the bed in a wave of despondency. Willow manages a couple of shoulder pats, and then Marion encourages me back to my feet and into the new clothes. It's another humiliation when I have to remove the underwired bra I'm wearing in view of them both and place it in the stupid cardboard box that is quickly collecting the sum total of my life.

But I'm not going to go into the bathroom. Bathrooms have mirrors. All of them. So I turn my back on them and slip the new t-shirt over my head. It's surprisingly soft. I had images of them boiling the clothes of all the patients in a large vat and stirring the whole thing with a long, wooden stick. I can't get those old horror movies about 1960's mental asylums out of my head. The sweatshirt fits loosely, and I cross my arms over my unsupported boobs.

I join Willow at the side of my bed and watch her pile belongings into the infernal cardboard box. In goes my iPad and all of my clothes which I won't be needing now that I have a very *attractive* blue tracksuit. At least it isn't prison orange.

Willow opens my toiletries bag. Out comes the razor. "It's alright, sweetheart. We'll bring you a safety one," she says. Her fingers hover over the compact mirror. It's the only mirror I tolerate. I can't look in any other. It's my most vital possession. It ensures that my eyebrows, even though they're fair, don't take over my face, that mascara goes on my eyelashes and not my eyelids, that my pale, pink lip balm remains on my lips, not smeared into the small crevice above.

But most importantly, I can see what I look like, who I am, the woman I'm becoming. Small glimpses, anyway. The compact isn't big enough for a full-on frontal view of my entire face. And that's the way it needs to be.

Willow glances surreptitiously at Marion who is busy arranging my possessions in the box. The lanky nurse puts the mirror back into my toiletries bag and slides me a secret smile. She's probably figured there isn't much harm to be done with a mirror. And after all, I'm the one with the mirror phobia, it's probably ther-apy. But I'm grateful for her small action nonetheless, and her secret smile makes me realise I might have an ally here—if I play my cards right.

Willow picks up the photo of Bart and me I dropped on the bed. She stands it up on the bedside table. "He's a handsome chap."

"My brother," I say. "He's ten years older."

"Is he now?" Willow finishes positioning the photo.

The last item in my suitcase is a two-litre bottle of vodka. It's the only thing that numbs the nightmares. Marion chortles when Willow pulls it out.

"Nice try, kid." Willow pats my shoulder. "But we believe in clean therapy here."

"Only a few more items on the checklist," Marion says. She gestures to Willow who shoves a hand into a gaping front pocket. She pulls out a bracelet. It looks like one of those rubber sport watches. As if the school-like bells I've been hearing since I arrived aren't enough to keep the girls to whatever schedule is imposed upon them. But then I realise it isn't a watch. It's a tracking bracelet.

I look from the bracelet that Willow holds in her hands, open, waiting for my wrist, to Marion. They might as well just give me ankle shackles and a cell door.

"It's more of a health and safety thing than an invasion of privacy," Marion says. "We had a spat of runaways during unsupervised outside time. We need to be able to locate you." I frown. "Your parents did agree to it in the paperwork they signed."

I take one more look at the white tracking bracelet and relent to Willow's encouraging face. Why not? My dignity has already been stripped from me, what's one more small humiliation? The bracelet closes around my wrist with a sudden snap, like powerful jaws around prey. Willow places her thumb on a small bio screen and the bracelet locks with a soft click. No escape. No combination code to crack in the dead of night. I rub at my wrist, feeling part of my identity dripping away to become just a number. Or a diagnosis. Free will, privacy . . . gone.

Willow wraps a blood pressure cuff around my arm while Marion opens a little box with rubber gloves and a syringe. She turns to me. "Are you ok with needles, sweetheart?"

Rolling up my sleeve, I nod and sit down on the bed. Mirrors, no. Needles, no problem.

Willow finishes with the blood pressure cuff and jots down something in a notebook, then a sharp prick stings my other arm. The vial quickly fills with my blood and I wonder if there's anything in there that will explain why I see shadows. Some kind of mutation. Something I can see in black and white on a piece of paper that will prove to everyone I'm not crazy. Despite the contrary evidence.

"That about does it." Marion holds the cardboard box tucked under one arm and my empty suitcase under the other. "You'll meet your roommates soon enough. You share the bathroom there." She points to the closed ensuite door. "We'll leave you to get acquainted with your new surroundings. Willow will come back for you in a bit and take you on a tour of the facility."

"Wait," Willow says, thrusting a plastic cup in my direction. "We need a urine sample."

I look from the cup to the bathroom door. "Can't you get what you need from my blood?"

Willow taps the cup. "Different kind of tests."

I look at the bathroom door again, then back at both nurses. "I'm not going in there."

"What do you do at home?" Marion asks.

"All my mirrors are covered, or they've been taken down." I can't control the tremor in my voice. The thought of going in there gives me the urge to pee, but I can't, I can't face a mirror.

Willow lowers the cup. "Tell you what, sweetheart, as you haven't started your therapy yet, we don't know what the doc is going to do, so, why don't I cover up the mirror for you and you can go in there and do your thing. Would that be ok?"

I let out a great shuddery breath, the relief streaking through my limbs. The nurses aren't so bad, nothing like what I had built up in my head. "Thank you."

Willow disappears inside the bathroom. I hear shuffling noises, and when she comes out, the mirror over the sink is completely covered with a white towel. I take the plastic cup from her and tiptoe towards the small ensuite. Leaving the door ajar, I don't spend any time analysing my surroundings. I don't even squat over the toilet, but pull my trousers down, fill the cup and yank them back up again. The whole time I feel the presence of something evil behind that white towel, waiting for its moment.

"A few words of advice," Marion says, accepting the cup in a gloved hand. "It's not a great idea to share stories with the other patients. Sometimes it gives the girls new ideas. So save it for your therapy sessions. Touching isn't allowed. And certainly no romantic liaisons."

"Also—you're allowed up to an hour in your room per day. It's not great to wallow." Willow pats my shoulder. "Try and relax, sweetheart."

I'm not your fucking sweetheart.

I admonish myself; she's only trying to be nice. But that's what my Mum calls me, and she's not her.

Ninety days.

Marion ushers Willow out of the room and closes the door swiftly behind them, leaving me alone in the dare-to-be-miserable yellow walls and singular overhead light. I'm tempted to open the blind. But I know the weather outside is still gloomy and all I'll see is my reflection in the darkened glass. That, and other things.

FOUR

I'M JUST SETTLING down on the bed for a good wallowing session when the door bursts open and I think Marion is back to perform some final humiliation. But it isn't Marion, it's Paul. He opens the door and wheels in a gurney carrying a sleeping girl. He shoots me an apologetic smile and pushes the gurney over to the middle bed and I catch a faint whiff of stale cigarettes.

"This is Liz," he whispers. "She's one of your roommates."

He lifts the inert bundle from the gurney and lays her gently on her bed. He pulls the covers up to her shoulders. Liz remains asleep, long, dark hair trailing over the sheet. Her face is turned slightly towards me, her pale lips parted, and I can hear her slow breaths. A large padded bandage peeks out of the top of her sweatshirt.

"Is she ok? What happened?" I point to the bandage.

"Bit of an incident," Paul says. "Things got a bit on top of her. She had to be sedated."

"Sedated?" I gulp. They had to do that to me in the shop. After the broken mirror thing. The paramedic stabbed me right in the butt with a needle. I can still feel the spot where it pierced my skin. Booty juice, they call it. I read about it and knew they did it here too. I'd been hoping it had been given up along with electric shock therapy and lobotomies.

"Does that happen often?"

"It depends on the patient. Liz doesn't normally cause problems."

"How long will she sleep?" I ask, leaning over the gurney to inspect my roommate. A narrow nose divides her pale cheeks. Acne reddens her chin, and her mousey hair could use a few highlights. But they probably don't allow that in here. I guess her to be the same age as me, sixteen.

"She'll be out for the day, probably most of the night too."

Paul moves to sit beside me on the bed and pulls out some forms clipped to the bottom of the gurney. I recognize the mood assessment questionnaire that I've filled out a million times before. But we go through it again anyway. No, I'm not depressed. Yes, I am high on the anxiety scale.

So would you be, if you saw the shadows.

The form is easy to answer until we get to one particular question.

"Hallucinations?" Paul asks.

I don't know how to answer that. To me, the

shadows are real. Is there a possibility it's all in my head? I guess there has to be; I'm the only one who sees them. How can I be the only one who sees them and call myself sane? The alternative isn't a path I want to follow. I don't feel crazy. But isn't that what crazy people think? I go round in circles with this train of thought all the time, and it never gets any clearer.

"Is it a fear of breaking mirrors or apparitions inside the mirror itself?"

My head jerks. No one has ever asked me that before. No one has ever specifically questioned what it is about a mirror that scares me.

"They're not apparitions," I mumble, forgetting my promise to myself to never speak of the shadows here.

Paul puts down his pen. "Spectrophobia. So it's not the mirror itself."

"I don't want to talk about it."

"That's ok." Paul gets up. "I've got your notes. I'm only trying to get a jump start on understanding you."

I laugh. "That will take longer than ninety days."

Paul smiles. "Maybe not." He pushes the gurney toward the door.

"Paul?" I question. He turns back, his hand on the doorknob. "Can I call my mum? Just once." Tears threaten again and the awful lump in my throat is back. I bite down on my lip, hard.

"I'm sorry, Georgia, it's just not possible. You need to get accustomed to your surroundings." He offers a sympathetic smile. "You will, quicker than you expect." He shuts the door with one quick tug.

Hugging the pillow against my chest and squeezing

my eyes closed does nothing to quell the tears. Will I ever stop crying today? I need tissues, but there are none on any of the bedside tables. I look at the closed bathroom door. Snot runs out of my nose. I wipe it with the back of my hand and am rewarded with a disgusting, smeary yuckiness stuck to my skin. Pushing myself off the bed, I approach the innocuous bathroom door. Standard light wood. Nothing unusual. Willow removed the towel from the mirror when she left the room.

With a hand on the doorknob, I close my eyes. In one or two fluid motions I open the door, stumble inside like some unseeing zombie of the night, fumble around for the toilet paper, grab it from its roll and retreat back into the room. I shut the door behind me with my right hand. Then I touch the doorknob with my left. As the door is wooden, I knock on it gently with the knuckles on my left hand three times, then three times with my right. I repeat the ritual with all three wooden bedside tables. Finally, I slump back down on my bed and blow my nose loudly.

After I cry out all the liquid my body contains and blow all the snot out of my nose, I finally calm down and crave nothing more than the oblivion of sleep. But as soon as I lift the hole-riddled blue blanket to my chin, and I feel the foreignness of it, a new shot of loneliness slices through my heart. I'm not in my own bed at home. I'm in a miserable grey hospital with a whole bunch of crazy people. Myself included. Sitting up, I rest my chin on my knees and press the heels of my hands into my eyes to quell any further tears. I don't even have my iPad to distract me. My only personal possession in the room stands on my bedside table; the picture of Bart. My heart lurches as the slice of loneliness cuts deeper.

In the corridor, footsteps creak by. I assume other patients or nurses. And I imagine all those portraits, watching, waiting. Above my head a weird squelchy, skittering noise comes from the ceiling and the wall behind my bed. An inconsistent, wet scratching. Must be squirrels or rats stuck in the walls, but it does little to ease my nerves.

Blocking out the creepy noise, I pick up the photo. Bart wears a suit. His top button is undone, and his tie hangs loosely around his neck. His jacket is draped over a shoulder with one hand, and the other is around my shoulder, an empty, crystal tumbler dangling from a casual two-finger grip. He was captured by the lens while laughing at someone off camera. The sun had set, but the sky hasn't darkened to night yet. His eyes dazzle with mischief, and the stubble lining his jaw shows him to be a bad boy who scrubs up well. In the picture, I'm looking at him and laughing. I always feel lighter when he's around. It's my favourite picture of him. He looks grown up. In control. Strong. When did he turn into such a man?

So much more of a man than my stepfather, David. After the mirror incident, he stopped talking to me. He was gentle and caring at first, but now he is bewildered and distant. My mother cries all the time. She doesn't know how to help me and she's stopped believing my stories. Over the last few months I caught her staring at me, a watery look in her eyes, a helpless look that broke my heart.

I learned to hide my problems. Panic attacks and shadow creatures accost me daily, in equal measure. But I learned to cope. I avoid mirrors as much as possible, and I didn't go shopping with my friends—not that I had many, I managed to scare off most. I bought myself the compact mirror.

Now, I put a finger to Bart's face on the photo. Then the finger of my other hand. He was drunk last night, and I know he will have gone back to his flat in London and popped the top off something as soon as he left me. And find a way to get me out of here. He's going to try. He is. If he can stay away from the bottle long enough.

"I'm not crazy," I shoot through clenched teeth. But how can I possibly explain it to anyone? I'm here to get better, I'm here to be fixed once and for all. But no one will be able to take the shadows away. And no one else can see them either. And then what? Archaic forms of therapy? Permanent tranquilisation? A lobotomy? Or will they just throw away the key?

My heart lurches again and I bite back another wave of emotion. I won't cry anymore; I won't give them the satisfaction. No matter what the shadows do.

Willow opens the door and sticks her head inside. Her long hair is fastened in a low ponytail and hangs over one shoulder. Winding it round a finger, she glances at the sleeping Liz and then looks at me. "How are you doing, sweetheart? Are you ready for your tour?"

I nod. I put the photo of Bart back on the table with

two hands and add two gentle taps. Climbing off the bed, I tuck my hands into the sleeves of the navy sweatshirt. If my hands don't come into contact with anything, I can avoid performing the rituals.

I follow Willow out the door. She leads me down the corridor to a back set of stairs. Once we're in the stairwell, she points up. "The floors above contain more patient rooms. There's a nurse sub-station on every floor where you can get medication during the night. The top floor is the attic. It's used for storage of old files. It's locked, and patients are not permitted inside." She stops curling her hair around her finger while she waits for me to respond.

"Ok, no going to the top floor," I say.

I follow her down the stairs.

"Down here is the common room." She opens the door with a flourish, and I follow her into a brightly lit room with a grey linoleum floor and what I'm now coming to think of as the go-screw-yourself yellow walls. The windows are large and square. Through the slatted blinds, I catch glimpses of heavy rain and sudden flashes of lightning. A hit of acrid cleaning fluid is barely muted by an automatic air freshener pumping out fake lavender in the corner. Willow leads me through the room before I have a chance to inspect the patients in it. She points to a door on her left. "Main nurses' station. This is where you'll collect your medication every day. There are various bells signally medication and meal times. Try not to be late." A big observation window gives the nurses a view of the common room.

Another door to her right leads to the cafeteria and

the kitchens. There are bathrooms just off the common room. She leads me down a corridor, and we end up in the grand entrance foyer with the sweeping staircase and terrifying bird statue. The similarities between it and the shadows in the mirrors are entirely disturbing. I swear its crumbling, granite eyes watch me as I walk across the room.

"All patients need to use the back staircase, no matter how inconvenient," Willow says. "Some have had the idea of sliding down the banister. It didn't end well." She chuckles at me conspiratorially. "You'll need to come this way when you have your therapy sessions with Dr. Zaleski. There's also a swimming pool and gym, but you need to gain privileges for that. You're welcome to come and go between here and your room, but only an hour in your room per day."

"You're permitted outside in small, accompanied groups when it's not raining." She points to a window where a glittering rain pounds against the manicured hospital gardens. Rose bushes make a boundary and worn, wooden benches stand sentry under the windows. "Plus three cigarette breaks a day, which you'll have to sign out and in for."

I didn't think to bring cigarettes with me. I don't consider myself an addict, but judging by the way I'm craving a drag, maybe I'm more addicted than I think.

"There's also the sensory room. It's a great place to relax and one of the most popular areas, so book in early. The register is held at the nurses' office." Willow leads me back to the common room. "If there is anything you need, please come to the nurses' station.

Otherwise, listen out for the bells, and the orderlies will fetch you for your therapy sessions."

She leaves me in the common room. A couple of orderlies are posted in the corners, and I spot Paul in the nurses' office standing in front of the observation window. He twitches like he needs a smoke and his watchful eyes scan the room, back to front, again and again.

I take another look around the large, rectangular room. Windows, almost as bad as mirrors for reflective properties, always need to be inspected first. On further examination, I don't think they'll pose a problem. The slatted blinds will protect against the shadows appearing in the reflective surface and judging by the thick layer of dust built up I don't think they've been raised in weeks. Thank god.

The common room houses about twenty other patients, all girls, dressed in identical navy-blue tracksuits. Their ages seem to range from as young as ten to as old as seventeen. I know they can't be older than that as they would graduate to an adult facility.

A group sits on plastic, yellow chairs that have been drilled into the ground, and stare at a TV hanging high in the corner of a room. "Saturday Kitchen" blares from the TV; James Martin is pan-frying a salmon fillet in a pound of butter. I doubt they ever change the channel. I'm already missing bad boy Jamie Lang and his playboy antics from Made in Chelsea. And sweet Sam that never catches a break and makes me wish I was a few years older.

A few tables and chairs are shoved in another corner

of the room, also drilled into the floor. Stacked on a nearby bookshelf is a multitude of board games. The frayed titles read "Monopoly" and "Sorry". I'm sure the dusty collection won't contain one game that doesn't have half its pieces missing. A pile of dog-eared, cover-less books, supporting at least an inch of dust, takes up all the space on another lopsided shelf.

I check the nurses' station. Paul is still standing here, one hand clasping the other, his finger tapping the back of the other hand. Maybe I can bum a cigarette from him.

I hesitate between the group of girls watching TV and the empty tables at the other side of the room. The yellow bedroom with the comatose Liz laying in the middle bed holds no allure, but equally, I don't quite feel like befriending a whole new bunch of crazies either. Opting for an empty table and chair, I slouch as best I can and keep my hands tucked in my sleeves. On "Saturday Kitchen", James Martin continues frying the salmon, adding a sprinkling of spring onions and salt and pepper, but all I can smell is the bleach used to mop the floor and my own fear pooling under my arms.

I cross my arms over my chest and wish I can fast forward my life. Or rewind. Or swap lives with someone.

Please.

Pretty Please?

With a cherry on top?

A faint banging noise interrupts my thoughts. A girl stands near the door that leads to the back stairs, staring at the wall. She's barefoot and, as if to make up for the misplaced item of clothing, she wears a thick, black crash helmet on her head. Abruptly, she leans forward and smashes her head into the wall. Then she stands straight again as if nothing has happened. She repeats the manoeuvre five seconds later. I leap out of my chair and dart over to her. I'm about to reach out and touch her when Paul appears beside me and shakes his head at me. "She doesn't like to be touched."

Crash.

I wince as the girl rebounds a foot into the room, stares at the wall, then goes at it again. And again. And again.

I creep back to my seat and watch, bewildered as she continues to smash her helmeted head into the wall every five seconds. Her timing is so precise I could set my watch to it. I'm also sure she'll be lucky to have one intact brain cell left in her head. All those American football players with brain damage and severe mental health issues isn't because they didn't wear helmets. It's because of the way the brain sloshes around inside the skull with each impact.

No one else pays her the slightest bit of attention. For a few minutes, I jerk every time she does it, then the banging becomes a rhythmical metronome and fades into the background.

The girls watching TV haven't moved. They watch with intense interest and *ooohhh* and *aaahhh* when the audience steps up to taste the final product. Others appear more docile, as though they've been drugged within an inch of their life. Paul walks between them, asking muted questions and offering comforting smiles, but they don't seem to care that he's there.

On the other side of the room, looking out over the front drive, another girl sits in a wheelchair. Skeletally thin, her head lolls to the right as though her neck muscles are too weak to support it. She stares out the window, despite the slatted blinds obscuring her view from the image beyond. But every once in a while, when a cloud momentarily covers the sun, I catch a hint of her reflection in the glass. She wears a wide-eyed expression that makes me think she's been frozen in fear. Saliva dribbles out the corner of her mouth. I avert my eyes before I can catch a glimpse of something darker.

A burst of noise snaps my attention to the empty chair beside me. A girl with dark punk hair slams into the chair and shoots me a dimpled grin. Feisty brown eyes lock on to mine. "Don't let it get you down."

She juts her chin at the girl in the crash helmet and taps short, stubby nails on the tabletop. "Some of them have been here for a long time. They can't deal with it anymore." I catch a flash of a tattoo on her forearm. Something written in Latin. "That's Crash Helmet Annie," she says with a twisted smile. "Back when she was still talking, she said it was to get rid of the dreams. She used to talk about aliens, that they were eating her soul, and she didn't know how else to get rid of them." She wraps her hands around her neck and mimes being strangled, performing a dramatic death fall to the floor.

"How does banging your head on a wall help?" I ask as the girl reclaims her seat.

"It's a good a way as any." The girl shrugs. "Now she doesn't talk anymore. But she must still have the dreams because she still bangs her head."

Hands still tucked into my sleeves, I lean my elbows on the table, cursing the fact that I can't pull my chair in. "Has anyone tried to stop her?"

The girl snaps chewing gum loudly and works it at the side of her jaw. "They did, in the beginning. She used to scream and kick and punch and scratch. Paul still has the scars." She nods towards him in the office where he twitches with the need for nicotine. "I think she actually bit part of his ear off. The doctors tried an aggressive cognitive behavioural therapy for three years. Then they gave up. She got her helmet back plus a whole bunch of drugs."

"Jesus," I mutter.

Willow appears in the office window and Paul scooches out the door.

"Smoke break," the girl says, shifting in her seat. "He can smoke as many as he wants, lucky sod. I'm June by the way. I'm one of your roommates." She snaps her gum again and takes up the nail-drumming routine once more.

"Georgia," I say, relieved she doesn't offer me a hand to shake. Then I'd have to shake both of them, and it can get tricky explaining my idiosyncrasies.

"Nurse Marion's asked me to keep an eye on you until you get settled in. And not that I'm in any way partial to doing what I'm told, but you look like a decent sort, and this place could use some fresh blood. You don't have any smokes on you, do you?" I shake my head. "Never mind. They say it's bad for your health." She barks out a short, sharp laugh, which flares open a hole in her nose. There are three more in her right ear and two in her left. June, my new roommate. The very sort I've been hanging around with of late, getting fake IDs and drinking cheap plonk under the bridge during school hours. She seems the sort to know all of the rules —and how to break them. She seems like my kind of girl.

A bell rings and June skitters to her feet. "That's the lunch bell. I'll show you the way." She tugs on my sleeve and drags me down a corridor, speeding around other girls and sliding against the walls to get past them.

Behind us, a whole bunch of crazies shuffle to their feet and form a haphazard line. Some of them mutter about not eating carbs. Others claim they aren't hungry. Monitors line the dining room, inspecting the girls' plates, making sure they eat enough. We are to be weighed weekly, whether we have a history of Anorexia or not. There's no dignity in this place. But there is June —a bright spark among the other girls who blend into one navy-blue mass with haunted pupils and dark circles under their eyes.

I follow June in the general direction of the dinner ladies. June hands me a plastic tray and a plastic plate, muttering about the lack of eco-friendly materials. One of the dinner ladies heaps a mound of oily cottage pie onto my plate. When it's June's turn, she moves her plate at the last moment, the mound of slop falling onto the floor at her feet. She shoots the dinner lady an apologetic smile when she pins her with a look of fury.

"I'm vegetarian. And I have issues. If meat touches my plate . . ." she lets the threat dangle. I stifle a giggle when the dinner lady turns her furious look on me.

The dinner lady stabs a finger at the salad bar, muttering under her breath. I accept a small portion and a spoonful of chips before I join June. I can never turn down a plate of chips. At the salad bar, we load up on lettuce, cucumber, tomatoes, mushrooms, sweet corn, and salad dressings. They even have a cold pasta salad.

"I'm not really a vegetarian." June winks. "But I'm not going to eat that stuff." She points at the congealed, indescribable mess on my plate that leaches into my lettuce leaves. "Stick with the salad. At least they can't put anything in it."

FIVE

I SIT down beside June on a foldable bench and stare at my plate of semi-familiar food. It's not the roast chicken with trimmings Mom makes every other Sunday. I tense against a pang of homesickness. "Put anything in it?"

June doesn't answer. She shrugs and piles food into her mouth with a plastic fork. All of the utensils are plastic. I sigh with relief and pour myself a cup of water.

June scrapes her plate clean and wiggles out of the bench. "Catch you later. Need to go do the zen thing."

"Zen thing?"

"You know, spend time with my inner thoughts. Think about the healing process. Saturday's are pretty dull around here. Not that I think lessons during the week are much better, mind you."

I take a sip of water while I search for the right response. Has she gone all new-age, crystal-wielding, chakra-hunting, Namaste on me?

"Kidding!" She punches my arm. Could I ask her to punch the other one, just to even things out? The untouched limb hangs heavy from my shoulder, stinging with the need for balance. "But I do like my own space. They've got a great sensory room here with twinkle lights and ocean sounds effects. I try and book a session every day. I kinda need it sometimes."

I smile. "Or you'd go crazy, or something."

"Ha. Exactly! Stark raving!" Her brown eyes flash. "Cool?"

"Cool."

June scurries away, giggling to herself about something. I have pause to consider just how alone she needs to be. She was joking, right?

After lunch, I settle back in the chair in the common room and watch Paul through the window. He stares at us and sometimes makes notes on a clipboard. I have the urge to tell him it's not a two-way mirror, that I can actually see him hovering there, but as the hours drag by and his nicotine twitch intensifies, I mellow. He makes me crave a cigarette so bad I start tapping out a rhythm on the table with my fingers, making sure my touches are balanced, trying to stem the need. Crash Helmet Annie bangs her head for an hour and, when I can't bear it anymore, I creep to the nurses' station and tap on the door. Willow steps out of the office and sweeps an arm around my shoulder. The brief squeeze of human contact turns my mouth dry for a moment.

"I need to do something," I say. "I can't sit around here all day."

"Saturday afternoons can be a little dull. We don't force the weekend activities on anyone. Are you interested in art therapy?"

I shake my head. "I just need to do something."

She smiles and agrees to show me the swimming pool and the gym.

"If I could exercise now, it might help stem some of my anxiety." I give her my best hopeful face, resisting the urge to bat my blues.

Willow taps her long fingernails on a radiator covering and tilts her head. "We want to give you something to aim for, something to motivate you."

My heart drops. "Trust me, I'm motivated. I don't want to spend a single second longer here than I have to."

Her nails keep tapping as she looks me up and down. "Very well. I'll allow you to use the gym. Just this once."

"Thank you," I breathe out.

"You're a cunning one." She pats my shoulder, and again, the untouched one stings with the need to complete the ritual. I grit my teeth until the compulsion fades, which is most of the afternoon. The rituals keep me safe, and I'm already so unbalanced on my first day. What bad things are heading my way? But I know the answer to that. The very thing I'm here to confront will be my end. I can feel it. The omens are stacking up and I have little ability to thwart their insidious intentions.

Willow issues me with two bras, a navy pair of gym shorts and an additional navy t-shirt. I spend my very first afternoon in Brookwood Hospital pounding out my frustration on a squeaky cross trainer, ignoring the oily cottage pie that slides around in my stomach, and the sting of imbalance. The endorphins flow through me and I'm grateful for the few minutes that I can ignore the whisperings in my head.

A few minutes before the dinner bell rings, June finds me again and leads me to the cafeteria for take two. The main meal looks like they've tried to accommodate the leftover cottage pie into some kind of stew. I avoid it this time. Salad bar again, followed by a passable sticky toffee pudding.

The cafeteria is busier than it was at lunch. At least fifty girls fill the benches. Paul is there with a handful of orderlies.

"Where have all these girls been all day?" I ask.

"Some of them need constant supervision. A lot have all day therapy sessions. Many of them have visiting privileges." June performs a little cha-cha and gives me dramatic jazz hands, which makes me laugh. The last time I laughed was when Beer Can Barnaby crushed a full can of beer and it squirted up his nose and all over his face. But that was weeks ago.

I scan the room of navy track-suited girls. Some appear to be going about the usual machinations of eating and drinking and engaging in conversation with some semblance of normality and even some laughter. Others are fed with the help of an orderly. A few with red-rimmed eyes refuse to eat anything at all. But no one makes any kind of scene. Not today.

"Does anybody ever get better?" I circle my fork around my plate, trying to decide whether the stew or the overcooked carrots are more appetizing.

June cocks her head as she pours water into a cup.

"Sometimes." But she won't meet my eyes and shifts her gaze to her lap.

I think of my other roommate. "Where's Liz?"

"She's still sleeping."

Another bell rings. It's the end of dinner. Two hours after that, the bell goes again. This is worse than school. We line up at the nurses' station for our nightly medication. Marion has the pills dispensed in tiny plastic cups with our names on them. She holds a clipboard in one hand and crosses names off her list as girls come and take their pills.

Willow hands June hers. Her cup contains at least five different brightly coloured pills, and for the first time, I wonder what she's here for. She swallows them down in one and opens her mouth for Willow to examine. Satisfied, Willow moves her along and turns her attention to me.

She hands me a plastic cup with two, round, white pills.

"What are they?" I ask.

"A sedative," she replies. "Dr. Zaleski is still finalising your medication. So for now, it's just a mild sedative to help you sleep. If you want it."

"You'll save us all a lot of trouble if you learn to take your medication well now," Marion pipes up without looking up from her clipboard. "It can be quite unpleasant otherwise."

Paul leans against the wall with his arms crossed. A couple muscly orderlies stand beside him. An implicit threat. I stick a finger into the plastic cup and ignore the lengthening line of complaining girls at my back. I pop the pills in my mouth and swallow them down with the offered water. Willow doesn't bother to check.

"That's the way to do it," Marion says, briefly patting my shoulder.

Her comment brings back a memory of a Punch and Judy show I saw when I was little. That's the way to do it, or you'll be battered with a stick.

"You'll fit right in here," she calls out as I retrace my steps to the back stairs. I wince. I don't want to fit in. I don't want to belong or become part of the wallpaper or one of those apathetically docile girls that barely blink underneath the bright fluorescents of the common room. I'm not a conformer; I'm a fighter, a survivor. But everything is so much worse when I don't sleep. A little medicinal help to keep the whispering away in my dreams doesn't seem like a bad idea. Haven't I been doing it to myself with alcohol? At least this is legal.

In my room, June lays on her bed, reading a book by the light of her bedside lamp. Liz remains sleeping between us.

"Are you a morning showerer, or do you prefer the evenings?" June asks, without looking up from her book. I hadn't thought to bring books with me. I usually download them onto the Kindle app on my iPad, which is now sitting in a square cardboard box in the nurses' station. I'll have to grab one of the tattered ones from the common room tomorrow.

Standing at the foot of my bed, I contemplate June's question and realise I will, at some point in my stay here, have to have a shower. In the bathroom.

Where there's a mirror. I glance towards the closed door. Behind that solid wood, my future waits. The shadows.

June raises her gaze from her book and looks me over. I'm still in the gym shorts and spare t-shirt I changed into to use the cross trainer. I've been sweating. I ought to have a shower.

"Morning," I mumble, walking around my bed. I busy myself with the drawer, pretending there's a wealth of personal possessions inside to occupy myself with. June doesn't comment on my lack of proper hygiene. Instead, she opens the little door of her own bedside table, removes another book, and lobs it over the sleeping Liz towards me. It lands in the middle of my bed.

I pick it up. It's Louisa May Allcot's *Little Women*. My mum read it to me when I was little. I would have preferred something like *The Hunger Games*, but it beats staring at the walls.

"Lights go out at ten," June says. "We have an hour to read."

I run my hands over the worn cover of the book. "I didn't pick you for a reader."

June looks up from her book again. "Well, you could go to the common room and watch the night anxiety turn all the girls into unreasonable bitches instead. Reading's better than listening to the them, or the ghosts."

"Ghosts?"

June turns her book around and presses it face down on the bed. "The ghosts of Brookwood Asylum."

"Oh, come on now." I flick the pages of the book from top to bottom with my right hand, then my left.

She cocks an eyebrow. The corner of her mouth quivers and I can't tell if she's joking. "That's right, you haven't been here for a night yet. Check back with me in the morning. Tell me what you heard."

I laugh. Then remember the eerie wet scratching noises coming from the ceiling when I was here earlier. Squirrels, surely. Not ghosts. But suddenly I'm not so sure.

June picks up her book again, snuggles deeper, and turns to the wall.

Tension winds through the air. And as if on cue, a series of squeaking footsteps run by the closed bedroom door. Then a burst of laughter. *Just some of the other girls*, I tell myself. But I can't get my shoulders to drop.

Looking for a distraction, I open up the book and begin to read about the world of Jo March and her poverty-stricken family. In a world so far removed from my own, I lose myself for a little while.

The hour passes quickly, and I'm surprised when the hall light flickers its five-minute warning.

"You go ahead and use the bathroom. I brushed my teeth already," June says.

I put the book on my bedside table and tap it with my left hand, which is unbalanced now that the tracking bracelet adorns it. Maybe I should give it an extra tap with my right hand, to account for the added weight on my left? But then I will really be uneven. Fingering the bracelet for a moment, I wonder if I can pull it off. I yank at it, but it cuts into my skin.

Ignoring the ongoing battle warring inside my head, I get out of bed and face the bathroom door, which is a much bigger problem. Today I've been touched twice without the opportunity to even the balance. Twice. Balance is my protection against the shadows. Don't ask me why or how, but so far, it's been working. They've stayed inside the mirror. But now I'm unarmed.

The door looms tall and solid, seeming to increase my dread. Snatching a breath, I will my hand to reach towards the knob.

"It's not going to bite, you know." June's voice is an amused jangle.

How do you know?

I suck in a second deep breath and throw the door open. Snapping my eyes shut, I shuffle into the room, feeling for the light switch. I flick it on. Tilting my face to the floor, I dare to open my eyes. I stare at my feet. The pedestal of the sink stands a few inches in front of my toes. Out of my peripheral vision I sense the mirror above the sink. Like it's a live entity, or a giant hole to an unknown land. The toilet is on my left, the shower on my right. No curtain, no door. It's a wetroom.

My washbag has been placed on a shelf above the toilet. Hunching my shoulders, I take one step on the white, tiled floor and grab my bag. Taking out my toothbrush and toothpaste, I brush my teeth with my eyes closed. Finally, I turn my back on the mirror and face the door. With the mirror behind me, I'm free to open my eyes.

Someone whispers my name. Someone in that small

bathroom with the door closed and the mirror behind me, whispers my name. Right in my ear.

"Georgia . . . Georgia . . ." Taunting me.

The shadows have never called my name before. They've never spoken actual words. Just sibilant whispers. With trembling hands, I stuff my toothbrush in my washbag and shove it back on the shelf.

The shadows are behind me. In the mirror. Reaching towards me. Wanting me. I can feel them, their sinister presence, their malicious intents, their wish for me to die a slow and horrible death. I can feel their red eyes staring at me and their sharp beaks wanting to tear into my flesh. I snap off the light.

"Georgia . . . Georgia . . ."

My vision swims in the pitch-black room. Bile rises in the back of my throat. I stumble to my knees. Clutching at the door handle, I tug and fall out of the bathroom and onto the carpet of the bedroom. I slam the door behind me. Then tap it with my left hand. Then knock on it three times with both.

"Everything ok?" June snaps her book closed.

Gasping for breath, I crawl to my bed and pull myself up. My knees shake and sweat pools at the small of my back.

"Georgia? Are you ok? You look like you've seen a ghost. I did tell you there were ghosts." Frowning, June leans forward in her bed. "But they don't usually appear in toilets."

I inject some attitude into my voice. "Can't a girl have any privacy?"

June's frown deepens. "Not in this place."

I turn off my light and dive under my covers, turning my back on June and Liz. A few seconds later, June turns off her own light and darkness plunges into the room. She shuffles around in her bed for a minute and then silence falls over the room. A thick, eerie silence full of the worst kind of imaginings.

Stop it, Georgia!

The shadows are bad enough. I don't need to picture beheaded ghosts and beady eyes from oil paintings of soulless devil children. I squeeze my head between my hands, willing the rolling images of the macabre to stop.

They whispered my name. They whispered my name! What does it mean? I'm not crazy. I know I'm not. There's no reason for my phobia or hallucinations to get worse. Except that there is; I'm here, in a place I don't want to be, and countless doctors have told me how powerful stress can be, how it can cause physical side-effects.

But the shadows are real. I know they are.

The deep, even breathing of Liz and June occupies the room. That and the rain outside. It pours and thunders. Lightning flashes against the closed curtains. The storm presses against the building like it's trying to find entry somewhere in the crumbling brick walls of the hospital.

A deep, mournful groaning through the air, like the whine of a rusty door, or an angry wind trying to unearth a tree. But it's closer than that. Right above my head. The wet scratching sounds come back, and something about them unnerves me. A wet sucking, squelchy sound. I've never heard a squirrel make a sound like that.

"June?" I whisper. "You awake?"

"Yes," she whispers back.

"Do you hear that?"

"I do."

"What is it?"

Neither of us talks as we listen to the faint squelchy sounds. It's hard to hear, and I have to strain my ears, but it's there, sometimes above my head, sometimes in the walls.

"The ghosts." Her voice quivers.

"I don't believe in ghosts."

"Maybe you should start."

"Can't you tell someone?"

June laughs. "Who would believe me?"

I roll onto my back and notice a weak light shining through the window above the door. Staring at the light, I grab the photograph of my brother and clutch it to my chest, wishing he was here. Bart, my brother. The lawyer. The solicitor. The alcoholic. The hit and run driver.

SIX

I WAKE up sometime in the middle of the night. The rain has stopped. It takes me a moment to realise where I am. The weak light above the door. The stupid yellow walls. The closed bathroom door. Brookwood Hospital. How can I have forgotten?

The sleeping shapes of June and Liz melt into the dark. Liz has rolled onto her side during the night and now she faces me. Her eyes are open.

A burst of loud clanking in the wall makes me sit bolt upright and wrap my arms around my ribs. Pipes. Just pipes. But then a series of footsteps run by in the corridor. Heavy and purposeful. Ghosts?

I hold my breath as my heart skitters around in my chest. I turn back to Liz. Her eyes are wide and dark. She doesn't blink, and her breathing remains deep and even. But she stares and stares at me.

"Liz?" I whisper across the dark divide.

She doesn't reply.

"Liz?" I lean towards her. Maybe she's been lobotomized. Or she's actually an AI waiting for primary instructions. Or the shadows have come from her. But I suspect if the shadows come for you, they won't leave much behind.

She opens her mouth wide and screams. I erupt out of bed and slam against the far wall. That's what I get for not staying even, for not making sure all the touches rebalanced.

Her eyes peel back, the whites gleaming in the dark. She pounds small fists on the mattress and weeps into the duvet.

June rolls out of bed and creeps over to Liz. "Shhhh. Shhhh. It's ok now." June strokes her hair.

"Don't let them take me," Liz mumbles, her hand going to the bandage at her shoulder.

"Shhh."

"I thought we weren't allowed to touch each other," I say.

June frowns. "I don't know about you, but I could use the occasional hug. It gets lonely in here."

I WAKE AT DAWN STILL ON THE FLOOR, HUDDLED IN A ball with a blanket wrapped around me, as the weak light sneaks in around the cracks of the blind. Liz's scream echoes in my brain, sending tension skittering through my limbs. Today I will not forget the rituals. I will be strict, no matter how embarrassing they might be. Double tapping both my hands on the ground, I push myself to my feet.

Both Liz and June are still and sleeping. I know I'm

not going to get back to sleep, so I pick up June's book and immerse myself in the story of Jo March falling in love.

An hour later, Liz shifts and stretches her hands above her head. She arches her back, causing the bandage on her shoulder to pucker. Underneath the gauze, I spot three long scratch marks. Like claws. Despite the weak light pouring into the room, I shudder.

Without looking at me, Liz slips out of bed and shuffles to the bathroom. June stirs, throws back her covers and sits up with a grin and an exaggerated stretch. I change out of the hospital-issue gym clothes and back into the navy tracksuit. No one comments on my lack of shower.

"Breakfast time." June pats her stomach.

Liz tiptoes out of the bathroom dressed in her own navy tracksuit. Bloodshot eyes emphasize her pale skin. She might have been crying. She looks as though she's just gone ten rounds with the shadow creatures rather than been in bed for almost twenty-four hours. As she closes the door, she offers me a tentative smile.

I smile back just as tentatively. "I'm Georgia."

She nods at me, fixing me with wide, dilated pupils, filled with nothing but my reflection. Her irises are a milky brown.

She inches around my bed and sits on her own. "Sorry if I scared you last night. I get bad dreams." She places her hands in her lap and looks at June as if awaiting instructions. Maybe she is an AI.

June pats her shoulder. "We all get bad dreams."

I suck in my bottom lip. "Yup."

June grabs Liz's elbow, and the three of us make our way to the cafeteria. Before we can join the line for food, our blood pressure and weight are taken by a couple of young nurses I haven't met yet, who note things down on the ubiquitous clipboards. In the cafeteria, the smell of bacon has my stomach grumbling. I accept two rashers from the dinner lady and heap a pile of scrambled eggs on my plate.

"Thought you were vegetarian," the dinner lady snaps at June when she piles three rashers of bacon on her plate.

June smiles sweetly. "Depends on the day."

The dinner lady frowns at us and we scurry away. We find an empty table and sit down together. June pulls apart a square of buttery toast and stuffs chunks into her mouth. Then she wraps her hands around a steaming black coffee. Liz pushes her eggs around her plate, her wide, brown eyes staring vacantly.

I wonder if I should ask Liz something, maybe get her to talk about her dream, but a commotion on the other side of the room snaps my attention away. An orderly stands above a girl about my age. He holds a forkful of eggs in front of her face. She crosses her arms over her chest. She shakes her head at the orderly, and her quivering long, dark curls emphasise her refusal to eat.

"That's Kiara," June whispers to me. "She has anger issues. She's a classic ASBO. We get at least one outburst from her a day."

"I don't eat eggs!" Kiara shouts in the orderly's face.

I watch the dark-haired girl. Her tracksuit hangs off

protruding bones as though her body is no more than a hanger. Anger isn't her only issue. Suddenly, she leaps to her feet and hurls a series of expletives at the orderly. The orderly holds out his hands for her to calm down. She spits in his face, leaps onto the table, pulls down her tracksuit bottoms, and urinates on the table all over four other girls' food.

"Oh . . . wow," I say, trying to hold back a reflexive giggle.

"Told ya," June says, turning her mug in circles. "But that's an impressive display, even for her."

The orderly grabs the semi-naked Kiara and carries her, baby-kicking and screaming, out of the cafeteria.

"She'll be in solitary for that," Liz says.

But the commotion isn't over. One of the girls who was sitting at Kiara's table starts crying. The crying turns to loud, wretched sobs, and a nurse at her side can do nothing to console the mounting, emotional volcano.

"Shut up!" June yells across the room.

The girl scowls at her. "I can't eat that!"

June smirks. "Urine is sterile. Might be good for you."

"June!" one of the orderly's snaps.

June holds up her hands and turns back to us.

"You really shouldn't goad them," Liz says, winding a curl around her finger.

"Gotta do something to get my kicks around this place." June sticks a finger in her coffee and swirls.

"We'll get you a new plate of food," the nurse says to the sobbing girl.

But the girl won't be cajoled. She backs away

from the table, pointing at the urine dripping onto the floor from four corners. "It's dirty! It needs to be sanitised!"

Another nurse approaches her and talks in soothing tones. But the girl sticks her fingers in her ears. Even though the clean-up crew are already in attendance and sopping up the mess, the girl creeps away from the table as though it's about to explode.

She backs away, one small step at a time, her plimsoles squeaking on the polished floor. A dinner lady brings her a new plate of food, but she upends it, and it lands all over the floor. The nurse sighs and rolls her eyes.

"That's Sarah," June says. "She's got hygiene issues. Severe OCD. And Kiara knows it. This'll set her back for a week. Doc's not going to be happy."

Sarah, with a long immaculate ponytail streaming behind her, flees out of the room. June flicks out a hand to grab her coffee. I catch another glimpse of her Latin tattoo, and this time I make out the words:

Fortitudo

Virtute

One word under the other written in a curly script.

"Georgia." Paul stands behind me. "It's time for your session with Dr. Zaleski."

"It's Sunday. Is that normal?"

"He always comes in when there's a new arrival."

My hands fist inside my sweatshirt sleeves. "Ok."

"Follow me."

"Da-da-da-daaaaaa." June feigns playing the organ with grandiose gestures. I stifle a giggle, accidentally touch the tabletop with my left hand and have to touch it with my right. No more mistakes.

"When I get back," Paul says to Liz. "I'll change that bandage."

Liz nods, her hand floating to the gauze, a faint grimace turning the corners of her mouth.

I dump my tray in the rack and trail after Paul, stuffing the last piece of toast in my mouth. I glance back towards June; she has her eyebrows raised in parody of an undead, demented organ player. She swivels stiffly in her seat, still tapping her fingers against the table.

"Good luck!" She mouths at me.

"Thanks," I mouth back and then hurry after Paul.

"You'll be having some sessions with me, some with the psychiatric nurses, and some with Doctor Zaleski. He's going to assess you now and put together a therapy program," Paul says, as we wind our way through the building.

Dr. Zaleski's office lays off a corridor I haven't been down before. Paul opens the door for me and ushers me into a large, square room with heavy oak panelling. The stale stench of years-old cigar smoke clings to the carpet, competing with the more pleasant scent of a jasmine diffuser propped on the windowsill. The doctor himself sits behind an expensive oak desk positioned in the centre of the room. He has a hand to brow and hasn't yet looked up despite my entrance.

A window overlooks fields of unused land that leads to the canal. Droplets of last night's rain glisten on the end of grass blades under the shining sun. Signs of the storm will soon evapourate.

Behind the doctor, shelves line the entire wall. Heavy, hard-backed books with the spines glittering in intricate, gold lettering overwhelm everything else in the room. They are scientific journals and encyclopaedias. I spot the DSM-V. Another on psychosis. Bipolar Disorder. Anorexia Nervosa. Obsessive Compulsive Disorder. It is a particularly thick volume. No doubt he'll be referring to that one for me. The titles stretch on. It seems all aspects of mental health is covered on those shelves.

"Please sit, Georgia." Dr. Zaleski peers at me through bold, black glasses. The lenses are so thick his blue eyes appear twice the normal, human size. Like he's been invaded by a body snatcher from outer space and his human frame can't contain the parasite. He holds a hand towards one of two vacant, brown, leather club chairs positioned in front of his desk.

"I'd thought there'd be a chaise lounge," I say, a lame attempt at humour to loosen my nerves.

Dr. Zaleski clicks his ballpoint and smiles at me. "Can't have you falling asleep during therapy." He has a round face to match his round eyes and the beginnings of a double chin that wobbles when he speaks. Mostly balding, but grey tufts of hair stick up over his ears like a five-year-old has decided to glue cotton balls to his face. All he needs is a moustache and he'll look just like Fat Blue from Sesame Street. That, and blue skin.

I sink into the club chair and cross my legs. I scan the

room for mirrors or other reflective surfaces. Nothing. Nothing in the room save the books on the shelves and the dust motes dancing in the sunlight coming through the slatted blinds. There are slatted blinds in every room I go in; institutional, unfriendly. But I'm not going to complain. Windows can become mirrors too. A gold-plated name plaque sits on the desk. Dr. A. Zaleski. A multitude of smudge marks extinguishes its reflective properties.

"Why can't I talk to my mum?" I ask, bracing myself against the loneliness the question evokes. I've never been apart from my mother for longer than a week.

"We find it helps the patients to settle in better." Dr. Zaleski watches me from behind his desk. "When girls arrive here, it's common to see both the patients and families at breaking point. The few weeks with no contact will help both of you gain some distance. A chance to catch your breath. Does that make sense?"

I nod, but really, I want to cry. It's not like I can rely on Mum to help me with the shadows, but it would be nice to hear her voice, to know she's there. And Bart, I've never had the guts to ask him if he believes me. I just can't go there. My stepdad . . . well . . . he's never even tried to understand.

"How was your first night?" Dr. Zaleski gets up from his desk and walks over to the chair next to me. "It can take some time to get used to this place. Many patients are far worse off than you. I imagine you feel like you don't belong. You'll see things you never expected."

"Kiara," I say, thinking of the scene at breakfast.

"Yes. I heard about that incident. How did it make you feel?"

"I . . ." I begin to reply. But I'm not entirely sure. Did it scare me, seeing behaviour so outlandish, so uninhibited, so defiant in the face of authority? No, not so much. But I don't want to be brandished by the same brush either. All those movies I watched and all the websites I read trying to prepare myself for my stay here covered the whole spectrum of behaviour and incidences, and yet, nothing is as I expected. But so much if it feels familiar.

"We don't expect you to be the same as everyone else." Dr. Zaleski carries on. "Everyone is here for a very different reason. No two people or two therapies are the same. Don't worry about that. I just want you to concentrate on you. Here, you can take the time to relax and focus on you. You don't have to think about anything else, just getting yourself better."

I nod. Just as is expected of me. Compliance is key.

"Sound good?"

"Yeah."

Dr. Zaleski rises from the second club chair and goes back behind his desk. He rummages in a drawer for a moment until he comes up with half a pack of chocolate chip cookies.

"I knew I had some around here. Want one?"

"No thanks."

Dr. Zaleski shrugs. He pulls a cookie from the pack and eyes it suspiciously, as though it's just a figment of his imagination and might suddenly crumble away. He ingests it with two bites, flicks the crumbs from his mouth and wipes them from the top of his desk and onto the floor.

"Tell me about why you're here. In your own words, not any of the fancy diagnoses that your previous doctors have spoon-fed you. What is the crux of your problem?"

I look around the room as if the answer is a fact to be plucked from one of the serious, hard backed books on the shelf behind him.

"The mirrors . . ." I mumble without thinking.

Dr. Zaleski's fluffy eyebrows shoot to the top of his head and disappear over his bald head somewhere.

"Ah. The mirrors. Yes. Everything is connected to the mirrors. Not an uncommon fixation, believe it or not. There are others here who are afraid of the mirrors. Even my own son . . ."

I look for a photo. For some reason, I pictured Dr. Zaleski as an aging bachelor. Something about the way he ate the cookie and was actually aware he'd sprayed crumbs all over himself and the desk. There aren't any photos of a smiling family in the room. There aren't any pictures at all. Just the brown monochrome painting of a landscape over by the door. When I peer at it a little closer, I realise it's the scrubland of the fields between here and the canal.

"But anyway," he continues. "It's a common phobia. One we will tackle in two ways. Firstly, with medication . . ."

"No!" And be like all the other patients glued to the TV twenty-four-seven? A few reacted to the incident at breakfast, but most were too sedated to notice or care.

"No?"

"I don't like drugs. They change me. They change who I am. I've tried them before, and they've never helped."

"But that's why you're here. To find the right medication for you. I really wanted to try a new SSRI with you. It's very effective at combating the obsessive-compulsive behaviour. If we can take that out of the equation, we can get to the crux of the real problem." He looks at me from under his eyebrows again, his magnified blue eyes expectant.

SSRIs. Serotonin re-uptake inhibitors. I've tried three before. One made me gain weight—and did nothing for the shadow problem in the mirror. Another made me lose weight—and did nothing for the shadow problem in the mirror. The third made my eyesight blur and gave me crippling headaches. Not to mention, again, doing nothing for the shadow problem in the mirrors.

"I've seen the patients in the common room. I don't want to turn into that."

"Georgia," Dr. Zaleski says slowly, as if he's learnt my name for the first time and is rolling it around his tongue just to understand the feel of it. "Those patients are far different from you. I know this place can be a little scary. But I can't imagine a situation in which you would need . . . sedation. Those patients are prone to harming themselves, or others. It's for their own good. We're giving them a break from their reality, a chance to relax and reset their thinking. The medication will help, Georgia, it will open up your mind to the possibility of recovery. You've been struggling for so long."

"For as long as I can remember." My voice breaks. My entire body aches. It isn't until that moment I realize how tightly I've been holding myself. The tension in my limbs is a constant reminder that I need to be prepared at all times, prepared to fight for my life. Because one day, the shadows will step out of a mirror, and medication won't do a thing to kill them.

Dr. Zaleski presses his lips into a thin line. "Exactly. Let the medication help."

It won't help.

But I nod, already capitulating to his suggestions, too tired to spend the energy on arguing. Otherwise, I know I'll have the orderlies forcing them down my throat. Or I'll be sedated with worse.

"I'm here to help, Georgia."

"What's the second way? You mentioned two methods?"

"Yes, yes I did." Dr. Zaleski steeples his fingers under his chin. "Exposure therapy."

"No!" This time I shoot to my feet. My hands, hidden away in my sweatshirt's sleeves, fist at my sides. No one can make me look in a mirror.

Dr. Zaleski leans back in his chair and glares at me reproachfully. "I can't help you if you don't try. You'll never get over it if you don't face it."

"But you don't understand," I say. "The mirrors . . . it's not the mirror . . . it's . . ."

"What is it, Georgia?" He leans forward again, pen hovering over his notes.

Can I tell him? Can I really reveal that, within the mirror, I see shadows? Evil, threatening shadows that take on the shape of human-sized crows, with red eyes and wide, gnashing jaws that open from a black nothingness. Can I really tell him all that? And that they've been whispering at me, and I know they want to harm me if they can just figure out how to climb out of the mirror. And that last night one called my name. Can I tell him all that? Or will they stick me in solitary and throw away the key? Pump me full of drugs and write me off as just another statistic?

"Georgia?" Dr. Zaleski questions. "You were saying something about the mirrors?"

"I don't know how to explain it." I grit my teeth.

Dr. Zaleski nods as if he didn't expect anything more profound. "We'll get to the bottom of it. Together. That's our job. You and me."

I slump back in the chair, a wave of despondency rushing over me and quashing my urge to resist.

"The mirrors, the OCD, the panic attacks. Sometimes these things become part of our normal life, for so long, that we don't know why they started to begin with."

I remember why it began. The panic attacks because I was afraid. The OCD because I could think of nothing more to stop the shadows. It isn't a habit, isn't just some mental illness: it's a life-saving manoeuvre. And Dr. Zaleski isn't going to be able to vanquish the shadows. He won't be able to save my life.

SEVEN

I STARE at the mound of five-year-old National Geographic magazines, trying to decide if I care about the indigenous population of a remote tribe in Brazil or if the avalanche on Everest, killing thirty people, will pose more of an enthralling story.

I sigh, put the handful of magazines back on the shelf with my left hand—I've already touched them all with my right—and thumb through the old paperback novels again. Then I thumb through them with my left hand. Most of them are missing at least the cover, usually the first ten pages too. Maybe it'll make it more interesting, not knowing how the story starts out. I can invent my own beginning, and ending, I realise as I turn one book around and see the last chapter is missing too. The one I'm currently flicking through seems to be a detective story set in 1960's London. It'll have to do.

"There you are!" June rocks into a chair beside me. "Fancy a game of chess?"

She pulls the board from beneath a mountain of tattered games.

"I can't imagine all the pieces will be there."

"A-ha!" She removes a plastic bag from the waistband of her tracksuit bottoms and lays it on the table. Inside are all thirty-two wooden pieces needed for a game of chess. "Black or white?"

"Black."

June begins setting up the board.

"I haven't played this in years," I say.

"But you've played?" June asks.

I nod. "My brother taught me." At the mention of Bart, my throat tightens. He'll be in the city, going about his day, getting drunk at parties every night, trying to numb the memories of the girl he put in a wheelchair. And hopefully remembering he promised to try and find a way to get me out of here.

"White goes first," June says and moves her middle pawn forward two spaces.

The game commences, initially with tentative pawns taking single steps to protect the wealth of the empire at their backs. June doesn't comment when I have to repeat each move with the opposite hand. She doesn't even raise an eyebrow. I'm thankful for that. I dare to release a knight. June exposes her bishop, and I take it with my queen. I smile when she curses.

"How long since you played?"

I laugh. "Years."

June leans back to contemplate her next move, her lips puckered in thought. Some of the other girls watch TV—a reality chat show with family members yelling and cursing at each other. Sarah, the one who got so upset with the urine all over the table, stands by a window. Her perfect ponytail trails down her back and immaculately manicured nails split a gap in the blinds. Maybe she wishes she could be outside in the brightening day. She brings her hand away from the window and examines a thick line of dust on her index finger. Her eyes widen and her mouth drops open. Her hand shakes, and she holds it a few feet away from the rest of her body as though it doesn't really belong to her and she can merely shake off the suddenly unacceptable limb.

"No . . ." she groans.

She clenches her other arm around her waist and doubles over.

"No . . ." She attempts to wipe the dust back onto the offensive, slatted blind but only proceeds to come away with two more fingers tipped in grey.

"Ah, here we go." June grins.

"No!" Louder this time.

Paul scurries into the room and whispers in her ear.

"But it's dirty," Sarah says.

Paul holds her by the forearms and looks into her face. He talks to her in soft, dulcet tones.

"No!" Sarah says again.

Tears fill her eyes and stream down her face. A few of the girls notice the altercation taking place and turn their faces towards Sarah, desperate for something juicier than the mother currently slapping her son around the head on the TV eight feet above our heads.

Sarah holds out the offending fingers for Paul to

examine. She wipes them on her sweatshirt and visibly relaxes. Then she inspects the smear on her sweatshirt and the *no*'s begin all over again.

"This is not going to end well," June says, snapping a piece of gum in her mouth.

Sarah backs away from Paul and his placating words, holding her hand out like Lady Macbeth, clawing at the mark on the sweatshirt with her other hand. Finally, she squats on the floor, drops her head in her hands and cries great, heaving sobs. All ten fingers tremble. Her tears splash onto the floor.

Marion and Willow storm into the common room. Marion hoists Sarah back to her feet. In one swift movement, Paul goes to Sarah, plucks her off her feet and carries her out of the room.

"Solitary?" I ask June.

"Nah. She'll be taken to her room for a while. If she doesn't calm down, she'll be sedated." She takes my knight with her remaining bishop.

Marion and Willow remain in the common room, checking each group of patients for signs of civil unrest. Wouldn't it be funny if we all just stood up and started having our issues at the same time? Maybe we can all storm out of here.

Who am I kidding? Most of the kids are barefoot and subdued. I wouldn't be able to lead them out of here with a rope. And where would we go with our tracker bracelets signalling our positions to the nearest metre? It would be just a matter of time before we were all collected again. And there will still be the shadows.

Crash Helmet Annie starts banging her head on the

wall. Marion looks up and frowns. She watches Annie for a moment, a medley of pitiful expressions on her face. She hands Willow the clipboard and marches back into the office. Willow remains in the room, watching us from a corner, an almost serene expression on her face. Her chin is raised and her eyes are partially closed, as if the cacophony of the noise in the common room—Annie banging her head; girls laughing and pointing and screaming at the now semi-violent chat show; another skittering across the floor on all fours, her hands and knees dirty despite the lino being mopped twice a day—is some kind of symphony to her. When she catches me staring, she winks at me, her bright, blue eyes magnifying the small, tender gesture.

Paul comes back. He sidles up to Willow, their arms touching as they stand side by side. They exchange a whispered conversation. He props his foot on the radiator and flexes his muscles as she flicks her long hair over her shoulder and leans into his ear. I doubt the patients here would care if they suddenly stripped naked and did it right here on the dirty lino floor.

Willow fixes him with her blue eyes and lays a hand on his forearm, the nail of her index finger tracing a line down his arm. Even from across the room, I can see how hard she presses. Is it some kind of sadistic foreplay? Will they be wildcats with whips and chains in the bedroom? I giggle at the thought of the demure Nurse Willow going all tigress between the sheets. But then Paul takes a step back and a flicker of unease travels across his face.

"Let's get down to it," June says as she takes one of my pawns. "What are you in here for?"

I snap my attention back to the punk rock girl. She keeps her eyes on the chess board, a sour expression on her face as if she suspects she's made a wrong move. When I don't answer, she looks at me, pins me down with those dark, feisty eyes.

"It's really none of your business." The staff might think I'm crazy, my parents too. But I don't need the pitying looks and whispered asides revealing the truth will bring. Except I don't have a ready lie at hand either. "And we're not supposed to talk about our stories."

June snorts and leans over the chess board. She flicks a glance towards Willow in the corner and lowers her voice. "Don't be like that. We're all in this together. We don't have anyone else. Most of us abandoned by famous or wealthy parents that don't want to be embarrassed by their kid who's gone a little crazy and managed to get themselves in the newspapers."

"My parents aren't famous. Or particularly rich. My stepdad is a self-made man and my mum has a trust fund." But she's used most of it on hiding Bart's secret, on paying off the girl in the wheelchair so he won't lose his lawyer's licence. And I'm pretty sure the rest is dwindling fast, paying Dr. Zaleski's bills. A hard brick of guilt settles in my stomach. Then a flash of anger. Why wasn't Bart ever committed? Why do I have to be the one in a hospital? The answer is well rehearsed: because Bart is a lawyer and lawyers can't commit crimes. "You make it sound as if I've committed a crime."

"Haven't you?" Her eyes flash at me. "Many here have. Not because they're criminals and not because they wanted to hurt others, but because their conditions gave them no other choice. The newspapers sensationalise it: little rich kid gone wild on drugs and money. But that's not your story, is it? That's not why you made the newspapers."

"How did you know that?" I snap my eyes towards her face, searching, trying to determine if she genuinely cares or if I'm just the next bit of juicy gossip.

June looks me up and down. "I can read, you know. And despite the line of pills I swallow down every night, I do actually have a brain in my head. You're the one who broke all the mirrors in the shopping mall."

I advance on her queen. "I was having a bad day."

June grins. "We've all had a few of those."

She doesn't hesitate; moves her queen out of harm's way and manages to put me in check.

"Damn," I mutter.

She fiddles with my captured chess pieces. "Is that why you're here? Because you broke all of the mirrors?"

I keep my eyes on the board. "Sort of."

It really had been a bad day. I went to the mall with friends—old friends who extended an olive branch and invited me to go shopping with them. I thought if I could just have a normal day with my old friends, girls I'd known as long as I can remember, perhaps the rest would follow. But it didn't happen that way.

They wanted to buy dresses for prom. School was over. Most of us were enrolled in the local college, and the dance was going to be our big celebration. We traipsed through shop after shop. I fingered the fashionable clothing, enjoying the feel of the comfortable cottons and soft silks on my skin, wishing I didn't order everything I owned online, wishing I could face the mirror, watching as my friends pulled dresses off racks and slipped them over their heads. They would prance and pose and jostle for position in front of the temporarily benign mirror.

For the first hour, I saw nothing, but that might have been because I kept my head down and stared at my feet. I was hesitantly hopeful the shadows were decent enough not to accost me in this very public mall. But then when Karen looked over at me from where she was standing in front of a full-length mirror and asked my opinion on her eye-catching, guy-catching very red dress, I looked towards her and into the mirror. A shadow totally blocked her reflection. It didn't flicker, it didn't streak across the surface as they usually do, making me think it was just my imagination. It just stood there, staring at me with its hungry red eyes, swallowing Karen's image.

"Karen! Get out of the way!" I barrelled towards her.

Her mouth dropped open. I shoved her away. She tumbled to the ground in a split of red clothing and flying blonde hair. I screamed and slammed my fist into the glass. But it didn't break, and the shadow remained. Mocking me.

Karen got to her feet and held the remains of the ripped dress around her. "Georgia . . ."

I grabbed one of the wheeled-clothing racks and rammed it into the mirror. With an enormous crack, it split and shattered into thousands of pieces. As they cascaded to the ground in a tinkling cacophony, the shadow finally disappeared, snorting at me in derision as it departed.

Karen's mouth hung open and her fiery gaze scorched my cheeks. "What is wrong with you?"

I became aware of a stinging sensation in my hand. Looking down, I saw the jagged sliver of mirror squeezed tightly in my palm, blood dripping in a surprisingly forceful flow. The staff in the shop crowded around me. My other friends grouped around Karen.

"Easy now . . ."

I swished the shank back and forth. My heart beat wildly. There were a thousand pieces of mirror and now a thousand potential shadows. The flicker of harsh fluorescent lighting drilled into my head. People spoke, but their voices were distorted. I couldn't make anything out. I glanced at the broken mirror pieces. Darkness loomed within them. Someone grabbed me and I stabbed out.

I hurt someone. An ambulance was called—and the police. But before they got there, I managed to break every other mirror in the shop. After my hand was bandaged at the hospital, they kept me in the psych ward for a night. A hearing followed. The ten-year history of my mental illness was exposed, and the shop agreed not to press criminal charges if I underwent inpatient therapy. Welcome to Brookwood Hospital. Retreat for the crazy. Not surprisingly, in the weeks between the incident and hearing, I never heard from Karen.

I block June's offensive move with a castle. "They tell me I have OCD and a panic disorder."

She scrunches up her nose and her empty piercing flares for a moment.

"They tell you? What do you think?"

"That I have OCD and a panic disorder." That's the line I've been fed for years. It's the line I use. It's the line that makes me sound like I have normal mental health problems, not supernatural ones.

June raises an eyebrow and snorts. "Panic disorder doesn't make you attack people with a shiv made of jagged mirror. Neither does OCD. Most people in here aren't violent and could be managed while they live in the great outside."

I grip hard to the chess piece in my hand. "So why are they here?"

June shrugs as if the point is irrelevant. "But *why* did you break the mirrors?" She ignores the game between us and folds her hands on the table.

I mimic her shrug. But mine is defensive. "I don't like mirrors." I can't bring myself to lie to her face. Something about the way she stares at me makes my scalp prickle. Has she guessed there's more to my story? I've lied about the shadows for years; surely she can't see through my iron façade. Opening up to a person I've only known for twenty-four hours isn't an option, even if she claims to be just like me. She's not just like me. No one is. No one else sees what I see.

"Fair enough," she says, lowering her eyes. "Everyone's got their demons."

Never has a truer word been assigned to the shadows.

"What about you?" I ask, after I rescue my king for a second time. "Why are you here?"

June ignores my question for a moment, posing at being preoccupied with her next vital move on the chess board. When she moves forward to take my castle with her queen, her wrist tattoos flash again. A faint red line underscores the area beneath them. A scar. Only one kind of violence results in a red line like that.

"Sure you want to know?" She asks, her lips stretching into a mischievous grin.

"It can't be that bad."

"They say I killed my sister."

I suck in a breath. I didn't expect that. Shouldn't she be in jail? Or a facility for the criminally insane? Or something? But she doesn't seem insane to me, not even the slightest. In fact, she appears very, very shrewd and cunning.

"Did you?" I stare into her dark, challenging eyes.

"They never found her body." She says it as if there could only be a murder if there's a body. She finally puts me in checkmate with one small move of her queen.

"Did you?" I ask again. Are there worse threats in here than the shadows?

"Would you ever hurt your brother? Your older brother who you look up to and admire and who just wants to protect you?" She props her elbows on the table. A tear slips down her cheek, which she quickly wipes away.

"Of course not."

"Just because I don't talk about it—the event, the incident—it doesn't mean I'm guilty of a crime. She is my sister. They think I did it because of my diagnosis, because of what's wrong with me. But did it ever occur to them that I'm ill because of what happened to my sister?" Her voice is low and gruff, filled with the agony of a lifetime of pain. She plays with the chess pieces, twiddling her queen around her fingers. "Whatever. It amounts to the same thing. I'm here now, probably always will be."

June catches me staring at her scars and tucks her hands into the sleeves of her sweatshirt.

My heart softens. We are the same. Although I haven't been accused of murder, my problems started after the shadows appeared. Just like June. Anyone could have accused me of trying to hurt someone in that shop on purpose. I know how it feels to be falsely accused, never believed, totally alone.

Maybe June and I aren't alone anymore.

EIGHT

"GROUP THERAPY!" June calls, skipping down the corridor. She drags me after her, and I manage to hold onto her hand with both of mine to keep the balance even. When we reach the end of a gloomy corridor, June throws a door open to reveal a bright, sunny room with three other patients draped over armchairs: Liz, Kiara, and Sarah.

Marion whisks in a moment later carrying an armful of files and a packet of cookies. June leaps on her right away and takes three custard creams before passing them to me. What is it about biscuits in this place?

"You all know the drill," Marion says as she shifts her weight into a swivel chair. "Apart from you, Georgia. We start by introducing ourselves and saying something positive about our week."

"There's nothing positive about this place." Kiara glares at the offending packet of biscuits spilling crumbs onto a side table.

Marion sighs. "Now, now Kiara, that's exactly the

attitude we don't want. We must maintain a positive outlook."

June giggles and kicks her legs over the arm of her chair. Marian swivels her gaze to June. "And we don't want to take it too far the other way, either. We must adopt a professional commitment to recovering."

"We?" Kiara snorts. "Are you a patient too?"

Marian clears her throat. June giggles again. Liz smiles at me, her thumbs chasing each other in her lap. When I return her smile, I realise her eyes are hazel. Weird. I could swear they were a milky brown this morning. And her hair seems a little lighter too. Maybe it's the light. The September storm has cleared to reveal a cloudless day and light streams in through all the windows.

"Maybe we should start again," Marion says. "Sarah, would you like to start?"

Sarah raises her chin and flicks her ponytail over her shoulder. "I'm struggling to find a positive. Kiara pissed all over my breakfast and then the dust from the blinds . . . all over my hands." She holds them up for us to see. Judging by the redness, I guess she washed them at least a hundred times since.

"Yes, you did have quite an ordeal. But how did you cope?" Marion asks.

Sarah tilts her head. Twin pink dots form on her cheeks. "I did have to wash my hands, but I didn't do it as many times as normal."

Marion nods several times. "Good. Good. It's all about breaking the chains of the rituals. Excellent work, Sarah."

Sarah beams.

Kiara laughs.

Sarah pivots towards the bigger girl. "You peed on my food."

"I was making a point," Kiara says, crossing her legs. "The food is terrible. We need to make a stand."

"Did you have to use my food as an example?" Sarah says, her ponytail quivering as she bangs her clenched fist on the table.

Kiara slouches in her chair and crosses her arms to match her legs.

"Girls!" Marion holds up a hand. I'm almost sure she'd blow a whistle if she had one.

"What about you, Liz?" Marion peers at her, opening a standard manila folder.

Kiara tuts. "What about her? She barely ever opens her mouth."

June shoots her an evil eye.

Liz raises her brown eyes. "I slept really well last night. I know I was sedated . . ." She touches her bandage. A flicker of a frown crosses her face. "I don't really remember why. But I feel much better today."

"And do you feel in control of the others today?" Marion asks her.

Liz looks at me, colour flooding her cheeks, then gives a subtle nod.

"Oh for God's sake!" Kiara erupts.

"Sit down!" Marion says.

June claps her hands, a slow condescending clap that seems to approve of Kiara's outburst.

"This is such bullshit. We've all been here for

months and no one is any better." Kiara tips her chair over and storms out of the room.

Marion presses a finger to the bridge of her nose and inhales deeply.

"Good riddance," Sarah mutters, shifting in her chair.

"Is there anything anyone is struggling with?" Marion asks.

Liz raises her hand. "Despite sleeping well last night, I'm worried about other nights. I know I can't take the heavy sedatives all the time . . . and then I just can't relax enough to let go."

"No one can sleep in here," June says. "All those ghosts walking around in the middle of the night?"

"Oh, shush," Marion says. "What are you talking about, child?"

"The older patients who were lobotomized and given electric shock therapy. The unwed mothers who had their babies taken from them." She leans forward, kicking her feet over the arm of the chair. "The ones who died here, unhappy. Now they want revenge."

"I don't believe in ghosts," I say. But I do believe in shadows.

"Nor should you," Marion says as she gives June a scalding look.

June shrugs. "Maybe you should start." There's a mischievous glint in her eye. I'm almost sure she's joking. Almost. The wet, squelchy sounds. It has to be rats. Or squirrels. It has to be.

Marian focusses on Liz. "The normal sedatives don't help?"

"No." Liz places her hands on her chair, gripping tightly. "They make me dream . . . horrible, terrible things." She shudders and rubs at her puffy eyes.

"Maybe we should try a week of the stronger sedatives, to get you back into a routine." Marion scrawls some notes in the folder. "How does that sound?"

"Just enough so she doesn't hear the ghosts," June says. "Not too much so she can't defend herself."

I look at her expecting a laugh, but her face remains neutral, and I can't read her expression. Does she really believe in ghosts?

"June! That's enough now!" Marion says. "There are patients here who have spectrophobia." She glances at me.

"I'm not afraid of ghosts," I protest. Shadows aren't ghosts. There's nothing remotely similar between the two.

Marion holds up a hand. "It's the fear of an apparition in a mirror. I'd say that includes ghosts?"

June sucks in an audible breath and Liz offers me a worried smile.

"I'm not afraid of ghosts. And I don't want to talk about mirrors." My jaw aches with tension all the way down my throat to my clavicle.

"Please try not to get upset," Marion holds up a hand again. "We're here to help." Then she turns a patient smile on Liz. "It's not unusual for patients to dream. Sometimes it's a side-effect of medication, sometimes it's your subconscious working through your problems."

Liz's hair falls over her face and she tucks it behind an ear. "Sometimes they don't seem like dreams."

"I don't sleep well either," I say. "Never have." Not since I was six-years-old—when I first met the shadows. And now one has called my name. I've tucked that new development deep inside and refused to look at it. I'm good at avoidance and denial—in fact, they're kind of my superpowers. But now the subject of night-time has been raised and I can almost hear the shadow's whisper in my ear.

"Well done for sharing, Georgia. Hopefully, the sleep will improve while you're here." When the clock chimes one o'clock, Marian sighs and checks her watch. "I think some outside time for you all with Paul will do you some good."

"Like a walk?" I say, my limbs aching at the thought. I've never been much of an outdoors person, even though I'd do anything to get out of here. But the brief reprieve will be all the worse for knowing I have to come back through the heavy doors, past the terrifying bird statue, and accept my life here. Like holding a bone just out of reach of a puppy's mouth.

"Not all group sessions are held indoors," Marion explains. "I think it's time for a different kind of therapy." She stops me before I get up. "You're going to be ok, Georgia. You can get better, if you want."

Paul arrives and leads us out of the room, down a dark corridor and into the great outdoors. I blink against the glare of light. Raindrops cover the grass and leaves and they sparkle under the sun. The fresh smell of the recent rainfall surrounds us. We walk for a few minutes towards the canal. My heart soars for a moment with the intrepidly foolish idea of escape and then I feel the weight of my tracker bracelet. Paul stops just inside the tree line that borders the canal. He drops a box of tools on the ground.

"Den building," he announces with his hands on his hips and a satisfied smile lifting one side of his lips.

"I left the Brownie's a long time ago, Paul." June rolls her eyes, but she crouches and fingers the tools in the box.

"Hands off the saw." Paul grabs the potentially dangerous weapon. "We don't need a repeat of the Texas Chainsaw Massacre. Anything you need cut, let me know and I'll come and help you. Otherwise, I want you to start collecting big sticks, anything long and not rotten."

"Big, long, hard sticks." June giggles, and stares at Paul's crotch. Paul turns tomato red and splutters a retort.

I scan the area, resigned to the fact I will be spending the afternoon outdoors with the worms and the birds and getting dirt under my fingernails. At least there aren't any mirrors.

The four of us set to work, fetching sticks and twigs and the occasional complete branch with the help of Paul's brawn. June works quickly and efficiently. Surprising, considering her disdainful Brownie comment. She even seems to have a skip in her step as she wanders about the woods and she shoots me a genuine smile when we catch each other's eye. I claw through the dirt, looking for the right kind of stick, accumulating mud under my fingernails.

We stack our finds in a clearing at Paul's feet. After

an hour of heaving and sweating and sawing and piling, we're all hot and breathless, but we have enough raw materials to build a den. Paul hands us cups of water from a plastic bottle. June goes to relieve herself in a bush somewhere. Perhaps I'll do the same before we head inside, so I won't have to face a mirror. June's voice rings out from behind a clump of ferns, singing a creepy chant from a horror movie. It gives me chills, and I find myself looking around the woods waiting to lock eyes with one of her ghosts. Or to see the glint of light as sun reflects off a binoculars' surface, proving that we're being watched. June comes skipping back into the group, still singing her creepy song until Paul frowns at her and tells her to shush.

"I thought the whole point of being here is to learn to be happy," she says.

"There are a lot of reasons why you're here, June." He picks up a couple of the largest sticks and measures them against each other. "And we know being overly happy isn't a good thing for you."

June pouts and sticks her tongue out at Paul's turned back. I giggle. Even Liz laughs from where she sits on a patch of grass, plaiting her long hair. She ties it in a knot at the end and picks up June's song, her voice sweet and pure, further exaggerating the creepiness of the words which tell the story of a murderer coming up the stairs and coming for you. It's from an old, famous horror movie I'm glad I've never seen.

The break doesn't last long before Paul begins issuing more instructions. I hold the first branch ready and Sarah brings the next one carried between the tip of her thumb and index finger. We connect the tips and June winds the stem of a fern around it in a makeshift knot. Slowly, the four of us add more branches and sticks in this fashion until we create what looks like a wooden tepee. As I step back to admire our handiwork, I catch sight of another structure deeper in the woods, half crumbling and rotten. The evidence of a previous group bonding experience.

"Now we need ferns," Paul says. And I was just about to sit down on a very comfortable looking log, thinking our task was finally over.

June and I venture deeper into the woods, ripping ferns from the undergrowth.

"How's the therapy going?" June asks, pausing to look at me. "Do you know what the doc has in store?"

I glance at her earnest expression as I pile ferns together. Not talking about my problems hasn't helped so far. The bottling it all up method creates such a sense of loneliness that my thoughts often go to very dark places. But I can't tell her about the shadows either. "He wants to put me on a new medication. Exposure therapy. And lots of group stuff."

"You don't sound convinced."

"I've kind of run out of hope."

June walks up to me, takes my hand in both of hers, and sandwiches me between her tattoos. I can feel the faint line of her scars pressing into my hands.

"Would you mind doing that with the other hand? I'm not good with imbalance . . ." I wince.

She smiles and clasps my other hand, with just the

right amount of pressure. Her feisty eyes sparkle with kindness. "I didn't hurt my sister."

"I know."

Her head drops and she winds the stem of a fern around her finger. "We went to a funfair after hours. I couldn't wait for it to open the next day. I was only eleven, and my sister followed me to make sure I was safe."

"You don't have to tell me this."

June's lips purse. "Who else can I tell?"

I lead her deeper into the woods where the smell of damp grass and rain gathers around us. We sit down on a mostly dry log and June starts chipping at the bark. "We went into the hall of mirrors."

"Mirrors?"

"I know you don't like them." She blows her cheeks out. "But I've always been fascinated with how they can change your shape. Make you fat or thin, tall or short. But not anymore; I've haven't been to a funfair since." Absently, she fingers one of her scars.

"Becca came after me. She called and she called. And I ran, thinking it was all a game. I didn't realise her screams were real. Not until she was gone." June raises her brown eyes to me and now they're filled with sadness. "She never came home."

I edge closer, but not so close that I'm touching her. "Why is that your fault?"

"Rebecca would never have gone after me if I hadn't run away. They never found her body and I was the only one at the scene. I was already exhibiting signs of my illness—so my parents thought. Hell, I don't know what they thought." Swiping at her cheeks, June leaves muddy tracks. "And now I'm here." Her hands tremble. "I would never have hurt her."

I double tap the log we're sitting on then take both her hands. "I know."

"It feels better, talking about it, to you, not to them." June slides her glance at the hospital.

"I know what you mean."

A piercing whistle startles us both and I spot Paul with his fingers in his mouth. June and I get up and, armed with a heavy load of ferns, we return to the others. I dump my pile of ferns on the ground and collapse next to them. Paul shoots me a smile which warms me up on the inside. I never thought I'd be so pleased to receive a simple smile.

"The great out doors, huh? Good for the soul." Paul reaches for a couple of ferns. He lays them over our branches while the others plop to the ground and watch. Pretty soon we have a camouflaged tepee den. It's been years since I've done something like this. Bart and I used to play in the woods behind our house, but we never built anything as elaborate as this. We'd get bored halfway through or catch the trail of an imaginary bear.

Paul refreshes our plastic cups. I pick out a small aphid from a tiny whirlpool in the centre of my water. Sarah blows her fringe out of her face and runs a finger around the lip of the cup.

A crow caws from a nearby tree. Sarah leaps to her feet, upsetting the cup of water all over her tracksuit bottoms and the ground. The crow rustles in the branches over our heads and streaks down to the ground, not five feet from Sarah's petrified pose. The crow looks at Sarah. Sarah looks at the crow, or rather, she stares at it in abject horror.

A shiver runs through me. The bird stands perfectly still. Watching. Waiting. Waiting for what?

The shadow-like bird and Sarah size each other up. I look up at the tree, trying to dispel the sudden, intense feeling that more crows are perched above our heads, staring down at us. A gust of wind sweeps through the empty branches, and I try to laugh off the irrational sense of impending doom. The cold smell of approaching autumn hangs in the air, wound through with a reeking stench of damp soil. I look back at the crow. Its eyes are red. I blink. Three times. No, not red. Black.

Fear freezes me. The bird is no more than four feet from the tip of my plimsole and I can't move. My throat turns dry and my tongue sticks to the roof of my mouth. A sense of ominous expectation winds through me so thick it sticks in my throat.

An eerie silence hovers over the group. Paul, with his hands on his hips and his head cocked, watches the crow. The black bird stands in the centre of us, swivelling its head, taking all of us in. Sarah backs away and then yells at the bird.

"Go away! Go away, you filthy animal!" she shouts.

The crow tilts its head and studies her one last time before it flaps its wings and takes to the air. As it flies higher, it is joined by a couple of others, then a few more until there must be at least fifty birds making up the murder. Their caws are ear-splitting and my limbs tremble and give way. I wrap my arms around my knees and give myself a moment to catch my breath.

"Well that's weird," June mutters.

"You thought so too, huh?" I frown at the ground where the bird was standing.

"It's just a crow, Sarah," Paul says. "Just a crow."

"But it's so filthy," she says. "Birds carry so many germs. And look at me! I'm filthy too." She wipes her hands on her tracksuit bottoms, picking at the green moss that has rubbed off on her from the branches, and at the dirt on her hands.

"But look how well you've done, Sarah." Paul takes both of her hands and makes her stand still. "We've been out here for hours and you've only just noticed that your hands are dirty. That's a real improvement."

"Yay, Sarah!" Liz claps her hands.

Sarah offers us a triumphant smile, but it quickly turns to a frown when her gaze returns to her hands.

They've all turned their attention to Sarah's hygiene issues. But what about the crow? The way it watched us —almost like it knew something, like it wanted something from us. The chill at the back of my neck refuses to abate and I have to physically shake my head to get a grip. *It was just a bird, Georgia.*

NINE

THE CROWS ARE LONG GONE, and silence is restored to our small group. I scan the immediate area and step further away from the opaque windows of the distant hospital.

"Come on," Paul says, clapping his hands. "Let's go inside the den." He pours water from the bottle over Sarah's hands and manages to abate her panic.

Checking the bushes and branches for more crows, I creep after the others into our small den. They all grin at each other, but my effort is weak at best, until June catches the sleeve of my sweatshirt and yanks my hand into the air in a triumphant pose. She balances me with the other hand and some of the tension leaks out of me.

This is our secret clubhouse. Now we just need a bottle of cider to really enjoy the experience and to numb the memory of shadowy birds. Paul flips open a pack of cigarettes and offers them around with a wink and a promise not to tell the nurses. I grab one, and after they're all lit, am immediately thankful for the calm the nicotine restores in me.

June grabs a torch from Paul's box of tools. She flicks it on and holds it under her chin, all campfire style.

"Are you ready for a ghost story?" she asks with a dramatic flair.

I pull on my cigarette. "You and your ghost stories."

"Is it even a real story?" Sarah asks as she tugs on her long ponytail.

"Let her tell it," Liz says. "I like this one."

June waggles her eyebrows. "I'll let you decide for yourself. But don't say I didn't warn you."

I giggle and clamp a hand over my mouth. I've never been camping, but I loved the idea of roasting sausages on a fire, telling stories so scary that the wind might frighten us and send us scurrying to our tents. I love horror stories, because they aren't real, not like the shadows. But there's no fire in our small den and the world outside is decidedly damp still, ticking with dripping raindrops.

"The one with the crows and the pecked-out eyes?" Sarah asks, rubbing her arms as if she is cold, or frightened, or both. Perhaps the staring contest with the crow didn't affect just me.

"Not this again," Paul says, frowning at her. "June, are you entering into a manic stage?"

"I'm taking the meds, Paul," June replies. "How could I be having a hypo episode when I'm taking the meds?"

Paul stares at her hard, unblinking, letting his

cigarette dwindle to ash. Finally, he relents and gestures for her to carry on.

"I saw her just the other day," June continues.

"Whatever." Sarah flicks her ponytail over her shoulder using the back of her hand, which is mostly clean.

"Haven't you heard the footsteps? The rustling in the walls?" June asks.

"Of the nurses on patrol?" Sara counters. "Yeah, of course."

"Not those footsteps." June smiles devilishly and two dimples spring onto her cheeks. "The softer ones. And the moans of anguish. There are no elderly patients here, but an old lady has been spotted by several patients before."

"Yes," Paul agrees with strained patience. "By the patients."

"It's not like we're suffering from some mass delusion," Liz says. "I've seen her too."

"You could be," Paul says. "Hallucinations are a common side effect of the meds that many of you are taking. And June, she could have been anyone's grandmother paying a visit."

I stub my cigarette out in the dirt. "I thought we weren't allowed visitors."

"Depends on the patient and settling in periods," Paul replies. "Most aren't allowed visitors for the first thirty days."

"Grandmother's don't float towards the canal a foot off the ground with five birds on each arm and disappear into a spooky fog." June keeps the light under her chin, a wide grin lending her face a demonic look.

"You'll frighten the new girl," Paul says, his voice edged with wariness.

"I'm not scared," I say. Not of an elderly ghost anyway. Shadows? Check. Old oil portraits with staring eyes? A little. The idea of never leaving the grounds of Brookwood Hospital again? Definitely. But of a harmless old ghost? No, not really. A ghost story is just a cake walk in a realm where monsters in mirrors exist.

Paul lights another cigarette, cupping his hands around the small flame. "As I say, mass delusion, or perhaps the gullibility of young minds together under one roof."

June tilts her head to an awkward angle, pinning him with an unreadable stare. "You think I'm gullible, Paul?"

He blows smoke upward where it circles inside the top of our den. "Not usually."

"What's the story anyway?" I ask.

June rests her chin on her knees. The flashlight reveals the excitement in her eyes. "She was a patient here once. Back when having a child out of wedlock was a crime. Back when this hospital had a working farm and nursery."

The flashlight flickers and Sarah and Liz both go *oooo* at the same time.

June slaps the flashlight against her palm until it shines brighter again. "She used to run the nursery, taking care of the babies and children of the patients who gave birth here. That is until her own child was adopted, and she went mad with grief."

June pauses and flicks a glance towards Paul.

"Yes, she had a child who was taken away from her," he says. "But that doesn't make her a ghost."

"Well," June continues, unperturbed. "After she went mad, longing for her child, she was no longer allowed to work in the nursery. She was assigned to the fields instead. In particular, she was in charge of making scarecrows, and she spent the day walking the rows of crops, shooing away birds and rodents from nibbling at the seeds and saplings. Every day she turned crazier with grief, until she no longer shooed the birds away, but began to talk to them instead. They started following her on her walks, perching on her outstretched arms, cawing at her as if in conversation. She sang to them—a lullaby she used to sing to her son. She fed them spare seeds from her palms. Some say her eyes turned black, just like the crows." June lowers her voice and we all lean closer. "She was never released. She died here, an old lady, never knowing the fate of her son."

"That's terrible," I say. A heavy silence falls over the group as we contemplate the life she led. At least I have a way out of here; my mother would never leave me in here indefinitely.

Ninety days.

"It doesn't explain how she became a ghost," Sarah says.

The sky clouds over and the light in the den dims. Sarah gives up on picking the dirt out of her clothes and flicks her fingernails against each other instead, rhythmically, one after the other. It reminds me of when Bart took me to see the musical *Stomp* in London. Making music out of everyday materials. When we got back to his apartment that night, he grabbed a bunch of empty beer bottles from the recycle bin and filled them with different levels of water. We had such fun tapping them to see the different sounds they produced. It's one of my best memories.

June taps the flashlight. "I'm getting to that."

"June . . ." Paul warns, but she ignores his cautionary look and continues.

"They say she was so maddened by grief that although she died and her body is buried in the hospital cemetery, her spirit never left, always searching for the son that was taken from her. She stayed bound to the place she lived and died, walking with birds perched on her arms, calling for her son, singing to him. But if you follow her, and some have, you best avoid her gaze as her eyes have been pecked out. Her sorrow is stored in those empty sockets and if you look, you'll go crazy too." The flashlight sinks the hollow of June's eyes into shadow until her face resembles a skull.

I laugh, trying to shake off my nerves. "Aren't we all crazy already?"

"Maybe. But do you want to take that risk?" June flicks the flashlight off and we're thrown into the gloom of the den. "Most have been maddened by the grief they see in her eyes. It's a brave and foolish soul that risks looking upon her eyeless face and feeling the full weight of her anguish."

Paul chuckles. "And that's where this story turns to fantasy."

"Did you not see the crows earlier?" June asks.

"She walks the grounds at night," Liz says, writing her name in the ground with a twig. A curtain of hair falls over her cheek. "You can hear her crying for her son." She says it matter-of-factly, as if the existence of ghosts is indisputable. "It's so sad."

"It's just a story," Paul says, tapping his fingers against his cigarette box. "Most old hospitals have equally eerie stories. While it's true that some of the patients had tragic lives, they died and were put to rest. Peacefully."

Liz shrugs, and digs the letters of her name more deeply into the soil. Then she adds an *E* before the *L* and an *A* after the *Z*. Eliza? Is that her full name?

June snorts. "You don't know what you're talking about."

"And you do?" Paul shoves the cigarette pack into his breast pocket. A sliver of tension hangs between them. I pick up on some kind of unfinished business.

June doesn't reply right away. She lets her gaze fall outside the den, towards the brick of the hospital, almost as if she's expecting the old ghost lady to appear this moment and prove her existence to Paul. And I'm halfway convinced. The gloomy weather and the old building and the creepy bird add to the ambience. Weird shit happens all the time. I count to ten, but everything remains still.

"I know what I know." She leans close to Paul, so her nose is only inches from his. "You need to salt and burn the bones, not bury them under six feet of earth. Only then will you get rid of a ghost."

"Oh, come now," Paul says. "I've worked here for two years, and I've never seen an old lady ghost with no eyes and a bunch of pet crows."

June laughs, short and sharp. "Of course not, Paul. You're not a patient."

"Enough of this, you don't need to be giving yourselves nightmares tonight." Paul clicks his fingers to declare the conversation over. He pops up on one knee, brushing the dirt from it with his hand, ready to move us along.

We trail after him through the damp grass in a loose line towards the hospital. June sings her creepy song again. The dampness seeps into my bones, and my socks are damp from the wet grass. Paul opens the door for us, and the musty smell of the hospital comes rushing at me. We weave our way through the dark corridors towards the main entrance. There's the bird statue. I lift a hand and trace the rough stone of its beak, then do it with my other hand. The other girls file past me towards the common room.

Paul stands behind me. June hovers at his side. She uses a finger to trace her own line over the rough stone of the statue. And then she transfers the finger to Paul's bicep.

Paul removes her hand. "What are you doing, June?"

She seductively shrugs one shoulder and pokes it through the neck of her sweatshirt. The pale skin seems so naked. Her eyes smoulder with salacious intent. I almost laugh at her obvious moves.

"I'm feeling some urges." She bats her eyelids at him in the parody of a 1950's movie star.

"Well," he says, taking a step back. "You won't be finding that kind of action in here."

"I'm so bored. And horny." She sticks her bottom lip out and steps closer to him. This is proving more amusing than the talk shows in the common room. June winks at me. The common room door opens, and Willow comes out. She pauses in the threshold, sizing up the situation with reptilian consideration. It's not difficult to read; June standing intimately close to Paul, her eyes all dark and wanting. Willow frowns. June smiles and Paul blushes bright red.

Willow grabs June's wrist and yanks her towards the common room, muttering something about sexual promiscuity and upping her meds.

"I'm only looking to fulfil my womanly needs," June says, as the nurse tugs her away.

Quiet returns to the ornate foyer. The grandfather clock ticks away the seconds. Together, Paul and I stare at the bird statue. My mouth goes dry. It looks so much like a shadow. But if I can face it here, maybe I can face it in the mirror.

"I call him Bert," Paul says. "He used to live in the old cemetery, looking out for all those who had passed."

I shiver. There's nothing benign about this statue. "Like the ghost lady?"

Paul chuckles. "It's just a story."

"Just a story," I repeat. Bird statues, crows, shadows,

and ghost ladies who walk with black birds. Is there a connection?

"Are you afraid of birds, Georgia?" Paul says in my ear. "It's supposed to symbolise protection."

My hand rests on the bird's beak. I almost laugh out loud. There is nothing about this stone shadow that offers any semblance of protection.

"That would be nice," I say.

"What would be nice?"

"To feel protected." I stroke the weathered beak.

"What do you need protecting from, Georgia?" Paul's voice is soft and gentle.

I jerk my hand away from the rough stone when the grandfather clock gongs a quarter hour.

"I don't know," I mumble. I think of the crow outside, how unperturbed it acted around us. And naturally, my thoughts turn to the shadows. Why does no one understand? Why does no one else see them? "It would be nice to know that someone, somewhere, is looking out for me, for all of us."

"That's what the doctors and nurses are here for," Paul says. "And me." He lays a hand on my shoulder, which makes me jump about five feet away.

"Sorry."

I nod. "S'ok. Just a bit jumpy."

Paul sighs. "June and her stupid stories."

My gaze falls to the dark carpet. "It's not that. Stories don't scare me."

Paul steps a little closer. "What does scare you?"

I look at him, so tempted to tell him, yearning to have someone, just one person, who might understand. I bite my lip and quash the urge to speak. No one will ever understand.

"The usual stuff," I say.

Paul looks me up and down. Can he see the lies on my face? Can he see the fear in my eyes? "You can talk to us. We're here to help."

If only that were true.

TEN

THE SMELL of fried onions and stewed meat hangs in the air as I eat dinner with my roommates. Sparse conversation interrupts the clang of plates on tables and the scrape of plastic forks. June keeps her eyes on her plate, watching her fork dip in an out of a puddle of gravy. Maybe Willow stunting her obvious come-on to Paul hit her more deeply than she's willing to admit. Human contact is a basic need. Love is primitive. Desire, lust, companionship are the things we seek the most. The yearning to be held, wanted. I've seen it before with the friends I drank with under the bridge; the quick shag behind the mouldering brick just to feel connected for a minute or two. But it never works. I tried it once and felt more alone than ever.

June blows out a breath and scratches her fork across the gravy until lines of the green plate underneath can be seen. The orderlies lining the room lean back against the walls with their ankles crossed and their impressive muscles on display. Perhaps it's part of the job description, to be able to bench an inexorable amount.

"You settling in ok?" Liz asks, fixing me with her pale hazel eyes. I detect a hint of an accent I haven't noticed before.

I nod. "But night time is always the worst."

She rolls her eyes. "Tell me about it. All those gurgling pipes. And when the wind blows it sounds like June's ghost."

"They're not my ghosts," June mumbles.

I push out a laugh. I'm pretty sure neither of them believes in June's story, but there's a certain wariness around their eyes that has me questioning what they really think the wet, squelchy noises are. Pipes. Could be. Maybe. Probably is. It's an old building. But I've never heard pipes make wet, squelchy sounds before. What else could it possibly be? I circle back to the idea of squirrels and rats. Nothing else makes sense.

June's gaze flicks from window to plate. Window to plate. Five times in quick succession. Maybe something more than her rejected flirtatious efforts is bugging her. Or maybe she really does believe in ghosts. Maybe she's latched on to the idea because she can't put the death of her sister behind her. Looking through the high windows at the scrubland beyond, I can well believe a wronged patient might be haunting the dismal grounds.

The eeriness that seeped into the den earlier has followed me inside. A prickly anticipation settles into my shoulders, burrowing in my bones. I find myself analysing her story, wondering if it could be true. When I think how the shadows appear in every mirror I walk by, why could I not believe in ghosts too? But that would presuppose the shadows are real. And since I've been here, a niggle of doubt has seeped into my logic. What if it really is all in my head? And now I'm believing in ghosts too. Soon it will be vampires, werewolves, witches, and any number of other mythical creatures.

I try to shake off the panic that I might be getting worse, not better, and tap the fingers of both hands a lucky twelve times.

Maybe June feels it too, or maybe mood swings are normal for her. I've only known her a short time, and I have no idea what the inside of her file—or her mind—looks like.

Shaking the perturbing thoughts from my mind, I sop up the remnants of my oily gravy with a passably fresh piece of bread.

"Don't take the medicine they give you, Georgia. Promise me." Liz reaches out a hand and grabs both my arms, hard. Her arms shake with the effort.

"Why not?" I ask, shooting June a sidelong eyebrow.

"Because," she says, shifting her eyes down to her plate again. She wraps her fingers around her tray. "Because it's not too late for you."

The medicine bell rings. Without another word, Liz stands and carries her tray to the stack. She follows the line of kids out of the cafeteria. It's a full five minutes before the hairs on the back of my neck decide to leave me alone. But I still feel an icy hand clasping the base of my spine. Maybe the ghost lady has found her way indoors after all.

"That was weird," I say

June gives up on swirling patterns of gravy and chucks her fork on her plate. "She's not wrong."

"I thought the medicine was supposed to help?" Not that I believe it. I mean, maybe it helps with normal mental health problems. But it doesn't do a thing to get rid of the shadows. My shadows. Or June's ghosts.

June laughs her classic derisive laugh. "Open your eyes, Georgia. Does anyone here look like they're ready to get out of here anytime soon?"

As we stack our trays, I look around at the line of docile girls trudging towards the nurses with their plastic pots of medicine. Crash Helmet Annie has to be swivelled around and pointed in the right direction. A small handful engage in conversation, potentially unaffected by tranquilising medication. Like June and me.

I stare at June's tattoos and piercings, the short hair, the fight in her eyes. "How long have you been here?"

"A long time. A really long time." Her brown eyes are flat and dull, utterly devoid of their usual liveliness. "Too long." She looks as pale as the ghost in her story.

I narrow my eyes at my new friend, studying her. "And what happens when you turn eighteen?"

June's gaze drops. "Then they'll send me to one of the adult facilities. Until the money runs out. After that . . ." she shrugs

Ninety days. I need to get out of here in ninety days. I'm holding on to that.

"My parents don't want me back, not to remind them of everything they lost." She juts her chin out and blots her eyes with the heel of a hand. No tears escape. "This way, they can ignore my existence and try to pretend my sister never died."

I want to comfort her, but my instinct is she isn't the type to take comfort from a hug. She's more likely to skewer you with her stiff, spiked hair. And all that attitude. If she really has been here for ages, surely the medication would have done something for her? But then again, the meds have never done anything for me. We all just need some human contact, some under-standing, some validation that we are still worth loving.

"You're not taking the medication, are you?" I realise aloud.

June eyes the line of girls waiting for their pills. "No, I'm not."

It will be our time soon. Liz is a few people ahead of us, and I watch as Willow hands her a pot with an extra sedative. Liz examines it for a moment and then swallows it down. As we approach the nurse, I smell the chemical odour of the tablets and the soap on Willow's skin.

"How? How do you get away with it?" I whisper.

"I cheek it." June leans into my ear. "You hide it between your upper teeth and your gums. Do it tonight. Take the pills back and practise. Liz is right, it's not too late for you."

"What does that mean?" An undefined sense of danger looms over me and I can still feel the place where Liz gripped my arms. "What about you? Liz?"

We shuffle forward another couple of feet. June

drags her fingers along the wall. Marion's voice gets louder as we near.

"Liz has been drugged for so long she's lost the will to fight. As for me, I don't need the drugs. But they think it will open me up. I go along with things until a certain point. Sometimes I take the sedative. I wouldn't sleep otherwise; I have terrible dreams." Her eyes lock on mine. There are so many emotions in her quivering pupils, it scares me to my core. "We all have nightmares. But as for the mind-altering pills—"

"Anti-anxiety," I break in.

"If that's what you want to call it." June raises her eyebrows and looks down her nose. "They change you. If you want to go out the same way you came in. Don't take them. If you want to leave at all. There aren't many who have learned to cheek them, but you can tell."

June has punk rock hair and lots of empty piercings. Tattoos on her wrist and a thin red scar. Perhaps she's prone to being overdramatic. Maybe I'm making a snap judgement. Maybe it's just part of her diagnosis—whatever it is—but I also know she believes every word she just spoke. You can't fake honesty like that, not when you stare at someone right in the eyes and they don't even flinch.

"Kiara," I say. Her name pops into my head, her feisty, combative nature not mellowed by pills because she isn't actually taking them.

"Yes," June whispers back.

Then it's her turn and she seems to gulp down her pills. She opens her mouth wide and Willow smiles like she's pleased with her star pupil.

"Here." Willow hands me a plastic cup. A new, blue pill sits alongside the two white sedatives. "The sedatives are entirely your choice, but Dr. Zaleski has described a new anti-depressant for you to start taking today." The scent of honey and vanilla oozes out of her skin, as though she's just applied hand cream. Her gentle fingers press the back of my hand, unbalancing me, causing the skin on my other hand to electrify.

The three anti-depressants I've had experience with thus far have all been round, white pills. As I pick up this new blue one, there's something in the quality of the colour, some unnatural brightness to it that makes me question whether it really is an anti-depressant—or something much stronger that might turn me into one of the unemotive girls at my back.

I try to shake off the foreboding feeling. June's ghost story has seeped under my skin and made me see the weird and unusual in something as mundane as a tablet. Add June and Liz's caginess about the medication . . . I mentally slap myself. Brookwood Hospital is not conducting illegal experiments on its patients. Liz is not some cutting-edge AI experiment. Ghosts do not live in walls. I attempt a laugh, but it comes out hollow and not like a laugh at all. I feel like the mad women on the street corner, giggling hysterically at something only she can see. For the second time in half an hour, I wonder if the shadows really are a figment of my imagination. Maybe I really am crazy. Proper crazy. Maybe June and Liz are too. Who's to say? This hospital possesses an entirely different rule stick of normality, and I'm not sure how to judge it accurately anymore.

Willow pats my other hand and I immediately relax. I roll the small, blue pill between thumb and forefinger, examining it for signs of its inner mysteries. I try to shake off my self-doubt, but something about this place has me feeling creeped out, and I don't trust myself to decide what's real or normal anymore. June's ghost story, Liz screaming in the middle of the night, the sounds in the walls—it's all adding up to something straight out of a horror film. Within thirty-six hours, I've been made to question my own sanity when I never doubted it before.

Maybe June and Liz are right. Maybe I should avoid the medication all together. I've never been a fan of drugs. The headaches, the nausea, the dizziness, the subdued reflexes that leave me unprepared for a swift attack by the shadows. I want to get out of here as fast as possible, but I know pills aren't going to take the shadows away. Faking it seems to be the only option. I have to believe the shadows are real. I have to. The alternative is something I just can't handle.

"I'll skip the sedatives tonight," I tell Willow.

It's best I try cheeking one pill at a time. I'll work up to more, like June. I pick up the small, blue pill in my left hand, transfer it to my right, and pop it in my mouth. Taking a sip of water, I manage to lodge the pill between upper teeth and gum. It fizzles against my skin, dissolving.

"Let me see, sweetheart." Willow shines her light in my face.

I open my mouth. Tensing my cheek against my teeth as much as I dare, I try to prevent the pill from slipping. Willow examines my mouth. She makes me move my tongue around. Then she shines her LED flashlight in my mouth.

"I'm sure Georgia isn't going to give us any problems," Marion says, without looking up from her clipboard. "No need to give her the third degree."

Willow shines the flashlight around once more. She hesitates a moment. But then she smiles, a new brightness making her blue eyes warm. She sneaks a glance at Marion, delves a hand into the deep pocket of her uniform and removes a chocolate bar. Without any of the other girls noticing, she slides the treat up the sleeve of my sweatshirt.

"Well done, Georgia." She pats me on the back. "You're doing well to fit in here."

As soon as I round the corner, I spit the pill into my hand. Then I transfer it to the other. It's mostly intact, the edges a little rough from dissolving in my saliva. But I'm less worried about ingesting a small amount of the medication and more worried about the fact that I'm sure Willow saw the pill in my cheek. And then she gave me a chocolate bar, too, like it is a reward for flouting the rules. But why?

ELEVEN

CURLED UP IN A FOETAL POSITION, Liz lies inert under her blanket.

I shut the door behind me. "She's asleep already?"

"The strong sedatives are quick." June stands in the bathroom, in front of the mirror. She applies cleanser and toner to her face and wipes it off with a cotton pad. A small shadow flits from the top to the bottom and I quickly avert my gaze. "Did you manage it?"

I hold up the offending, blue pill. "I think so."

She claps her hands together. "Well done!" Then she peers into the mirror again and swirls on her moisturizer. She smiles at me in the mirror, but the veins in her neck stretch tight, like wire. A pulse throbs in her temple.

My heart pounds a little faster, waiting for the shadow to come back. "But I think Nurse Willow saw."

The shadow appears again, bigger, and flies from the bottom to the top, fading from view right under June's cheek. I brace myself, half afraid its needle-like teeth will bite her.

June stumbles and catches the edge of the sink to steady herself. She comes out of the bathroom and frowns at me.

"You sure?" She holds out her hand for my pill. I transfer it to my left hand and pass it to her. She goes back to the bathroom and throws it in the toilet. Flushes it.

"No. I'm not sure." I can't bring myself to look at the mirror again, so I move away from the door. "I just don't think I hid it that well. And she gave me a choco- late bar."

June comes back out of the bathroom, still wearing her frown. She watches me tapping the bed with both hands, then Bart's picture. Everything needs to be even, symmetrical. Otherwise, I feel overbalanced in one direction. Unprotected, as if the side I haven't performed the double action with will be the one attacked by the shadows when they come for their reck- oning. I know it's silly. I know it's superstitious. I know it won't really help when it comes down to me versus an ungodly creature from some alternate reality which just might exist only in my head. But I can't stop all the same.

"That means she likes you. Or she's trying to buy your submission." June hands me my toothbrush with toothpaste already applied. "I used to get chocolate bars."

"Thanks." I accept the toothbrush with my left hand and transfer it to my right.

"I know you don't like mirrors." June hikes a thumb over her shoulder, indicating the bathroom with all of its glistening, reflective surfaces.

"No, I don't," I say around my toothbrush. When I'm done, June brings me a cup of water and takes my toothbrush back to the bathroom.

She stays in the bathroom, pottering around, re-apply moisturizer another three times. Ten minutes later, she emerges, her face gleaming and her upper lip beading with sweat. Earlier, Paul asked her about a manic episode. Do manic episodes involve excessive hygiene routines?

"G'night." June crawls into her bed and turns off her bedside lamp, even though it isn't yet ten o'clock.

"Good night." I flop down to my bed.

In the small triangle of light emitted from my lamp, I pick up *Little Women* and find my page. Ignoring what's going on behind the closed bathroom door, I lose myself in the story of Jo March and her insistent refusal of considering Laurie an appropriate suitor.

"Georgia . . ."

I look at Liz, but she's already been asleep for an hour. June, not so long, but her body lays still beneath her blankets and the deep, even breaths are a sure signal that she isn't the one whispering my name. Perhaps it's the ghost lady walking the grounds of Brookwood Hospital, having given up looking for her son and searching for me instead.

"Georgia . . ."

My head snaps towards the closed bathroom door. An insistent need to pee presses against my bladder. I haven't been for hours. I've curtailed my drinking in an effort to minimise my bathroom experiences. But the lack of fluids causes a headache to knock around my temples and I still have to put a hand between my legs to stop myself having an accident.

"Georgia . . ." Louder this time. Distinctly male. And distinctly insidious. It drips with malevolence.

No way am I going in there.

Crossing my legs, I read another sentence in *Little Women*. Five times. I can't concentrate on the story. Breath held, I wait. My ears prick up, tingling with the anticipation of an ominous event I just know is coming. Like when the water is sucked out from a beach and you know the next thing you'll see is a mammoth tidal wave. But here, in Brookwood Hospital, there is no wave. There are shadows. And I know they want me to go in the bathroom. To the mirror.

I stare at the door handle of the closed door, *Little Women* abandoned on my lap, and my hands tucked tightly under my legs to stop me peeing myself.

My bladder becomes painful. I hold my breath and only dare to breathe when it's absolutely necessary. Twenty minutes pass. There hasn't been a single further whisper. Maybe the shadows have given up on me for the night.

Footsteps quieten in the corridor outside and one by one, lights snap off until mine is the only one remaining. A soft knock on the door, a signal that it's now time to turn in. I switch off my lamp and sit there in the eerie gloom of the faint light leaking in through the top window.

Abruptly, breaking the descending silence, shouts peel through the corridor. Muffled shouts.

"No . . . please . . . no . . . please . . . not the m—"

The voice cuts off. Images of chloroform covered hankies plastered over mouth and nose fly into my mind. Eyes wide with terror as the hapless victim is dragged off and shoved in the back of a minivan. But I've always had a wild imagination. Or perhaps I just see the things others don't; the thin veil between the world we live in that separates normal people grounded in the roots of reality from the strange and unusual. For me, that veil doesn't exist.

"Georgia, someday I'm sure you'll be a writer. Or make movies," Mum used to say when she found me playing with my Barbies in my room. I hadn't set them up on their horses or pink convertibles. I hadn't braided their hair or clothed them in their shiny, meringue dresses. Instead, I let their hair fall loose and tangled leaves in the ends. Half the time they were naked, or wearing strips of clothing to symbolise their desperate plight through the woods, fleeing a deadly attacker. I used my duvet to build a mountain, and in the middle of it was Alice's rabbit hole, which led to a whole new world. I had rocks and pebbles and stuffed animals and kitchen utensils all to add to my magical realm. Preferring to be lost in my mind, thinking, imagining myself in the story I read the night before, I rarely asked to have friends over.

My mum thought I had a vivid imagination. I think I just wanted to change my reality, swap the baleful shadows for something more benign. Or perhaps something known. The Queen of Hearts isn't all that pleasant, but I knew I could out run her. I knew, if I had a Vorpal sword, I could slay a whiffling and burbling Jabberwocky. The Wild Things would be tamed with my six-year-old stare. And if I were Hiccup, I knew I would be brave enough to befriend the dragons. But what I didn't know is what the shadows were or what they wanted. And I don't know if I'm strong enough to fight them. How can you fight a supernatural creature when you don't know what the rules are? How can you fight what might only be in your mind?

"Please . . . no . . . please don't make me look—" the cry becomes desperate and helpless.

I shuffle out of bed and crack open the door. The smell of wood polish recently used on the heavy oak panelling wafts through the gap. Down the corridor, in the dim light of an unseen lamp, a girl struggles against Paul. He holds her arm behind her back and shoves her forward. The girl kicks out a leg and tries to wriggle from his grasp. Willow stands on her other side. She gives a placating smile at the girl. The nurse holds an object in front of the girl's face, but I can't make it out. The girl shrinks back, turning her head away from Willow, hiding behind a curtain of hair.

Willow sighs and indicates for Paul to use the large syringe he holds in his other hand. I suck in a breath, close the door a fraction more, but keep my eye pressed to the gap. Paul plunges the needle into the girl's arm and she immediately sags against him. He catches her before she hits the ground and hoists her into his arms.

Willow opens the door leading to the stairs. Paul carries the limp girl and follows the nurse. He glances once down the corridor and catches my eye. I gulp and shut the door. Leaning my back against it, I wait a moment for my heart to climb out of my throat.

What the hell was all that about?

The desperate urge to urinate presses between my legs. I can't hold it anymore. Tiptoeing over to the bathroom, I lay my hand on the door handle. I'm half expecting an electric shock or a nasty surprise or to wet myself then and there. None of the above. I suck in a breath and open the door. When I catch sight of my dim reflection in the mirror, I close my eyes. Stumbling to the toilet, I relieve myself with a bittersweet release and scramble out of the room again.

"Georgia . . ."

I slam the door shut behind me. Then I tap the door handle with my other hand, wishing I had a key. I dive into my bed and pull the blankets over my head. Squeezing my eyes shut, I pretend I don't hear my name whispered a further five times. Each time the voice becomes more guttural and commanding until, with the last utterance, it isn't really a whisper anymore but more of an angry hiss. Either the shadows are getting closer to making a move, or I'm losing my mind completely.

I must have fallen asleep because I jolt awake in the middle of the night with my pillow over my head and *Little Women* digging painfully into my ribs. The night still reigns. That deep, heavy darkness of the middle of the night when the house is hushed with stillness and the expectancy of what tomorrow will bring. I listen for a whisper, thinking it's a shadow calling for me that might have woken me. Footsteps pad outside the door. Clangs and groans moan from the pipes. The hospital feels alive.

"No . . . !" June calls from her bed.

I sit up, the pillow rolling off me, and *Little Women* falling to the floor with a dull thud.

"Please don't take her!" June punches at an invisible attacker, her blanket twisted around her hips, sweat beading on her forehead, her teeth biting on her bottom lip. She swings and punches at the air. The whole thing ends in a supreme right hook. If the attacker was real, I'm sure it would have done him in. Then she collapses back on her bed and is quiet for the remainder of the night.

I retrieve *Little Women* and my pillow from the floor, do my double tapping thing and put the book on my bedside table and the pillow under my head. I lay back and stare at the ceiling.

I lay there for a long time, listening to the sounds of the night, straining to hear the low tones of the ghost lady singing to her son, or another shadow to whisper my name. The wet squelchy sounds come back. The sounds grate against my nerves. Raising my arms over my head, I pass my hands over the walls trying to find the source. But each time I think I've located an area, it moves, into the ceiling or a different wall. Scratching and sucking like a wet bathmat ripped out of a tub.

I give up and cover my ears with my hands. Lying

on my side, I watch June sleeping. Then I look at Liz. She stares at me with her big, dark, scary eyes. Just like last night.

"Liz?"

Liz frowns, a single furrow wrinkling the bridge of her nose. The scratching sounds fade to nothing, as if trying to listen in. I think I hear a distance scream. But it could be the wind howling outside.

I prop myself up on an elbow. "Liz?"

She stares at me, a penetrating, searching stare that raises the hairs on the back of my neck.

"Who's Liz?" she asks.

Who's Liz?

I'm about to say *you are* when I think better of it. If she doesn't know she's Liz, I don't want to upset her by telling her she is. I don't want to upset her at all.

"Georgia . . ."

The softest of whispers from the bathroom. I glance at the door.

"Don't go in there," Liz, or Not-Liz, says.

"No, I don't think I will." I turn back to Liz. But her eyes are closed, and she doesn't say anything else.

I hide under the blankets, pulling them up to my nose. Bringing my fingers to my face, I breathe in the comforting smell of lingering nicotine from the cigarette I had earlier. I can feel the mirror behind the closed bathroom door, like a magnetic pull, wanting me to come and look. And, what really terrifies me, is I want to. I want to march into that bathroom, turn on the light with a confident flick of the wrist, and stare unflinchingly into the mirror. I want to watch it reveal all it has to tell. It's a physical yearning, like a cigarette craving. My muscles are prone, ready to leap and perform this flurry of brave activity. Then, I have the good sense to laugh and remind myself there's nothing good in the mirror.

Perhaps the shadows are delving into the realm of mind control now too.

I double tap Bart's picture and bring it close to my chest. With the blanket pulled high and Bart's photo hugged tightly between crossed arms, I fall into a fitful sleep.

In the morning, Liz springs out of bed, stretches her arms above her head, and thrusts her hips to one side. She yawns happily and rubs her eyes.

"Morning," she says. "I had such a good night sleep."

"Liz?" I question, not quite sure how to respond.

She looks up from pulling on a pair of socks, her eyes a golden brown in the morning light. "Yeah?"

"Nothing. I'm just surprised." I swing my legs to the floor. "I thought you were awake in the middle of the night."

"Nope. Slept like a baby all night. And no dreams. The sedatives must be doing the trick." She stretches again and disappears into the bathroom.

A moment later, a scream rips out of the tiled room. A bloodcurdling, piss yourself, madman-with-an-axe coming after you kind of scream. I freeze. It's a shadow. I know it. And it's finally made a move.

June scrambles out of bed. I still can't move. I can't

go in there. I can't face the mirrors. If it's finally happening—if they've finally made it through—I don't want to know. I want to help Liz, I really do, but my feet will not move.

June rushes by me, deep, dark circles under her eyes, and pushes into the bathroom. A moment later, she bursts out laughing.

"It's just a spider," June says.

"It's a really big one," Liz says, a hand on her hip.

June pokes her chest. "Liz, please don't scream like that again unless there's blood. A lot of it."

I hear some moving around in the bathroom. June picking up the spider, opening the window and letting it go.

"But I'm afraid of spiders," Liz says. "It's one of my issues."

"You have arachnophobia?" June asks.

Liz nods.

"That was quite some scream," June says.

"A bit like the one last night," I say.

June and Liz come out of the bathroom and look at me blankly.

I sit down on my bed and pull my pillow onto my lap. "You didn't hear it?"

They both shake their heads.

"I suppose it was after you both fell asleep." I wind my hands into the slip of the pillow. "But there was quite a commotion."

Liz inches closer, a brush held limply in one hand. "What happened?"

"I'm not sure," I reply. "When I snuck a look into

the corridor, all I saw was Paul giving some struggling girl a syringe full of tranq."

"Was he alone?" June marches to her bed and yanks on her tracksuit bottoms from a discarded pile.

"No. Willow was with them."

Liz and June exchange a look that makes me feel like the piggy in the middle. I don't know them well enough to interpret the meaning, but I know it means something.

My fingers and toes turn icy, so I pull on a second pair of socks and shrug into my sweatshirt. "The girl was shouting about something. About making her look. But I couldn't make out the rest."

Liz visibly pales. June turns her back and makes her bed, all nice hospital corners with military precision.

Liz drags the brush through her hair. "It was probably someone just having a bad dream."

I watch June's jagged motions for a moment before turning to look at Liz. "Bad dreams get you a needle full of tranq? Bad dreams get you carted away in the middle of the night?"

"Carted away?" Liz asks.

"Yeah," I reply. "They were heading for the stairs."

June punches her pillow into submission and swivels to face me. "Up or down?"

A flicker of unease winds through my limbs. "I don't know. I couldn't tell. Then Paul saw me and I . . ."

June marches around the bed to me and stands close. "Paul saw you?"

Liz slumps down on her bed and chucks the brush at her bedside table, where it slides across the surface and falls off the other side. She brings her legs to her chest.

"Yeah." I lift a shoulder. "So what?"

June examines me for a moment, her short hair pulsing with her heartbeat. Despite the fact that I'm freezing, sweat forms under my arms. "What's going on? What do you guys know?"

"Hopefully nothing," June says.

Liz's thumbs chase each other in a chaotic cat and mouse game. "Maybe they took her to solitary so everyone else could sleep."

June snorts.

Fear tingles in my toes and for the first time I wonder if the shadows aren't the biggest problem in the hospital.

June goes to the door, opens it, checks outside, then closes it again and gestures me over to the far corner of the room. "A couple girls have gone missing."

"Missing?" I squeak.

Liz nods but doesn't elaborate.

"The line is they've been transferred to other facilities, or they've aged out, or they've graduated." June smirks. "But we never hear from them again."

"Ellie . . ." Liz mumbles.

June nods. "There was a friend of ours. Lived next door. Ellie. She was here for six months, then poof, disappeared in the middle of the night. Staff said her parents came to collect her for a surprise holiday."

"Maybe they did," I say. I'd love it if Bart came to meet me on release day and whisked me away to a warm beach for a weekend.

June's smirk turns disdainful. "She never wrote. Never called. Never visited. Nothing." She holds up her hand in the shape of a zero and the hurt rolls off her.

"Is that unusual?" I ask. "Maybe she just wanted to forget all about it, put this part of her life behind her. I know I would."

June stares at me, her bottom lip quivering. "She was my friend. She wouldn't just give up on me."

I don't know what to say, so I just tell her I'm sorry. "What is it you think is happening?"

June and Liz look at each other. "Ghosts . . ." they both say and trail off.

I want to dismiss them. Ghosts aren't real. But that's what people say about the shadows too. And If I can be so confident that ghosts aren't real . . . does that mean the shadows aren't either? But where are the patients going?

It's the twenty-first century. Hospitals do not kidnap patients. I read the entire website before I came, including the hundreds of testimonials. There has to be a simple explanation.

"You don't believe us?" June asks.

"I don't know what to believe anymore," I reply. "You really think the old lady with the crows is walking around?"

"Not her," June says, looking at the walls. "But something else. Something that comes out at night." I gulp. "You've heard it too?"

I nod. "Pipes. Squirrels."

Liz stands up, her irises a warm hazel colour. "That's what I thought, too, to start with."

. . .

BREAKFAST IS QUIET. IN THE LIGHT OF THE CAFETERIA, and surrounded by the other patients and orderlies, neither of my roommates seem to want to talk about what might be living in the walls. And I'm beginning to think there's a reason we're all here at the hospital: because we actually need help.

It must be the history of the ancient hospital that has me on edge, looking for danger around every corner and menace in every shadow. I'll just have to shrug off the foreboding feelings. That's what I normally do. Otherwise, I'll end up in a corner somewhere like Crash Helmet Annie and rock myself through life.

Ninety days.

I don't want to be here a minute longer.

June pushes her half-eaten bowl of cereal away and murmurs something in my general direction.

I lean over the table. "Sorry?"

June lifts her chin. "Sarah. She's not here."

I glance around the bustling room. "Ok?"

June drums her short fingernails on the table. "Was it her you saw last night?"

"I don't know," I reply. "It was dark. Hard to tell."

"I think it was Sarah." June turns to scan the cafeteria again. "She's usually the first one here. And look, there's Kiara, out of solitary. They're normally together."

"I thought they hated each other," I say.

"They're roommates. They look out for each other. Like us."

Liz stands and backs away from the table. Her gingerbread eyes turn all watery and colourless, and her hands tremble.

"Liz? Are you ok?" I put my spoon down and half stand, reaching out a hand towards her. She teeters.

Liz pins me down with her watery eyes. I gasp. I was sure when she was staring at me earlier this morning, they were brown. Ok, yeah, we'd been distracted by ghost talk. But still. I'm sure they were brown. How is that possible?

Liz shakes her head, dumps her tray in the stack and runs out of the room.

"What's with her?" I ask June. Icy fingers crawl up my spine, even though it's only half past seven in the morning, the time of day that's usually reserved for reality and laughing at nightmares from the previous night.

"She's not Liz," June says.

I stare at her. "Not you too. What do you mean she's not Liz?"

"Haven't you ever heard of dissociative identity disorder?"

"You mean multiple personality syndrome?" My mouth drops open. "You serious?"

June nods.

I look at the doorway where Liz disappeared. "That's a real thing?"

"Yup." June runs her fingers over her tattoos. "And Liz has it."

"Who . . . what . . . how many personalities does she have?" I stumble for a coherent sentence.

"That's a rudimentary way of looking at it, but I guess it amounts to the same thing." She catches me watching and tugs the sleeves of her sweatshirt over her wrists. "It's more like she has one personality that has been split into different characteristics. She's been here for a year. I've met four so far. I suspect there are more. The meds keep her from cycling too fast. They keep the more volatile ones away."

I'm not hungry anymore and drop my spoon into my bowl. "Volatile?"

June cocks her head and purses her lips. "Victims of dissociative identity disorder have usually suffered abuse. Severe abuse. But Liz wouldn't hurt a fly."

"What about when she's not Liz?" I tap out an even pattern on the bench with both hands, seeking reassurance.

"Hard to say. She didn't do anything violent to get herself in here. It's obvious she was suffering from the disorder without her having to get violent. She's a sweet girl." June pulls at the roots of her short hair. "She's on meds. Willingly. She knows it keeps her more aggressive characteristics at bay, especially the ones that don't like the Liz part of her. And she wants that, despite the consequences."

"What about her eyes? They changed colour."

June props her chin in her hand. "It's been known to happen, depending on what personality is dominant."

"That's impossible—"

"No, no it's not." June wags a finger. "Next time you're near Google, have a look."

Paul taps me on the shoulder. "It's time for therapy, Georgia."

Staring at June, I get to my feet. "How long have you been here?"

June's lips twist into a sad smile. "Five years," she says. "Five long years."

TWELVE

"I REALLY, really don't belong here." I slump into one of Dr. Zaleski's club chairs. I try to slouch, but it just isn't the chair for that. Instead, I lean forward, elbows on knees, and look at the doctor, waiting for him to agree.

"Really. I don't." I shake my head at the offered chocolate chip cookie. "Multiple personality syndrome? Girls wearing helmets because they won't stop banging their heads on walls? Urinating on tables? Screaming in the middle of the night and taken off to solitary? Seriously. I. Really. Don't. Belong. Here." I say it really slowly, really loudly, so he won't miss the point.

Now he will stand up, hoist up his belted trousers around his thickening waist, stare down his glasses at me and smile. He'll say: *Of course you can leave, Georgia. It's all a big mistake*. Or he'll admit that he's in on a joke. There will be an absolution. An apology. Something. Please.

"Did you have a rough night?" He remains seated,

his magnified eyes peering at me through his thick lenses.

Rough night? To put it mildly.

"That's beside the point." I cross my arms over my chest and then cross my legs for good measure too. Digging in. "I'm not like the other girls here."

Dr. Zaleski raises one grey, furry eyebrow. "Breaking every mirror in a shop? Your wrist bleeding so profusely that the medics didn't know if you were going to make it, and threatening a member of staff with a blade—"

"It was a broken piece of mirror!"

I hold my left wrist in my right hand. The scar sits there between us, ugly and real. I didn't mean to hurt myself. I wasn't trying to off myself. I was afraid.

"She's scarred for life. On her face. Almost lost an eye. Tell me, Georgia, where do you think you should be?"

I glare at the doctor. The guilt washes over me. I'll never forgive myself for hurting that poor girl. She wasn't much older than me. She reached out to me, tried to take the broken piece of mirror so I wouldn't cut myself again. I thought she was the shadow. I thought she was trying to hurt me. I reacted. Defensively.

Dr. Zaleski stares back at me. Waiting. I shift my gaze to the window. The slatted blinds are still drawn, but the slats rest in an open position. Outside, the sun shines. But it's a blustery day. The gusty air blows leaves off trees. The uneven grass lays flat under the insistence of the wind.

"I don't know," I mumble. "But not here."

"How are you getting on with your roommates?"

"Fine."

"And you took your medication last night?"

I snap my head towards him. Does he know? "Yes."

"But you still didn't sleep well?"

I tuck my hands in my sleeves and grip the armrests. "I didn't take the sedatives."

"Ah. It might help if you did." He takes off his glasses and gives them a wipe with the hem of his shirt.

"I can't," I whisper. "I'm afraid at night."

Dr. Zaleski looks up and props his glasses back on his nose. "Of the mirrors?"

"No. Everything else. There's a noise in the walls—"

"Pipes, it's an old building," Dr. Zaleski says.

I ball my fists in my sleeve and tap them both against the armrests twelve times. "They don't sound like pipes. It sounds like an alien octopus, sucking, sucking . . ."

Dr. Zaleski smiles patiently. "Did you hear what you just said? Use your logic. An octopus can't survive out of water—"

"But when you go through all the logic and are only left with the impossible or the insane, then it must be true!"

"I don't think we've exhausted the logic yet. Pipes sound differently in different places. The nights I've spent here, they've freaked me out a little too."

I sigh. I don't want to argue about pipes. Or noises or shadows or ninety days.

"June's parents think she killed her sister."

Dr. Zaleski smooths a stray clump of gray hair back to his head. "Is that what she told you?"

"It isn't true?"

"No. Yes, her sister went missing. Her parents don't think June did anything. But they didn't know how to help her with her mania. They didn't know how to help her talk about what happened. So she came here."

"For five years?"

"She doesn't really want to leave. If she goes back home, back to where her sister lived, she'll be reminded of what happened all over again."

"I guess."

"But we're not here to talk about June. We're here to talk about you, Georgia."

I frown and clench the hand rests with a white-knuckle grip. I know what's coming.

Dr. Zaleski reaches into his drawer again and brings up a mirror. Its reflective surface faces him. My heart pounds and my pulse throbs in my temples. My hands go clammy and sweat pools at the small of my back.

Dr. Zaleski peers in the mirror. He rearranges his glasses atop his nose and smooths down the tufts of grey over his ears.

"I can't . . . please don't make me," I beg.

"Georgia." Dr. Zaleski looks at me sharply. "Do you want to get better?"

"Of course, but I can't look in a mirror . . . I can't."

How could I possibly explain without making myself seem the very kind of crazy that belongs here for the rest of my life?

"Georgia, if you want to get out of here, you're

going to have to look in the mirror. It's obvious all of your problems come from your fear of mirrors. You're going to have to face it. And best do it here, in a safe place with the right kind of people around you to help."

We have a bit of a standoff. I glare at the doctor. He stares me down. I feel like he's one of those wild animal whisperers, staring at me in just that way that will make me suddenly cock my head, slip to the floor and stick all fours in the air, waiting demurely for a belly rub.

He looks in the mirror, then at me. "What is it you think you're going to see?"

Great, big, black shadows with nightmarish teeth and dinosaur-sharp beaks and insubstantial bodies that lend them an indomitable immortality. Shortly followed by my own agonising death. *Try telling me not to be afraid of that one, Doc.* But I'll never, ever voice my fears aloud and I don't have a credible lie that can get me out of this potentially fatal situation.

Bart, where are you? In that moment I want nothing more than my big brother to come charging through the gates and rescue me like some old-fashioned knight saving his damsel in distress. Any time now please, Bart. I even strain my ears to hear horse hooves on the drive. Or a loud engine drifting across the gravel, signally my epic rescue.

"Fine!" I huff after five minutes of mutinous silence. My pulse pounds in my ears. I'm not going to get out of this room without looking at a mirror. Adrenaline heats my face. My hands slip off the hand rests.

Oddly, in spite of my terror, part of me is excited. Ever since last night—since I heard them calling my name—I felt the urge to go into the bathroom and stare into the mirror. I want to see the shadow. I want to face it, to pound it to a bloody pulp, extract all its needle teeth with as much pain as I can inflict, stick my thumbs into its hungry, red eyes until they drip blood. I want to feel flesh give way to brain—if it has one. I want to maim it, kill it, vanquish it from existence. I just needed a Vorpal sword, but I don't know where to find one.

Maybe it's time to face my fears. Maybe I'm strong enough.

I don't think I have the energy to run from them forever. Perhaps it's better to get it all over with, come what may. And if it is all in my head, then I'll know.

"Here." Dr. Zaleski plants the mirror in my lap. It catches the light of something and reflects a tiny circle around the room, the perfect tease for a cat. But the darting light has me glancing into the mirror before I've prepared myself.

I snatch a breath. I haven't looked at myself in almost five years. Not properly. Maybe an eye here or a cheek there in my tiny compact. But as I peer into the large, rectangular mirror, I realise I'm no longer a kid; I'm a young woman. Profound, I know. But the last time I really stared into a mirror I was eleven. On that occasion, I saw so many shadows that I had nightmares for a month.

Now, I look into a foreign face. My skin is pale and smooth. A few freckles decorate the bridge of my nose. A button nose, my father called it. My blonde hair falls in shaggy waves just past my shoulders. Pretty standard as far as appearances go. Despite the dark circles, the crisp blue of my eyes reminds me of the sky on a perfect summer's day. There's a twinkle of confidence in them. I smile. My lips reveal perfectly white teeth, American-straight thanks to the braces I wore when I was twelve. Apart from my top front one, which is the tiniest bit crooked. Probably due to my refusal to wear a night-time retainer.

"See?" Dr. Zaleski stands next to me. "Not so bad, hey?"

I glance at him and see his smile is proud.

I look back in the mirror. I scream and propel it away from me. It doesn't break, miraculously, consid-ering I really hurled it. I throw myself towards the back of the office, as far away as I can get from the duplici-tous looking glass. I slam into the bookshelf, causing a couple of books to topple down. My head is in the perfect position to break their fall. With a hand clamped over a swelling bump, I squeeze my eyes tight and curl into a ball.

"Georgia?" Dr. Zaleski kneels at my feet. "Are you ok? What did you see?"

"I . . . I don't know . . ." I can barely talk; my tongue is so dry it might be an entirely different entity living within my mouth. So dry, drier than a pegged-out lizard in the middle of the desert at noon.

"Do you need something? Water? An ice pack?"

Wincing, I nod.

Dr. Zaleski leaves the office.

I curl my arms around my knees and stare at the edge of the mirror. What did I see? Not myself. Not a shadow, either. I had just been taking a small amount of pleasure from seeing my face in the mirror for the first time in such a long time. A confidence had bloomed in my chest; after looking in the mirror, I would know if I was crazy or not. A test for myself. There had been my reflection and nothing else. Then I looked up at Dr. Zaleski, and when I glanced down again, it wasn't my face that peered back at me. It was that of a boy. That's when I screamed.

Maybe it was one of Liz's personalities taken up supernatural powers and disembodied from her. Maybe it was the image of the kind, attractive boyfriend I always wanted and seemed destined to never find; my mental health diagnosis a large red warning siren keeping people away. Or maybe it was my imagination. It couldn't be anything else. But why would my mind plant the image of a boy within the mirror? And if the boy wasn't real—and I really don't see how he can be— then maybe the shadows aren't either. Test complete. I'm actually crazy. Properly. My body trembles as I process the thought.

But what of the boy? From the brief glimpse I got, he didn't seem to pose much of a threat, whoever he is. He looked about a year or two older than myself and was, I realised, quite attractive.

Ignoring the warmings in my head, I creep towards the mirror on hands and knees. I don't touch it, but slowly edge closer until my face looms over it and my hair touches the glass.

The boy is there, looking at me. Sweat prickles at my hairline, and I hold my breath, waiting for the image to dissolve. But the boy remains. He has dark brown hair. Blue eyes with a twinkle as if he's a magician and has just successfully pulled the notorious white rabbit from his black hat. He smiles at me and the hint of a dimple appears on each cheek. Apparently, the boy is real. Or I'm much crazier than I thought. I'm about to pose my first question when Dr. Zaleski bustles back into the office, spilling water from the cup as he comes.

I turn back to the boy. He lays a finger across his lips. *Shhhh*. And he winks. But then snaps his head over his shoulder and the smile falls from his lips. He frowns and his lower lip quivers. Without warning, he vanishes. I'm left staring at my own reflection again. No shadows.

"Georgia!" Dr. Zaleski stops in his tracks. Did he see the boy? "You're looking into the mirror again! Now that's what I'm talking about! Well done you!" He hands me the cup of water. Then the ice pack. Even those small actions seem to carry an exclamation mark. I gulp the cool but faintly salty water down, regretting the fact that of course, I will need to pee soon after.

Dr. Zaleski retrieves the mirror from the floor and picks it up. He puts it back on his desk.

He turns to face me and perches on the edge of his desk. "What did you see? What made you scream?"

I smile, going for sheepish. "I just haven't seen myself in such a long time. I almost forgot what I look like."

Dr. Zaleski barks out a cheery laugh. "Well, you've taken a huge first step. I'm pleased. For a moment there I thought you were going to insist on travelling the hard road. But now you see, it's not so bad. You've earned yourself some outside privileges. It's a little blowy, but the sun is shining."

"Thanks Doctor." With a trembling hand, I transfer the cup to my left hand and throw it in the bin as I leave his office.

I wait by the back door, peering through the window. Outside. I smile. Perhaps I'll visit the den again. Then a massive wave of compulsion almost has me running back inside the office to touch the mirror again. I realise, when I looked at the boy for the second time, I touched the mirror with my right hand. Not my left, ever. Now, my right hand feels too heavy and my left too light. I'm unbalanced. I stumble over my own feet and turn at the sound of heavy breathing, fearing a shadow in flesh.

But it's just Paul and June. I pant, and he asks if I'm ok. I nod, the wave of compulsion fading, the urge still present, but lessening. I stand there hesitating, trying to think of a viable excuse to return to the doctor's office and touch the mirror with my left hand. I come up blank, begin to panic, and then remember to breathe. Paul takes the ice pack, gesturing for us to follow him, and returns it to the nurses' station. I hesitate once more, the compulsion turning into an elongated leash connected to my chest and the doorknob of Dr. Zaleski's office. But with every step, it loosens until I can draw in a breath without feeling like I'm going to faint. Perhaps I'll get an opportunity later to right the imbalance.

Paul opens the door for us, and June and I slip outside.

"I'll be watching from inside," Paul says.

When I step out of the back door, the wind immediately accosts me. It takes hold of the ends of my hair with invisible hands and whips it around like the chains of the dead. But I don't mind. My sweatshirt is warm and the air is fresh. I didn't realise how musty the asylum smells. With its floral carpets and ancient oil portraits, it's no wonder it reeks of old people. Dying old people with spittle drooling down their chins and ripe farts that get trapped in the seat of their trousers and two-day-old stewed broccoli that somehow seems to turn their skin green. Perhaps they still have a roller vacuum in a storage cupboard somewhere. And the electric shock cables. The frigid, wet sheets.

I take a couple of hesitant steps on the back patio. My hands are still trembling from the experience with the mirror and the unfulfilled compulsion.

June makes a beeline for the den, and I follow as fast as I can, into the cover of the woods. As soon as we plop down on the damp earth, June releases a bottle of Jack Daniels from the waistband of her tracksuit.

"Where did you get that?" I ask.

She raises both eyebrows and grins. "I have my ways. Want some?"

Before I know what I'm doing, I reach out for the bottle and take a large swig. It will numb the effects of the compulsion still warring inside and maybe help me sleep better tonight. It burns as it goes down my throat, but I don't care, and take another. I don't know how to take the appearance of the boy in the mirror. I don't know what it means. Either I'm not crazy, and new things are happening, or I am crazy, and my psychosis is reaching a whole new level.

"Did the doc make you look in a mirror?" June asks, slugging her own gulp.

I nod.

"What did you see?

I hesitate. Can I trust June? She's told me her story, and if I want a friend in here, I'm going to have to even that up. But how will she look at me after? With pity? Screw it, I've got nothing to lose.

"I saw a boy."

June frowns. "A boy?" She leans towards me, curious, not the least perturbed.

I shrug. "I see things in mirrors."

"Not monsters?"

My head snaps towards her. "Monsters? What kind of monsters?"

June shrugs. "Figured you must see something pretty scary to make you avoid looking in a mirror. That's all."

"No monsters," I say. "Not today."

"So, this boy." June takes another glug with a mischievous glint in her eye. "Was he hot?"

I throw a pinecone at her and take the bottle. In half an hour, we put a dent in the whiskey and manage to get quite drunk, only realizing it's a bad idea when Marion comes to fetch us. She takes one look at the empty bottle and our giggling and marches us straight inside, upstairs, past our rooms and into separate solitary rooms. She makes me swallow my meds before she leaves me alone. The room doesn't seem so bad, even when the clink of the lock clangs into place, and I flop onto the unmade bed. I could use some alone time to figure out why I'm seeing a boy in the mirror. But then I see the small bathroom in the corner of the room, which doesn't have a door and a large mirror hanging above the sink.

There's nothing in there at the moment, but I can't stay in here a minute longer. I pound on the back of the door, screaming to be let out, for hours, until my fists are red and bruised and my throat is hoarse. No one comes.

I back into the room until I feel the edge of the bed digging into my calves. When the shadow flits from top to bottom of the window, I scream again.

THIRTEEN

I HUNCH in the corner and cover my head with my hands. It's the only place in the small room I'm not in direct sight of the mirror. But I can still feel the shadow in there.

"Georgia . . ."

It whispers my name, a persistent hiss of sibilant noise. I squeeze into the corner, pressing my back into the hard edges, wishing I could make myself smaller, or invisible.

I don't say a word as silent tears roll down my cheeks, and my trembling hands wrap around my knees, drawing them close to my chest.

"Georgia . . ."

What does it want? Why me?

And then I think of June asking me if I saw monsters. Why would she ask that, specifically? Her sister went missing in a funhouse of mirrors. Does she know something about the shadows and mirrors?

I think of the noises that we all hear, the wet sucking

noises I can hear right now coming from the small bathroom, and I know I'm not the only one. I'm not crazy, and the shadows are real.

"Georgia . . ."

Ice crawls down my spine and an intense fury pulses through my limbs. How dare the shadows do this to me. How dare they ruin my life and make everyone think I'm crazy. I stand up, ready to confront the shadow, no matter what the outcome, when I see the boy in the mirror again.

"Go away!" he yells at the shadow.

Both of them stand in the mirror, looking at me, then each other. The shadow opens its beak and roars and both images dissolve. My vision ebbs and I fall onto the bed. I don't wake until the next morning when my door opens and Paul is standing in the threshold.

"You had quite a night," he says, sympathy in his eyes.

I lift my head, but the hangover clamps on my skull and my mouth feels drier than a camel's hoof.

June and I aren't allowed outside unsupervised for another week. I almost don't care. I have other things to think about. The boy. And the fact that I'm not crazy.

That afternoon, after disturbing the nurses in the office one too many times, asking for chewing gum, a phone call, a new book, whatever it is I can think of to annoy them, Paul takes pity on me and whisks me outside for a smoke.

In front of me rolls flat fields of nothingness. In the distance, trees. Mostly pine and oak with the occasional silver birch thrown in, their skinny trunks anorexic against the fuller girths of the others. Beyond the trees is the canal. A means of escape. Potentially. If I want to think that way. But not with Paul by my side. And of course, there's the little problem of my tracking bracelet.

I slide into an old wooden bench, now grey with age and weather and stick my hands into my sleeves and tap each one on the bench. Paul lifts a foot and rests it on the seat of the bench. He taps his foot, whistling, twisting this way and that.

He offers me a cigarette. "What got into you yesterday?"

"Had a bit of a breakthrough."

Paul lights a match, managing to light his own before the wind steals the flame. He hands me the matches. I light a second. He cups his hands around the cigarette for me. The cigarette takes and I suck in the nicotine. I nod my thanks and pass the matches back to him.

Paul looks at me, my cigarette, and then the flimsy book of pub matches. "You keep them."

I flip the matches over. The Anchor is the name of the pub. I wonder if it's nearby.

"Thanks." I slip them into the cup of my new standard issue, non-wired bra.

"A breakthrough makes you drink booze?"

I nod. "I looked in a mirror with the doc."

"That's great. What did you see?"

I breathe in the cigarette, watching the glowing embers at the end. Throwing my head back, I exhale the smoke to the murky heavens. I actually have a head rush. The trees in the distance melt into one green mess. I see two of Paul.

"Ordinary things. My face." I'm not about to tell him anything.

Paul chuckles and finishes his cigarette, lights a second with the end of it, stamps out the original under his feet and sits down next to me.

"So why the drinking then?" His voice contains a surprising note of tenderness that makes my throat clamp shut for a moment.

I shrug. "Bad habits die hard."

Paul sighs. "There are going to be more strict room searches."

I shrug again. There's not much more they can take away from me. I think of finding June again to see how her night in solitary went, and then of Sarah and how she's not been around since the other night. I don't have the guts to ask Paul about what was going on, so I go on a different track. "Tell me about Dr. Zaleski?"

"The doc?" The cigarette hangs out the side of his mouth, and he rubs his square hands together to keep warm. "He's decent enough. Tries to help where he can."

"He mentioned he had a son. But there are no pictures in his office." I suck on my cigarette and watch the ash float away on the wind. Coldness settles into the tip of my nose.

Paul looks off into the distance, at the clump of green that seems to be advancing towards me with the effects of the head rush. Or maybe I've stepped in a rabbit hole and have fallen to Wonderland. The Queen of Hearts versus the shadows. Which is worse?

"Doc's been here for a long time. And since the divorce, he pretty much lives here." He flicks ash onto the patio, which is quickly whisked away by the wind. "Doesn't know how to take a holiday. Always thinks someone needs saving."

I take a second cigarette from Paul when he offers.

"He had a son." Paul leans back and straightens his legs out, crossing one ankle over the other. "Would be about thirty-six years old now if he'd . . . aw . . . anyway. The kid had problems. Doc didn't know what to do to help. That's when he brought him here. Doc stayed and took a job as a psychiatrist here too. He loved that boy more than anything. But the boy was too far gone. Unreachable."

I turn on the bench to face Paul and bring my knees up to my chest. "Too far gone?"

"Some say schizophrenia." He blows a perfectly circular smoke ring, but it's snatched away by a gust of wind. "They didn't have the meds back then like they do today. Not without the risks. Doc didn't want to take the risks. Not with the boy's life. But, well, it didn't matter in the end. One stormy night the boy made his choice. And that was that. Marriage didn't last much longer after that either. Doc's been here ever since, thinking he can save each patient, making it his life's mission."

Save, not help.

"Don't you think he can? Save us all?" I shiver as the wind creeps down the back of my neck.

I think of Crash Helmet Annie, June and her sister,

Liz and her bag of personalities, Sarah and her OCD, Kiara and her exhibitionism. Me and my mirrors. Can we be saved?

Paul stands and his eyes shift around the dark windows of the building. "Who's to say? Doc sure has his heart in the right place. But his heart isn't the only ball in the game."

What does that mean? That some of the patients are too far gone to help? That they don't have the will?

"I need to get you back now, Georgia. Marion will be cross if she knows I've taken you out after yesterday." A warm smile softens the hard edges of his face.

"So why did you? Take me out?"

"Therapy comes in all forms."

I stand and follow him back into the building.

He points me in the direction of the cafeteria and lunch. I start walking that way when I realise I need to pee. I think about the mirror. The boy. How he got rid of the shadow for me last night. He's in their world and maybe, with him on my side, I don't need to be afraid anymore.

Upstairs, in my room, I close the bedroom door behind me, and I breathe a sigh of relief. I double tap Bart's picture as I walk by my bed, thinking maybe I don't need him to rescue me; maybe I can rescue myself.

Marching to the bathroom, I throw open the door. The smell of bleach and lemon shower gel wafts out of the room. I look in the mirror. There's my button nose with the freckles and the crisp blue eyes. But my reflection disappears in a nanosecond. The boy returns, smiling tentatively at me, his head cocked slightly to one side, making him seem quizzical.

Staring into his eyes, I wait for him to disappear. I wait for the shadows to gobble him whole. I wait for the craziness to overtake my mind and body and send me running down the corridor screaming uninterruptible warnings about the end of the world. Like the dude at the beginning of every other sci-fi movie with dishevelled hair and a cardboard sign reading: *The end is nigh*, in bold, red letters.

But his image remains.

"Georgia?" The faintest of whispers, the merest of sounds, but I know it's come from the boy. I watched his lips move.

I step over the threshold, into the bathroom, closer to the boy. Raising a hand, I intend to reach out and touch the mirror, but he shakes his head at me and the word 'no' forms on his lips. A light shines from his side of the mirror. An aura, a saintly glow that outlines his body, making him appear like a cardboard cut-out.

The reflected image of my bedroom in the mirror fades, and behind the boy, a snowy landscape appears. Mountains rise in the distance, their peaks obscured by cloud. Snow falls in thick, heavy clumps. The boy stands on an untouched field of snow, buried up to his knees. Wearing jeans and a grey hooded sweatshirt, he wraps his arms around his waist, shivering, but continues to smile at me. He backs away from me, pulling each leg out of the snow, turning every so often to look towards the mountains at his back. His teeth chatter like one of those freaky vibrating pairs of teeth found at pound stores. Each laboured step takes longer and longer and his lips turn blue. I shiver, feeling the cold of his world leach into mine. He stumbles. At his back, a rock rises out of nowhere. A big, black, jagged rock partially covered in snow.

I follow the boy's progress like I'm directing a movie camera, closing in on him, examining the rock. A crevice appears in the rock. A glinting, reflective opening. As the boy gets closer, still walking backward, maintaining eye contact with me, I realise the opening isn't an opening, but a mirror. But the boy disappears into it all the same. The snowy landscape disappears, and I'm left staring at my own reflection.

Warmth floods into my limbs. I stand there for a moment, wondering where the boy vanished to, wondering how any of this makes sense, but know it's real all the same. Then a shadow fills the mirror. Its dark, shapeless face takes over the entirety of my reflection. It stares at me with its hungry, red eyes. They widen, murderous intent dilating its pupils. It opens its beak of a mouth, revealing its long, whittled teeth and screams at me.

It isn't a human sound. Hatred and venom and menacing threat pour out of that scream. It intends me harm. The scream erupts from the mirror, threatening to shatter it. A gust of wind blows my hair from my face. Its fetid and ancient breath, like of a monster from another time, long forgotten, primal, antediluvian, blasts over me. It roars, lifting its beak, opening it wide until I think it might break apart. Then the mirror shatters into a thousand tiny pieces. I put my hands over my face just in time.

I step away from the mirror, tiny cuts bleeding on the backs of my hands, away from the bathroom. The last of the glass fragments settle upon the floor with tiny tinkling sounds. Chunks and shards of glinting mirror cover the sink and the floor and the toilet. They catch the light of the fluorescent and beam rainbows throughout the room. The shadow is gone.

June bursts into the room.

"Catch." She hurls a bread roll at me filled with cheese. "You missed lunch. Did you get yourself into more trouble?"

"Thanks." I take a bite, looking for something normal to do, something to dispel the roaring silence that rushes around the room like a vacuum, sucking up all sound in the wake of the violent mirror explosion. I take another bite of the roll. My hands tremble and bleed. I wish for another of Paul's cigarettes.

"What happened?" Her eyes widen as she takes in the mirror shards.

"Funniest thing," I say, trying to keep the tremor out of my voice. "I walked in and the mirror just exploded. I'm lucky I wasn't hurt."

June eyes me up and down. "It looks like you were hurt." She steps close and points to my hands. The blood drips and the cuts sting. "I'll get some help."

Moments later, she reappears with Marion who carries a dustpan and brush and a first aid kit.

"Here." She hands June the brush. "Let's clean this up first, I don't want you cutting your feet too, then we'll see about your hands, Georgia. Why you girls keep breaking things in this place, I will never understand. Don't you have enough issues to deal with? And after yesterday with the alcohol? If you're that desperate for something sharp there really are easier objects to get hold of . . ." On and on she goes, huffing and puffing and emitting her general dissatisfaction from her pores like sweat. Then she sighs and looks at us both. "I know it's hard in here. You're away from your family and friends, but girls, please, if you follow the rules a little better, you'll get out a little quicker."

She holds the bin for June as she empties the shards from the dustpan. Neither of us responds to what she says.

"I'll have maintenance in this afternoon to fix a new one." A pair of glasses hang from a chain around her neck and she slides them up her nose. "If you can promise me you won't try and break it?"

I hold my hands up. "Promise."

"Very well." She gives me one more piercing look. Down her hook nose. Which reminds me a bit of a bird. A crow's beak. "Let's see about those hands."

She gestures for me to sit down on the bed next to her. She takes out antiseptic wipes and begins wiping my hands. I grimace at the sudden sting. Next, she slathers me in cream and wraps up my hands in a bandage. The whole thing is done in a couple of minutes, and not without tenderness. Then she puts everything back in the kit, snaps the lid closed with a flourish, and gets to her feet. She pivots on her heel and leaves the room, taking the bin with her.

"Now are you going to tell me what really happened?" June grabs my wrists, holding them tenderly.

I pull away from her and tuck my fists into my sleeves. I want to ask her about her sister. The hall of mirrors. What she saw. What she meant by monsters in the mirror.

"You were calling your sister's name in your sleep," I lie, changing the subject. I don't want to talk about the mirror or the shadow. The fact that it finally made a move. Finally broke free of its mirrored world. Now, it will come for me. No, I don't want to talk about that at all. Denial and avoidance are two of my more adept qualities.

June slumps onto her bed. "I'm not really in the mood to talk about it." She's not the only one. "It brings the nightmares back . . . every time."

"I wish there was something I could do to help," I say, searching for the cheese roll that I abandoned on my bed.

June looks up from her bed, runs a hand through her short hair. She wraps her arms around her knees and lays her chin on the bony points. "The person I love most in the world is dead. They took her."

I rush to her side. "Who took her?"

She holds up a hand. "Something . . . something so awful . . . I can't, please. I'll start crying, and I'm tired of crying. I promised myself no more tears."

"I know what you mean." I hover by her side, not quite sure what to do or what to say. "I thought you said her body was never found. How do you know she's dead?"

"I know," June says, her voice trembling, her eyes dim. "I was there. I know. There's no way she could have survived . . ." She drops her face into her hands.

I reach out a hand to stroke her back. "I'm sorry."

There's a knock on the door. The maintenance guy sticks his head around the door.

"Heard you had a little trouble with a mirror." He pops a piece of bubble gum. "Now a good time?"

I nod. He bustles into the room, humming a cheery tune under his breath. He goes into the bathroom, sets the new mirror on the floor. The shadow returns. In the new mirror. It fills the reflective surface and stares at me, not moving, breathlessly, as if it doesn't need to inhale to survive, right between the legs of the maintenance guy.

"Georgia . . ." it hisses at me.

The maintenance guy doesn't notice. Of course not. Normal people never see the shadows. It's only me. He measures up the wall. Then places the mirror directly in front of his face and drills into it with screws. The shadow remains there the whole time, deathly still and staring, one wide, red eye fixed on me. And it smiles— if birds or crows or whatever they are, are capable of smiling. The maintenance guy drills in the last screw and stands back to admire his handy work.

"That should do it," he says, oblivious of the shadow who stares at him, leaning closer and closer.

The maintenance guy shivers. "Got a window open in here? Sure is a draught." He shakes his head, not really expecting an answer. "Well, mirror's fixed. I'll be off." He leaves the room, chewing his gum and humming.

June has curled onto her side and pulled her blanket around her shoulders. I look back at the new mirror, but the shadow is gone. I catch a hint of snowy bleakness and then the shape of June's body under her blanket.

I touch her knee. "Are you coming to group, June?"

I'm met with a wall of silence.

"June? You're only allowed an hour in our room."

She snores softly. I leave her sleeping there and make my way to group on my own. The corridors are quiet. The younger kids have to go to class and work towards their GCSEs. But I've already completed mine, not that I passed many. And once you're officially finished school, you don't have to attend classes.

Leading the session is a new lady I haven't met yet wearing civilian clothes. She hands out pieces of paper and a selection of pastels. Art therapy. I roll my eyes. I've never been good at drawing, and no picture is going to make me feel better about the shadows.

Liz is already there, sitting with crossed legs across her chair. Kiara has her chair turned backwards and straddles it.

I slip into a chair next to Liz. "Where's Sarah?"

She looks at her hands resting in her lap. "She hasn't come back."

"I heard Sarah was transferred to another facility," the art teacher informs us. She puts down her sketchpad and looks at all of us. "It's hard when one of you moves on. Change is always hard for those who are more sensitive—"

"Sensitive, my ass," Kiara butts in.

The teacher doesn't react, just gives her a sympathetic smile which I'm immediately drawn to. "Different people need different treatments. I think it's great the doctors here recognise that. Instead of taking your money each week, they're doing their best to get you the right help."

Kiara scowls but doesn't say anything.

The art teacher picks up her pencil again and draws a few lines on her pad. "I don't mind what you draw. Anything. A dolphin, dragon, Easter egg party . . . whatever. Draw whatever comes out." Then she looks at me. "You're new?"

I nod.

"My name is Samantha. Call me Sam. Do you have any questions?"

I shake my head and pick up a pastel. Black. Thinking I might draw a shadow. Then I change my mind and picture the boy's face in my head. I begin to sketch his outline, smudging the lines where I don't get it quite right, but after a few minutes, I have what I think looks a little like him, and his snowy background.

Samantha plays some music from her cell phone, and for the first time since I arrived here, my mood lifts. Liz sits next to me. She hasn't picked up a pastel yet and her hand trembles near my paper.

"What's the matter?" I ask.

Her knee knocks against mine and she takes several short, shallow breaths. She throws me a nervous glance and a half smile that takes obvious effort. It's only a quick glance, but long enough for me to confirm that her eyes are indeed brown. For today anyway.

"I don't think Sarah went to a new facility," Liz whispers.

Ignoring the assignment, Kiara rests her head on folded arms. Dark circles bruise the skin under her eyes. Sarah was her roommate. She's been gone for two nights, and by the sounds of it, she's not coming back.

Samantha sings along to the song on her phone, ignoring our whispered conversation. Or maybe she thinks it's good for us and will report back later.

"Where do you think she went?" I ask.

Liz glances at the ceiling but doesn't say anything. Kiara remains pale and unresponsive. I don't think she's just tired; she isn't the type to let exhaustion get in her way. I've spent years watching the shadows, watching people, gauging their reactions. I can spot an angry glint in the eye from a mile away.

I finger the table while my brain ticks over, scratching at a dent in the surface. I keep coming back to the abrupt way Sarah left us. I thought there would have been an examination by the doc, lengthy paper-work to fill in and extended inspections of her behaviour in order to warrant a facility change. And shouldn't it occur in daylight, in the morning with a proper govern-ment-funded vehicle with the correct markings on its side transporting her away? And the rest of us would all hug her goodbye and wave from the steps. That's how it's supposed to work, isn't it? Just like that movie, "Girl, Interrupted". Or Maybe it's more of a "Shutter

Island," and everyone dies. Or "One Flew Over the Cuckoo's Nest" and the establishment really is evil. I've watched all the movies based in asylums, and while I don't think any of them come near to the reality of Brookwood Hospital, those three are my favourite. I watched them like a comfort blanket. First, as soon as I was old enough, in an attempt to find other people like me. Then later, as I sought to understand my "condition."

I thought Sarah had been making progress, with Paul and in the woods building the den. She didn't seem like the sort who needed a different facility and I can't imagine what that facility would be like. Unless, of course, her parents ran out of money. Maybe her quick strides to recovery were noticed and she was released to her home as an outpatient to a hospital nearby. Or maybe, and I don't really like to contemplate the matter too deeply, but maybe there was something ever so slightly dubious about the way she was carted away the other night with a needle-full of tranq.

And so I sit and I draw the icy rocks around the boy in my picture and I think about Sarah. When it gets near the end of the session, Samantha coos all over our drawings and doesn't make a single tut at Kiara's empty page. When she asks Liz to explain her drawing, I almost jump out of my seat. Sitting in the middle of Liz's page, drawn only with the black pastel, is a large bird-like shadowy creature.

My throat tightens as I suck in a breath.

"We saw a crow outside the other day," Liz says,

keeping her eyes on the page. "It stared at Sarah for ages and didn't fly away."

I look again at the black wings and the sharp beak. It could be a crow. But it looks more like a shadow.

Samantha makes us all lie down on the floor and guides us through a relaxation exercise. Liz slips down to a mat next to me and lays down on her back. As she closes her eyes, as per Samantha's instructions, I notice that her pupils are green. Who is Liz right now?

I close my eyes and try to concentrate on my breathing as Samantha instructs us into a meditative trance. But it just isn't working. With my shoulders hunched up near my ears somewhere, a tightness squeezes in my chest. Tension coils through my body. And the harder I concentrate on the breathing, the more tense I become.

I don't think Liz's drawing is of a crow. And I think June knows something about the shadows too. *I'm not the only one*. A shallow breath catches in my throat, and I panic, thinking for a moment I've forgotten how to breathe. My body is as taut as a guitar string. And then I realise Kiara, on the other side of me, isn't breathing either. And then she starts to laugh. At least I think she does. Some very strange, loud sound erupts from her throat. At the same time, she performs a fluid roll up onto her knees and then her feet.

"I am not going to sit here, or lie here, or whatever and be all hippy, new age, all Namaste, and pretend that my roommate is fine, that she really is taken to another facility, that everything is just hunky-dory!" She storms towards the door.

"Kiara!" Samanta shuffles to her feet and knocks a mound of paper from the table.

Kiara pivots on her heel, throwing her hand out at rapid speed. "What?"

Samantha flinches. I flinch. But Kiara's hand doesn't connect with Samantha's cheek. Instead, she picks up a chair and throws it across the room and then slams her hand into the wall. She could easily have broken a finger, but she doesn't even wince.

Samantha sighs and dips to her knees to pick up her papers. "Where else do you think she might have gone?"

Kiara narrows her eyes but doesn't reply. Instead she stomps towards the door and slams it behind her. It bounces violently off the jam and springs open again, but Kiara is already gone. I look at Liz, whose eyes are brown again. She frowns at the doorway. She gets to her feet and slips quietly after Kiara without a word of explanation.

"Well, we were almost done anyway," Samantha says, packing away the paper and pastels. "I'm sorry your first art session wasn't as peaceful as I'd intended, Georgia."

"S'ok." Art therapy isn't going to get rid of the shadows. Neither will relaxation exercises. Can you imagine coming face to face with a screaming shadow in the mirror and sucking in a deep breath, right down to your stomach, to make it all better? I snort a laugh. Samantha raises an eyebrow. I morph the snort into a cough and make my exit.

I spend the next two hours in the common room

watching Crash Helmet Annie bang her head on the far wall. If I don't think too closely about the circumstances of how she found her way into this hospital—or the dwindling amount of brain cells she has left in her head—I can find the rhythmical thud oddly comforting.

As I sit there, I think about the group therapy session. Does Kiara know something about where Sarah was taken? Kiara is angry all of the time. It would be weird if she weren't. But now she's suspicious, and I wonder what's going on in that acerbic head of hers. Maybe nothing. Maybe something.

Can I ask her about it without having my face slammed into a wall? I tell myself the niggly itch in the back of my mind can be ignored. The offered, plausible explanations are entirely conceivable. There's no need to consciously ponder the circumstances in which Sarah found herself the other night and what might have led up to them. No need at all. There are far more interesting things going on at Brookwood Hospital. Like the shadows. And how I'm going to get out of here if I can't find a way to get rid of them.

I pick up a book from the games corner and stare at it. Reading a sentence here or there, not really taking in the story. The first chapter is missing anyway. Paul gives me a brief nod of recognition as he enters the room and goes around the girls, talking to them, asking them questions, being his generally caring self. I smile back.

But more than Sarah's whereabouts and Kiara's anger and what Liz might have drawn on her paper, the most prominent thought occupying my mind concerns the boy in the mirror. So much has happened, is happening. Despite the shadow shattering my mirror into a thousand pieces, a tremor of excitement rumbles through me. A shift has occurred. The shadows have upped their game. But the boy appeared too, and I know, deep in my gut, he is good, and his presence might bring some answers. After all these years of waiting, wondering when the attack is going to come, I know I'm standing on a watershed, and soon, all will be revealed. But who is the boy? How did he get there? My thoughts circle round and round until I can think about nothing else except the strange boy in his snowy landscape.

Dinner passes without incident, and then I find myself in the queue for medication. Paul hovers at Willow's side, frowning at any disruptive girls. Marion hands out the medication. I accept mine, transfer the plastic cup to my left hand and pop the pills in my mouth. I manage to wedge them between teeth and cheek, and I'm prepared for Willow and her flashlight. But Willow doesn't check. She just gives me a faint smile, glances briefly at Marion, and waves me on my way. Doling out more pills and frowning at Crash Helmet Annie causing problems farther down the line, Marion doesn't notice Willow's failure to check my mouth.

Hurrying back to my room, I spit the pills into my hand. I take the stairs two at a time, because, for the first time in my life, I'm eager to face a mirror. When I get in my room, Liz isn't back yet, and June is still curled up under her blankets. I wonder briefly how she got away with hanging out in our room all day.

I tiptoe into the bathroom and close the door quietly behind me. As soon as I snap on the light, the boy in the mirror appears. He smiles and gestures for me to step closer.

I approach the mirror, my hands resting on the sink so I can lean in close. My breath should fog up the glass, but oddly, there is nothing. My nose is inches away from the boy's. In his world, snowflakes have ceased falling, but the crystals glisten on the ground. He smiles and I admire the dimples in his cheeks and handsomeness of his jaw. The unruly length of his hair and the way it hangs in his eyes. I haven't seen a boy my age in weeks.

Behind him, the settled snow stretches as far as I can see, without a single blemish to mar its startling beauty. No paw prints or child's footprints. No snowmen with stick arms and button eyes, scarves encrusted with ice. No igloos with caved-in roofs. The hushed cotton-ball silence of his side of the mirror seems to leach through time and space—if that is what separates us—into my small bathroom. I hear the expectancy of the world around him, the quiet waiting, the pre-whispers of the rocks and mountains biding their time until the snow melts and the world begins turning with the promise of spring and new life once again. The icy crystals glisten, invitingly, and I wonder what it's like on the other side of the mirror. I know there are shadows and I know there is the boy. Snow and ice and rock and cold. Is there anything else?

"Who are you?" I whisper.

"Elijah." His smile is slightly askew. "My name is Elijah."

Elijah. I like the way the three syllables feel in my mouth. Thick and tangible and exotic.

I'm wondering which of my many questions I should ask next when a shadow creeps out of the rocks behind him. It glides on the snow as though it has skis for feet, inching forward in jagged movements.

"Elijah," I say, pointing behind him.

Elijah turns away from me. He spots the approaching shadow, now only ten feet away. They stand there staring at each other, shadow and boy, sizing each other up. I can't see Elijah's face, but I sense his fear in the stiffness of his back and the shallow rise and fall of his chest. The shadow flicks a look towards me and grins with evil malice.

The shadow takes one more step towards Elijah. They share the mirror and Elijah stumbles toward me, his hair pressing against his side of the mirror. The shadow stretches out one long, feathery, winged arm. It has four fingers which end in wickedly sharp claws. Without moving any closer, the shadow reaches for Elijah and digs its four claws into his shoulder. It pushes Elijah to his knees. And then he screams.

"Nooooo!" I yell with him.

His scream echoes around the mountains, bouncing off the peaks and filling the snowy plain. Then it leaks into my bathroom, filling up the small room with so much fear and pain I'm worried the mirror will shatter again. I look away, shielding my eyes. The sound and physical presence of fear winks out. I stand there for a moment or two longer, with my arms over my eyes, before I dare to peek. It's my face in the mirror again. Elijah and the shadow are gone. The echo of his scream surrounds me, and I catch a faint stench of rotting breath. I tap the mirror to see if I can bring him back. Holding my breath, I wait, but Elijah does not reappear.

I stand there for a minute, adjusting to this new development. After a while, I give up on the hope of Elijah's return and relent to brushing my teeth. I cleanse my face, double taping every surface as I go, hoping Elijah is ok. What have the shadows done to him? I want to stay in the bathroom in case he comes back. But it might not be Elijah who returns, it might be a shadow deciding my time has finally come.

Eventually, I turn the light off and walk into my room. June sits on her bed, staring at me, one eyebrow raised. Her eyes follow me around the room.

"What?" I ask as I double tap Bart's picture, guarding against the physical pain of how much I miss him.

"Talking to yourself is one thing, but screaming in a bathroom is another thing entirely." June's lips twitch, but her eyes are serious. "Someone else in there with you?"

A blush creeps up my neck. "I told you I saw a boy in the mirror."

She smiles. "Inventing imaginary boyfriends now?"

I cock a shoulder. What good would it do to tell her he's real? No one ever believes me. "Something like that."

"You know talking to yourself is the first sign of

madness, right?" She grins, inquisition over. "Georgia, you're supposed to be getting better in here, not worse."

I genuinely laugh. "Do people actually get better in here or do they pick up everyone else's bad habits?"

"They get better," June says. "I think. Well, they leave anyway."

"Probably run out of money."

"Everyone apart from me. My parents will make sure they have enough money to keep me here. It's my home." Her voice is neutral, unaffected. She really believes her parents don't care. Pity blooms in my chest. At least I have a mother who loves me—even if she did stick me in here. June examines her unpolished finger-nails, scraping at the cuticles.

"Would you want to go home, if you could?" I ask.

June looks up, rummages in her drawer and brings out another bottle of Jack Daniels. Where she got one so soon after our last escapade, I have no idea. She takes a glug and puts it back in her drawer, hides it among the mess of other belongings. "I don't really have a home anymore."

"Oh, June." I wish I could take her home with me.

Shutting her drawer, she averts her gaze. "Don't forget to take your bandage off, give those cuts air to breathe."

I unwind the bandage. The cuts aren't deep or seri-ous, just multiple and sting when I expose them to the air.

"Don't do anything stupid," June says, as she snug-gles into her bed.

"You either," I say, thinking of her bottle of whiskey.

But alcohol isn't stupid. Numbing pain is a basic human right.

"Yeah, well, that can't be helped. I do stupid things all the time." She looks once more towards the bathroom. "Mind shutting the door?"

I left it open. I'm waiting for Elijah to come back, to make sure he is unharmed. Or, at the very least, still alive. I need him to come back. His presence in the mirror proves it's possible to exist alongside the shadows. His very existence shows I'm not the only person who sees the shadows. At least, that's the way I'm going to interpret it. He proves . . . I don't know what he proves, but something, definitely something. Whatever his presence means, it gives me hope. I'm desperate for answers, and I pray he has them. If he's ok.

I reach behind me and push the door shut. Then tap it with my other hand.

"Thanks," June says, and rolls onto her other side.

FOURTEEN

IT TAKES Elijah three days to come back to the mirror. I
spend seventy-two anxious hours peering at my own
reflection, ducking when a shadow flits from top to
bottom, waiting for him. Or a shadow to make a move.
Something.

He might be the key to the puzzle. The harrowing
harassment I've endured for the last ten years by the
shadows, with no explanations in any science book or
internet site or second-hand book shops dealing with the
ancient arts of witchcraft and Satanism—and believe
me, I've looked—has taken a step in an unexpected
direction. There is a human in the world of the shadows.
How did he get there and how has he survived? I'm so
close to finding out answers that only Elijah can give.
So close.

And I can't deny the immediate connection I feel to
him. Not just because we obviously share knowledge of
the shadows—and let's be honest here, a big plus is that
I'm no longer alone in this. There's something about

him, and I'm not sure whether it's the golden aura that surrounds him, or the hint of something mysterious in his eyes, or perhaps even that he is enduring what amounts to my worst nightmare with a bravery I don't possess. That kind of stuff bonds two people quicker and tighter than any shared blood. He is a kindred spirit.

I lost my real friends because of my issues. I swapped them for a crowd that never once asked me a personal question. It was all about the booze, or the smokes, or just getting completely zonked on pot together with a half-hearted grope in the dark. And it didn't even matter who they were, and I didn't really matter to them. We were all screwed up, just looking for some human companionship to share our lonely, miserable lives with, even if it only lasted for a fleeting moment. An illusion of compassion. And now, here, suddenly, in this screwed up place of all places, is this boy smiling at me in a secretive we-have-something-to-share kind of way, despite the fact his very existence must be a living hell.

But where is Elijah now? I'm starting to suspect the shadows have harmed him. Permanently.

On the third day, after I bite my fingernails down to the pinks in a very compulsively balanced way by nibbling on each nail five times before starting all over again, I have an evening therapy session with Dr. Zaleski. He hands me a mirror and asks me to describe, in detail, what I can see on the wall behind me—which consists of absolutely nothing because Elijah pops into the frame with his twinkling smile. On his side of the mirror, it's snowing. Gentle flakes this time, swirling fragilely to the ground. But the snow fades to the background as soon as I notice the large gash across Elijah's right shoulder. His hoodie is ripped and his shoulder sports a terrible wound; three jagged lines beginning to scab over. It looks deep and serious and painful. A pull of concern tugs at my heartstrings.

"Hi," Elijah says.

I nod in reply. It won't do for the doc to witness me having a conversation with an imaginary person in the mirror. I can't see the book titles anymore, and I hesitate.

"Don't stop Georgia, you're doing so well," Dr. Zaleski says.

"Yes, sorry," I reply. "Are you ok?" I mouth to Elijah when the doc glances at his notes.

Elijah nods and smiles a sweet, crooked half smile.

"Georgia?" Dr. Zaleski gets up from his desk and stands behind me. He bends over my chair to look into the mirror with me. "Can you carry on?"

Peering into the mirror, I look all around Elijah's head and into the snowy landscape beyond. Dr. Zaleski's bookshelf is completely lost.

I rise to my feet, gripping the mirror in two tight hands, afraid of dropping Elijah and shattering his image. "I need to use the bathroom. Female issues." Those are the two magic words. Never fails.

"Ah . . . yes . . . of course." Dr. Zaleski shuffles out the way. "We're almost finished anyway."

"Thanks, Doc."

He holds out his hands for the mirror. Elijah's image remains and I'm reluctant to let it go.

"It's ok," Elijah says.

I hand the mirror back to the doc and make my way towards the door.

"Georgia?" Dr. Zaleski says, as he settles himself behind his desk, telephone raised, ready to make a call. He lays the mirror on his desk, reflective side up. Elijah is still there, and the doc is totally oblivious. "You're doing really well. You should be proud of yourself. You might not be here as long as you expected if you keep up the effort."

Ninety days. Maybe less.

I nod, then leave his office.

I run down the hall, my heart pounding in my ears, and fly into the bathroom off the common room. It's only then I realise I haven't double tapped the mirror, or the chair that I sat in, or the door as I closed it. I almost run back down the corridor to perform the rituals when I realise I don't care. The compulsion to perform such actions that usually lands in my chest as a physical sensation, a great block of ice making it difficult to breathe, is oddly absent. As I pant for breath, I smile. Actually, I grin. The shadows might be real, and I might have met a strange boy in a mirror, but my OCD is retreating. I know I can't control the shadows or what they might do to me. All I can do is face my fears and fight. Each day I inch closer to some profound revelation and each day I shed my OCD like a skin, bit by bit, finally realising the routine of the rituals are powerless to change the course of my life. I mean, I knew that anyway—intellectually, logically—but something deep inside me finally accepts it. Sort of.

The bathroom is empty. Elijah waits for me in the massive mirror that scales the three sinks in a line.

"You're still here." I breathe a sigh of relief.

"I'm still here." He tucks his hands into the pockets of his hoodie.

I can hear him much better this time, as if the distance between our worlds has lessened.

"Are you ok?" I ask. "I was so worried when I saw that shadow grab you."

"I'm ok." His face is untouched by the sun. I doubt the sky ever emerges from behind the white, overcast clouds. The land and sky look as one. And it isn't just a bleak colour, it's the very hue of misery and loneliness, of isolation and dejection. Hopelessness.

"You don't look ok." I gesture to his wound and tattered clothing.

"It's not as bad as it looks." He glances at his shoulder and fingers the shredded clothing. "All I needed is a bit of ice. And thankfully, there's plenty of that around here." He chuckles, a low throaty sound that makes me want to reach out and hug him.

"I have so many questions." I place my hands on the cold porcelain of the sink and lean in close. He is so real. His breath plumes in the cold, and I spot a tiny scar just beside his right eye in the shape of an arrow. Although clean shaven, I make out tiny bristles along his jaw beginning to grow again.

"We don't have a lot of time," Elijah says, his smile disappearing.

I glance from one side of the mirror to the other. "Why not?"

Elijah mimics my actions on his side of the mirror. "The shadows are always nearby, always hunting me. If I stay in one place too long . . . they'll be here soon enough."

"You call them shadows, too?"

Elijah nods and sticks his hands in his pockets. "That's what they look like. Dark, fleeting, and insubstantial. They're not so insubstantial when you're on this side of the mirror, when they grab you. Then you know they're strong. Really strong."

"Have you also been able to see them? How did you get in there? What do they want?" The questions came tumbling out of my mouth.

He picks up a handful of snow and moulds it into a ball. "I don't remember a time when I couldn't see them. They've always been there. It took me a long time to realise other people didn't see them too. I mentioned them to my father when I was six years old. That's when I knew for sure I possessed a unique . . . ability. My father didn't quite see it that way. I learned to keep quiet about it." He grimaces.

"Snap." We are the same. I press closer to the mirror. "How long have you been there?"

Elijah frowns. "Months. I think. I'm not entirely sure. What year is it?"

"2019."

Elijah blanches. His face turns the same colour as the stark white landscape at his back. A pale colour, almost brilliant in its own right. The red of his blood flows through the veins under his pale skin. He stumbles but manages to steady himself.

"How long has it been?"

"Twenty years," he replies.

My jaw drops open. "But you don't look much older than me."

Elijah fiddles with the snowball. "I was seventeen when I was taken by the shadows. Time, in here, stands still. I could exist in here for eternity. I didn't realise it had been so long. I have no way of marking time. It's all the same here. The sun rarely sets, and it never burns through the clouds. It's always snowing. And it's so cold."

I immediately regret being the one to tell him he's missed twenty years of his life. And then I shiver, imagining the sub-zero temperatures of his world.

"Georgia?" Elijah draws out my name, a question in his voice. He squeezes his eyes shut for a moment and then snaps them open. "I need to get out of here. Will you help me?" His words rush into the room, surrounding me, hopeful and expectant.

"Of course."

Of course I will. And not because he's hot, or because I seem to be the only one aware of his presence —the only one who *can* help him—but because no one should have to suffer an existence on that side of the mirror. His reality is my worst nightmare. Cold and ice and shadows and monsters. Being hunted. I don't wish that on anyone.

Twenty years!

And ok, it's a little bit because he's hot.

"Thank you." All of the air whooshes out of him in those two small words. His face sags and he raises a hand to touch his side of the mirror. I mimic his actions and place my fingertips against his.

A vibration pulses under my fingertips. The mirror ripples. My fingers sink into the glass. Warmth presses against my hand. The warmth of Elijah's fingers under my own. The rippling increases to such a frenzied level and the reflective glass buckles under my touch. Elijah's image stretches out into a jigsaw puzzle with dozens of missing pieces. Dark shapes slide down the mountain and advance across the tundra towards him. The shadows glide down the craggy rocks so smoothly it's like they ride on tracks.

I snatch my hand away from the mirror. When I look at my fingertips, they are blue with cold.

"Elijah! Run!"

Dropping the snowball, Elijah turns and runs. Sprinting for the mirrored cave I saw him disappear into before. As he flees through the reflective entrance, dashing low to avoid the claws of a shadow, the snowy view winks out of existence. I stare at my face. My lips tremble and my nostrils flare as I suck in shallow breaths. Heat pools under my arms and my knees threaten to buckle.

"Run Elijah," I whisper. "Run—and be safe."

I leave the bathroom quickly, fearing the shadows might come for me. I stand outside the door, in the dark corridor, not quite ready to face anyone. Sucking in a few deep breaths does little to calm my pounding heart or ease the adrenaline jumping through my veins. I feel like a hunted rabbit in an empty meadow. Leaning against the wall, I prop one foot behind me and close my eyes for a moment.

Elijah was taken by the shadows twenty years ago, confirming my fears the creatures are a tangible threat to humans. Twenty years. How long have they been mounting their attacks? Are they as ancient as they look? Do they predate time? How many others have been taken? Has anyone else survived? I know so little. I curse my propensity for avoidance and denial.

I could be taken. I know that. I've always known that. But the fact that Elijah exists on the other side means something. You can survive. Hope is not lost. If I can find a way to bring him back.

The quietness of the corridor becomes unnerving, as if the shadows have found new portals to pass through. Perhaps in the eyes of the ancient portraits staring silently at me. I feel a strong desire to move, to be around light and people and laughter.

Opening the door to the common room, I squint against the bright fluorescents. I look for June. When I don't immediately see her, I seek out Liz. Or perhaps a book will be a better distraction.

Neither of my roommates occupies the common room, but it bustles with purpose. Several girls laugh at some sitcom on the TV. I note Kiara sits among them. Crash Helmet Annie stands in her corner, quietly, not banging her head. She faces the hard, right angles, watching the paint peel. Paul is perched in a corner and Marion is fussing over the shelves holding the books and games. She pulls out a couple of board games and remarks loudly about the plume of dust that rushes up her nose and causes her to sneeze four times in a row. She moves onto the next shelf, her frown becoming deep and irritated. She leaves the room momentarily and returns with a feather duster held together with duct tape, muttering scornful comments about the cleaning crew.

She sets on the games and books, her sneezing an accompaniment to her task. When she completes the chore, she put her hands on her hips and turns in a slow circle, surveying the room. Looking at one of the closed blinds, she steps towards it, runs a finger along one filthy slat, and grimaces. She dusts with fervour, and then pulls the cord and sends the blind soaring high towards the ceiling. My breath catches. It's night—dark. The lights in the common room are very, very bright. The windows become mirrors. And although I'm not quite as afraid as I used to be of what I might find in a reflective surface, the window is large, large enough to allow a shadow to crawl through into our world.

Marion attacks the next blind, and the next, and then the other side of the room until she's pulled all the blinds high, and the room and people in it are mirrored back to us.

I back towards the door, ready to run.

The girl in the wheelchair sits on the other side of the room, away from the group watching TV, positioned in front of one of the huge, square windows. Her head lolls to the side and she seems to be staring beyond her own reflection, out into the night sky and the driveway that might offer her an escape, if she was so inclined.

A shadow flies from the top to the bottom of the

window. With the reflective properties not as clear as a mirror, the edges of the creature are harder to distinguish, but the crow-like shape is unmistakable. It flies from bottom to top and then it comes back to the middle, hovering there, flapping its strong wings. I can almost feel its feathers against my cheek. I can almost hear the whoosh of air displaced as it moves.

I grip the door handle at my back with two hands, but I can't move.

A second shadow appears in the next window. A third in the one next to that. I risk a glance at the other side of the room. Shadows fly all over the freaking place.

The girl in the wheelchair screams. A scream so all-encompassing, it raises the hairs on the back of my neck as well as everywhere else on my body. With leaden limbs, I stand there. Watching. Waiting. Wondering what will happen next. The girl throws herself out of her wheelchair, lands on the floor behind the girls watching TV, and covers her neck and head with her hands. She sneaks furtive glimpses between spread fingers. At the windows. At the shadows. She sees the shadows. And she's afraid.

She sees the shadow.

The girls at the game's tables turn at the commotion, some of them half crouching, others craning necks to get a look at the wheelchair girl cocooned on the floor. Some glance towards the raised blinds. The windows.

Mouths drop open as they leap out of chairs. A series of gasps punctuate the TV show. Then silence.

Marion stands in the middle of it all with her hands

on her hips and her frown deepening to Grand Canyon proportions, still looking between the dust on the blinds and the girl huddled on the floor.

The girls watching TV finally notice the change in the room. They flick their eyes from the whimpering girl on the floor to the windows. One screams. Then another. Their eyes widen and fear licks the room with a thick brush. Pretty soon several of the girls are screaming until Marion covers her ears. With my heart pounding and my pulse thundering in my temples, I crouch by the door and watch. And wait. Trying to understand what it all means.

The girls run from one end of the room to the other. Some huddle in a large group, clawing each other for a position at the protected centre. Everyone screams.

Marion and Paul share a look, frowns on both their faces, not understanding, not seeing. How can they not see?

But everyone else does. All the patients.

They all see the shadows.

THEY ALL SEE THE SHADOWS.

What the . . .?

Marion runs out of the room, yelling something about getting help. Only Paul and Crash Helmet Annie remain unaffected as she continues to stare at her stark corner of the room. She can't see them from her position. But if she turns around . . .

Paul looks as frozen as me, his foot still propped in his favourite position on the radiator. But his muscles are taught, reading to launch. We share a look. Exchanging knowing and understanding. We move at the same time. Him down one side of the room and me down the other, grabbing for the blind cords, drawing them closed.

With each blind I draw, the shadows hiss at me. A sibilant sound of primitive menace, a promise that this is not over. But then all of the blinds slap into place, thunking against the sills, and the shadows disappear. One by one, the girls stop cowering and calm down. They take their seats and engage in their previous activities as though nothing happened. Just like that. As if the shadows appear to them every day. As if the presence of the shadows is normal. All except the wheelchair girl, who is incapable of climbing back into her chair on her own. Paul walks over to her and picks her up. He places her back in the wheelchair, smooths her hair out of her face and points her towards the TV, away from the windows.

Marion bursts back into the common room with an army of burly orderlies and nurses. They each hold a syringe of tranq in their hands, but they stop short when they realise calm and order has been restored in their absence. Willow runs in behind, eyes shifting all over the place, skin as pale as Elijah's. Once she registers the calm, she smooths down her skirt, sweeps her hair over her shoulder, and creeps out of the room again.

Marion and Paul engage in a brief conversation. The extra nurses leave. Another orderly, one I haven't seen before, takes up Paul's position in the corner. Paul marches over to me, grabs my shoulder, and ushers me out of the room.

"Feel like a cigarette?"

It isn't really a question. Once we're out in the corridor, he slows his pace and turns to face me.

"Thanks for your help back there." He jerks a thumb over his shoulder.

"Yeah. Sure." I can't think of anything else to say. I'm still reeling from the fact that I'm not the only one who can see the shadows. In fact, it seems most of the patients in this place can.

"Wish I could quit the smokes," Paul says, as he turns down the corridor. "But I got addicted somewhere along the way."

"Me too." I hurry after him.

"Balls." He stops suddenly and slaps his forehead. "I left my smokes in the doc's office. Quick detour."

We about-turn and hurry down another darkened corridor, those beady, portrait eyes watching our every move, and end up outside of Dr. Zaleski's office. He's left a table lamp burning. A pack of cigarettes sits on his desk.

Paul crouches and punches in a code to the electronic lock. 3-1-0-3. "Pretend you didn't see that."

I smile sweetly. "Sure thing."

Paul dashes into the office, grabs his smokes and then we're marching back down the corridor and towards the back door. We both pull up short in front of the large, black window in the door, look at each other for a moment, share a nervous laugh, and then he punches in the code to the door; 3-1-0-3 again. We tumble outside in the cool night air, the door banging shut behind us.

I suck in the autumnal air, tasting rain, and watch

my exhales plume in white clouds. I will my heart rate to return to normal. My legs to stop trembling. My hands to stop quivering. My brain to make sense of my thoughts.

Paul shakes out two cigarettes from the packet, lights them both, and hands me one. I accept it and slump to the wooden bench. I take a couple of quick inhales, waiting for the calming effects of the nicotine to combat the adrenaline playing havoc with my insides. My knee jerks up and down. Up and down. Seemingly of its own accord, like a possessed puppet.

"It's cold tonight," Paul says, looking out into the darkness.

That's all you're going to say?

"Yeah," I agree, my teeth chattering. But I don't really feel the cold, despite the iciness of the bench underneath me and the frost in the air. I feel wired.

I take a slower drag on the cigarette, breathing deep, letting the drug hit the very bottom of my lungs. I shudder as I exhale, the adrenaline finally leaking out of my body.

Paul stands beside me, staring into the darkness with interest, as if he can see something beyond the uneven ground pockmarked with rabbit holes.

I near the end of my cigarette. But I don't want to go back inside, even though I'm pretty sure there are a couple pairs of yellow eyes out there in the distance. Badgers? Foxes? Something else?

Paul hands me a second cigarette and keeps his eyes trained on the pitch-black distance. "You still have those matches I gave you?"

I pat the side of my bra. I carry them with me everywhere; I can't leave them in my drawer where they might be found by the scurrying fingers of the nurses. They offer a semblance of protection. Sometimes I dream up fanciful ideas of escape, involving fire and broken windows and a desperate run through the woods. But I need to get the tracking bracelet off first.

His chin juts and he taps a thumb against his cigarette packet. "Good. You never know when they might come in handy."

The laugh escapes from somewhere in the middle of my throat. It leaves a painful lump behind. "Handy? Like when your plane crashes in the middle of the snowy wilderness, and you have nothing on you except the matches that you keep stuffed in your bra?"

"It's happened." Paul chuckles right alongside me, but his laughter sounds hollow and his face is strained with the effort.

"Or if we're suddenly thrown into the dark ages and we no longer have electricity. Then I can pull the matches from my bra and set a pile of wood in the middle of the common room on fire to keep us warm from the coming winter?" I'm still laughing, sort of. I stop suddenly when I realise Paul isn't enjoying being teased.

"The discovery of fire. Or more to the point, of how to make it, was man's catapult into the age of intelligence. It's a primitive tool. An ancient one. But a powerful one," he says, his eyes still grazing the darkness. "It is to be feared. And revered. And wielded."

I'm not sure what to say to that, so I say nothing,

and picture caveman rubbing sticks together for hours on end until, hey presto, the first spark takes and ignites some kindling. Then suddenly they have light in their caves, cooked meat, warm water. I wonder how long it took them to figure all that out.

We both take another pull on our cigarettes. The silence becomes delicate, like that of a shattered piece of glass held together by one fragile thread, just waiting for that final tap to transform it into brutal violence. The yellow eyes remain in the distance. Lots of them. Rabbits? Foxes? Wolves? I chide myself for the last thought. But if shadows can exist in mirrors and I'm not the only one who sees them, perhaps it's possible for wolves to roam the quiet grounds of Brookwood Hospital.

"Paul?" I have questions and I'm now recovered enough to ask. And if he isn't going to bring it up, I will. He doesn't respond, but his body stiffens beside me. "What was all that about, back in the common room?"

Paul takes his time taking another drag on his cigarette. He stamps his feet on the ground a couple of times.

"Mass hysteria," he says. He still won't look at me.

"Really?"

This time he turns to face me. "What else would it be? Get a bunch of crazies together—sorry, no offense—in one place, and they share hallucinations, fears, dreams. It happens."

The disappointment of his answer stabs deep. "You've seen it before?"

His eyes swivel back to the distance. "Sure."

Another silence. A long one while we smoke our cigarettes.

"Paul?"

"Yes, Georgia?"

I push the words out. "Do you know something?"

His jaw clicks. He kicks at the leg of the wooden bench. Then he drops his cigarette butt to his feet and grounds it out with the sole of his boot. His hands go to the pockets of his trousers where they play with some loose change. It jangles far too loudly in the quiet of the night.

He cocks his head. "About what?"

About what, indeed? What do I really want to ask him? What do I suspect he might know?

"I better get you inside." He points to the door. "The medication bell will be ringing soon."

I stub out my own cigarette and follow Paul back inside. I don't miss the subtle way he scans the windows before he opens the door.

FIFTEEN

THE MEDICATION BELL RINGS.

As I line up, I realise I didn't double tapped a single object while I was with Paul. Although I don't feel a sudden compulsion in my chest urging me to run back and double tap everywhere I visited in the last hour, I'm not having an exactly comfortable experience either. An uneasy anxiety jiggles through my veins. As though the thread that has wound my life together thus far, the thread that offered me purpose and hope and explanation to my very existence—however limited—is slowly beginning to unravel.

I sense a purposeful event on the horizon and my chest tightens with anticipation.

Marion hands me my small pot of pills. I throw them in my mouth and wedge them between teeth and cheek. As Willow's intrusive flashlight shines into my mouth, one of the pills dislodges from beside my teeth and slides down the inside of my cheek. Willow's eyes follow the progress of the tablet. She plasters a fake smile on her face, chucks a covert glance in Marion's direction and then pats me on the shoulder like I'm a three-year-old who's just finished my first drawing, which is really no more than a scribble.

"Good girl, Georgia," she says, a little too loudly.

I don't move. She pats my shoulder again, this time with a little more force, and sends me in the direction of the stairs. As I round the turn in the stairs, I spit the pills in my hand. Looking back towards the nurses and the line of compliant girls, Willow shines the light into the mouth of the next patient. She must feel my eyes on her because she turns in my direction and frowns. She gestures with a hand to be on my way.

I walk up the stairs, slowly, waiting for the gavel of justice to come crashing down. But nothing happens as I pad along the hallway of portraits, and when I reach my bedroom, June and Liz are already there.

"What's wrong?" June asks. She is lying on her bed with her book propped in her lap.

I show her the two pills in my hand. "Willow saw me cheek them. One of them fell out. I know she saw it. Why would she let me get away with it?"

"Don't worry about Willow," June says. "She's one of the more sympathetic ones."

"Really?" I can still feel the force of Willow's hand on my shoulder, pushing me along.

"She's been through her own stuff," Liz says, as she comes out of the bathroom. She shuts the door behind her and plops down on her own bed.

"That's true," June says, swinging her legs. "She watched her stepfather rape her mother, repeatedly.

Then he turned his advances on her older sister. Her sister killed herself. Jumped off a bridge. Willow had a few years of imbalance. Was put in a facility like this for a while. She was pumped full of drugs and hated every minute of it. She just wanted some time to grieve. Anyway, when she made it out, she vowed to help others like herself, and so she became a psychiatric nurse."

"How do you know all of this?" I ask.

"It's not a secret." June pulls her legs up and sits cross-legged. "She told me about it once. Back when I first got here, and she was trying to make me feel a little less miserable. She shared her own experiences with me. She wanted me to know that I wasn't alone." She snorts and wipes her nose. "She used to share her story in group with us all of the time, cry with us, hold us. But she hasn't done that for a while." A slight frown spreads across her forehead.

"Talking doesn't really change what happened," Liz says. "I think it got too much for her."

"Maybe." June dog-ears her book. "But if you're worried about her seeing you cheek meds, don't. She was pumped full of them in her time, and she knows how awful it is to force this stuff on people that really don't need it."

I roll the pills between my fingers and lean against the wall. "You don't think we need it?"

"You? No, not you. I mean, yeah, you've got some OCD issues. I've seen your double-tapping thing. But lots of people do. Normal people who live out there in the big, wide, normal world." She circles her hand at the window. "OCD is actually quite common. Kiara came in with a bit of it, had to say the last word in a sentence three times. It was quite funny considering it was usually a swear word." She smirks, then lowers her voice. "During my manic times, I've been known to have obsessive thoughts. Usually about my sister, and what I could have done to sav . . ." She coughs, takes a swig of water from a plastic bottle and carries on. "Anyway. Even Liz here has OCD. Not as bad as it was before. She used to think if she cleaned herself regularly enough, she could wash away all those other personalities of hers."

"It's true," Liz says, watching me from her bed. "It took me a long time to realise it didn't change anything. The medication helps, but some of them still fight for dominance." She points to her head.

"You know about them?" I ask.

"Sort of," Liz replies. "I can hear them whispering around inside sometimes, waiting for their turn."

I walk to her and put my hand on her arm. "I think I met one of them the other night."

"Possibly. There's one or two who like the night, who aren't afraid like me." Her lower lip quivers. "At home, I slept with a night light to ward off the dreams. Here, they don't allow that, so I take the drugs."

"My point is." June places her book on her bedside table and swings her legs towards the floor. "Is that OCD can be treated outside of hospitals. It can be treated by your GP." She cocks her head at me and puts her hands on her hips. "Although OCD is the most obvious trait of whatever is currently eating you, that's not the whole story, is it?"

I don't say anything. June narrows her eyes at me but doesn't press the point. I already told her the truth; that I was talking to a boy in the mirror. She chose not to believe me.

"I don't think anyone in here is insane in the truest sense of the word." She turns to plump her pillow. "We've all just got a wire missing in our brains somewhere, or it's connected to the wrong section, or a synapse that won't fire, or a hormone that won't secrete. Whatever it is, it makes us see the world differently. It makes us experience life differently. That doesn't make us insane. Or bad. It doesn't mean we need to be fixed." Her voice rises with passion, as though she's trying to convince someone other than me.

"Some might argue that it makes us special," Liz adds, reaching for her hand.

June smiles at her and squeezes her hand, then turns her attention back to me. "You're one of the most sane people I've seen in here for a long time. And there are many others who don't need to be sedated. They just need a kind word here or there or an offer of understanding."

"I need the drugs." Liz wraps her arms around her legs. "It helps with the dreams. If I take the drugs, I don't dream and . . . well . . . it's just better that way."

"Well, I should probably take the drugs too," June says. "It might help with my more manic or depressive episodes. But it dulls the senses, and I feel like I need my wits about me in this place."

I sit down next to Liz. "What about the doc?"

"He's one of the good guys," June says, climbing onto her bed and lacing her hands behind her head. "But even he has to report to someone. He has targets to meet. He feels the pressure. Patients fall through the cracks."

"He thinks I might be able to leave sooner than expected." The words feel delicate, and I hope I haven't jinxed them.

June smirks. "That doesn't mean anything. It could be eighty-nine days."

"You'd think he'd want to tick all those boxes on his statistics and get people out of here as soon as possible." I move to my bed and re-arrange Bart's picture on my bedside table. Giving into the compulsion again, I double tap the frame.

June flicks a piece of lint off her duvet. I'm not sure if she's engrossed in the task or avoiding my eyes. "You'd think."

"What about Sarah?" I ask. "She left."

Liz's lower lip quivers more profusely until she bites down on it. June gives me a penetrating look that makes me want to put my name next to gullible in the dictionary. "Transferred to a more appropriate facility?"

"Yeah. So?" My shoulders hunch defensively. "What does it mean? You keep suggesting something has happened to her, but what? You never actually say."

"We don't know," Liz says, her voice barely above a whisper, her eyes fixed on the door. "But it doesn't feel right. Not with . . . not with . . ." She jumps as a loud clang from the pipes echoes into the room. The squelchy sounds arrive in the wall behind Liz's bed. All three of us look at the wall.

"Damn pipes," June mutters.

"Not with what?" I ask Liz.

"If I start talking about this now, I'm going to give myself nightmares," Liz says. "The drugs are getting to me, and I need to sleep."

All the patients in the common room saw the shadows. Liz must see them too, but she's too afraid to even talk about them. But then, I haven't been exactly forthcoming either.

"Sleep well," June says to her and tucks the blankets around her.

"What's going on, June?" I ask.

She walks over to me and lowers her voice. "Is the imaginary boy the only thing you see in the mirror?"

I stare at her questioning face. There's a challenge there, and a pleading. She's looking for an ally.

"I think you know it's not."

June sags against the wall.

"You see them too?" I ask.

She bites her lip and nods. "And Liz."

"We're not the only ones," I say and tell her about the common room earlier. But I leave out Elijah. She doesn't believe that part and there's no need to complicate things now. There's part of me that feels a special connection to him, that he belongs just to me. I don't know if that's stupid or selfish or naïve or something else, but the fierce protection I already feel for him urges me to keep my mouth shut.

"What do we do?" June asks.

I look at the closed bathroom door, then at the sleeping Liz, then back to June's worried face. "I have absolutely no idea."

The wet scratching noises come back, and June and I leap into each other's arms.

"Do you think it's them?" she asks.

I shake my head. "They live in the mirrors, not the walls." But her question makes me doubt my own words.

A COUPLE OF DAYS LATER, DURING OUR GROUP THERAPY session, Kiara gets a new roommate. She's been alone since Sarah moved on. Kiara's been quiet and sullen, her showy displays of defiance for once curtailed. I hear the nurses whispering they finally found the right combination of drugs. And when I look at Kiara, all of the fire is gone from her eyes. Instead, they're duller than a pencil tip, and she can barely raise them from the floor to look at whoever is speaking. And is that a dribble of saliva at the corner of her mouth, running down her chin? Did she get caught cheeking the meds and is now being force-fed them? Would they do that?

"Girls, this is Kim." Willow introduces the newest member of Brookwood Hospital during our group session.

She is young, perhaps twelve, with wispy dark hair caught up in a ponytail. Her eyes are red and puffy from crying. She wears the oversized navy tracksuit, no bra. I can see the twin points of her budding puberty pushing through the large sweatshirt. She gathers her sleeves in her hands and blots her eyes with them. Willow points to an empty chair, and the girl sits, sipping fragilely from a steaming cup of tea while alternately twiddling her tracking bracelet around her wrist.

June takes five custard creams from a plate and eats them all methodically, twisting them apart, licking the insides, then crunching the harder outer shells. We haven't spoken much about the shadows since the other night. Accosted by the spine-tingling squelchy sounds, both of us were too afraid, lest whatever was making those noises decided to reveal itself.

"You don't have to talk during your first session, sweetheart." Willow pats Kim's knee.

One by one, we introduce ourselves and present our labels.

"Dissociative identity disorder," Liz says. "My name is Liz. But I'm not Liz today." A mischievous twinkle shines in her eye. It takes me a moment to realise she's kidding. And then I laugh out loud, the first moment of genuine amusement I've felt for ages.

"June. Bipolar," June says.

"Kiara," Kiara mumbles, barely audible. "Victim of stolen roommates."

Willow gives her a sharp look. "We all know Sarah is in a more suitable place." She emphasises the word *suitable*.

"Do we?" Kiara says. I sense a bit of her defiance waking up. The flare of anger in her eyes is enough to turn someone to stone. "Which place is that, exactly?"

"Georgia?" Willow ignores Kiara's provoking question.

"Hi Kim. I'm Georgia." I wave. "I haven't been here long. I have an anxiety disorder, OCD, and an unhealthy obsession with mirrors. And no, I'm not vain. What I should have said was a fear of mirrors."

Kim nods, her eyes in her lap, one hand clasping the other. I imagine her thoughts are back with her family who left her at the imposing front doors.

Although I haven't kept Kim's attention, I gain sharp looks from Kiara and June.

"Mirrors?" Kiara asks, her tone now curious, her bright eyes flinting with suspicion.

I shrug and slide down in my seat a little deeper. The one time I decide to open up I'm going to get the third degree. "Dr. Zaleski says it's not an unusual fear. That there are several cases of mental health patients who fear mirrors."

"That's true," Willow says. "Spectrophobia or Eisoptrophobia."

"But what do you see?" Kiara leans towards me and gives a side-long glance to Nurse Willow. I don't remember her being in the common room the night the shadows appeared. Maybe she doesn't realize we all see the same thing.

"Yes, Georgia, what do you see?" Willow echoes. "Would it help to share?"

"See?" I question, looking for a way out. It might be an odd question if I didn't see the shadows. The obvious answer would be myself, but that wouldn't address why I'm afraid of mirrors. They're staring at me, waiting for an answer. But if I share my knowledge of the shadows here, right in front of Willow, perhaps

I'll be transferred to a facility more suitable. Even if I know I'm not the only one who sees them. "I didn't say I see anything."

"I heard there was a commotion in the common room the other night." Kiara moves to a chair closer. I shrink back. "That you were particularly helpful. What did you see?"

"What happened in the common room?" Liz asks.

I lean back from Kiara's looming curiosity. "There aren't any mirrors in the common room."

Willow talks quietly to Kim, but like a dog, her ears twitch. She's listening.

"Funny that, isn't it?" Kiara says, wiping a hand across the table as if it wasn't Dettol-ed just an hour ago. I can smell the disinfectant. Everywhere.

"Is it?" I swallow hard. My throat gurgles. Loud in the temporary silence. The three of them watch me. We can't talk about this with Willow in the room. "I would think the nurses would want us concentrating on getting better, not checking out our appearances in mirrors or looking for potentially viable weapons."

Kiara arcs her body so she is blocking Willow. "Yes, they told me that too."

There is another pause. Willow is trying to wrap up her conversation with Kim, but the poor young girl has started crying again. Willow gets up and retrieves a box of tissues from a shelf behind her.

"What did you see?" I ask Kiara. "Did you see something in the common room? In the windows?"

"A-ha!" Kiara claps her hands together and a triumphant smile spreads across her face. "You do know what I'm talking about. You see them too." She jabs a finger at me.

"Everyone sees them," June hisses. "And we can't talk about this now."

"The shadows?" Liz asks with a trembling voice.

"Agreed," Kiara says. Willow claps her hands together gently, signalling she is ready to carry on with the session. "But later."

Kiara perks up for the rest of the session, feeding Willow words she wants to hear about her recovery. It's like she is reading from a script. I actually admire her for it. She almost has me convinced she's getting better, that she doesn't see strange creatures in mirrors and windows. But I know otherwise.

Kim is quiet but manages to share a few words. Liz doesn't say anything at all. She slips behind her shield of silence. As for me, I barely hear a word that is said. During the days since the common room episode and the conversation with June, my thoughts have been windmilling. I've replayed my conversation with Paul over in my mind, sometimes convinced that he knows something about the shadows. Other times, I'm certain he's just been here a long time, has been witness to all sorts of craziness and that that night in the common room wasn't anything extraordinary. But I've seen the shadows and I know the other girls have seen them too. That is indisputable. But what does it mean?

Kiara wants to talk about it. So does June. Perhaps we can figure it all out together.

"There's been some good sharing going on today," Willow says at the end of the session. "I'm so glad that you've engaged in conversation while I have been dealing with Kim. That's what these group sessions are all about." She smiles perfunctorily and claps her hands just once.

As we get to our feet, I can't help but feel the metaphorical pat on my back, and I get caught up in a feeling of genuine pride, as if I've just completed a tricky school assignment and the teacher is ever so proud. The tracking bracelet digging into my wrist reminds me why I'm really here and that all the compliments and good work and feeling-sharing aren't going to take the shadow problem away. But maybe June and Kiara can.

"It's good to share," Willow says, as we file out of the door.

Yes. Yes, it is.

SIXTEEN

I SPEND the rest of the day excusing myself to the bathroom every half hour, trying to catch a moment alone with Elijah. One time, shortly after a lunch of spaghetti bolognaise that I manage to spill down my sweatshirt, June is in there. She sits on the counter, her back to the mirror.

"We're going to talk with Kiara later tonight. After lights out."

"We are?" I lean across the counter, take a paper towel from the dispenser and wet it under the tap. I try wiping at the spag bog stain but only proceed to disintegrate the paper towel and spread it across the sweatshirt. Sighing, I throw the wet wad of paper in the bin.

"Yes. We are." June swings her legs and cocks her head. "I think it's time the three of us sat down and had a little chat. Compared notes. Figure out what the hell is going on in this place."

Why does she make it sound as if we're opposing heads of mafias about to have a powwow, one that even though we've declared our guns with the impartial guard at the door of the corrugated tin warehouse, will reveal we still wear hidden ankle holsters? Of course it will be raining—in my little imagined scene—the *tap-tap-tap* drilling into the metal roof unnervingly. There will be a swaying ceiling light illuminating us all in grotesque shadows, emphasising the tightness in a jaw here or the twitch of a cheek there, but always leaving our eyes in the dark, unable to measure the integrity of each other's words.

"Tell me more about what happened in the common room." She drums her fingers against the counter top.

Elijah pops up in the mirror. I shake my head at him. He nods and disappears, taking the chill of his snowy landscape with him. June doesn't acknowledge his presence and I wonder why only I see him.

"I . . ." I think about the way the shadows appeared in every window, circling, like they were looking for a way in. The girls screaming like someone had walked in with a gun and started shooting. "It was weird. Scary. Awful. I don't know what the hell happened."

June jumps down from the counter. We stand side by side peering into the mirror together. "The shadows?"

I nod. Then swallow to work some moisture into my throat. "They were everywhere. And everyone saw them. Everyone." I catch her eye in the mirror. Her pupils widen and she grips my hand. "It's not just us."

"I knew it." June whispers.

"You've never asked anyone before?"

She shakes her head. "I've only talked about it with Liz. I didn't know everyone saw it too. I thought it was just us . . . that maybe we were really crazy." She covers her face in her hands and wipes a tear under her eye with a finger.

I put an arm around her, even though it imbalances me. "It's not just you. It's not just me. Thank God. This is real."

"What do they want?" June asks, some of the fire coming back to her eyes.

I look at her in the mirror. "I don't know. Nothing good."

"My sister . . ." her eyes water again.

"They took your sister?"

She nods.

"How? What did they do?"

June flinches, and I immediately regret my tactless question.

"They sucked her right into the mirror. She screamed . . ." her voice wavers. "She screamed for so long. I can still hear it."

"I'm so sorry, June."

We both look up as a shadow flies from the top left corner to the bottom right. It's a large one, and it moves languidly. We both stare at it. Maybe it heard us talking. Can they hear us? Do they know we know they exist? That we're forming a group? That we'll fight back? A group of mental health patients versus an army of shadows. I don't like the odds.

June heads towards the door muttering about talking tonight and then something else about wondering if perhaps the meds are the right way to go, that maybe Liz has it right all along.

I stay in the bathroom for a moment longer, holding tightly to the porcelain sink with two hands, feeling for the first time in twenty-four hours that my body needs to be balanced in what it's touching.

Elijah comes back.

"Am I the only one who can see you?" I ask as snow falls behind him.

"I'm not sure," he replies. Snowflakes land in his hair and eyelashes. He blinks and shakes his head to flick them away. "I think others have caught glimpses of me, but I've never be able to maintain contact with them like I do you. No one has been able to hear me before. Or if they could hear me, it's only faintly and they can't see me. And you're the only one I can see." He smiles the lopsided smile that makes me want to put my arms around him and hug him. He's been alone for so long. "Sometimes I catch a glimpse of another or hear a voice, but it's your image that's clear and visible to me. It's your voice that's brought me hope."

I smile and wish I'd washed my hair. "I'm just so special."

He chuckles and the warm sound heats my insides. "More than you realise."

"Why?" I lean closer, yearning to touch the mirror, but prudence holds me back. "Why can I see you? How can I hear you?"

"I don't know, Georgia. I don't know how it works." He shivers and hunches his shoulders. "I can only assume it's just who you are. Maybe it's because we're the same. We both see through the mirror to the other world so clearly." He stuffs his hands into his pockets.

"But I'm not the only one. The others see too. June sees. They all see the shadows. All the girls here. Maybe none of us are crazy."

"You're not crazy, Georgia. And neither am I."

I reach a hand to the mirror but pull back before I make contact. Some of the girls have been here a lot longer than me. The shadows will be coming for us soon. But how will we all fight if we're all so used to running?

"Are you having second thoughts about helping me?" His lips look slightly blue. The snow falling behind him is particularly heavy. But it's a gentle descent, a scene of Christmas promise, if it wasn't for the lack of sparkling tree or the shadow climbing down the mountain in the distance.

I point to the creature. "Elijah."

He turns and sighs. "It's ok. We have a few minutes—"

I tap the mirror, right over his nose. "I'm not having second thoughts."

"It might be dangerous." His lips compress.

"I'm sure it will be." I give him my bravest smile. "Elijah? If we're going to get you out of there, I think we should start with how you got in to begin with."

"I'm not really sure." He checks on the progress of the shadow to his rear. "Twenty years ago, I was standing where you are now. My father had me committed to the hospital."

I wince. "Eeesh."

"I don't blame him. Not anymore. He didn't understand. He was trying to help, trying to do what was best.

If only he hadn't been afraid. If only he'd accepted that science doesn't begin to explain all that is in our universe and that his own son might have an unusual ability." Elijah shakes his head wistfully. "There's a history of schizophrenia in my family. But it seems that's not the whole story."

"What is the whole story?"

"We have . . . a gift." He raises his hand, like he's going to touch me, right through the mirror, then lets it float back to his side. "I've been thinking a lot, but without anyone to discuss it with, all I have is a bunch of theories. People with mental health conditions see the world differently."

"Very differently." God, what would it be like to be blissfully unaware of the shadows? To be able to stare into a mirror for hours on end, to be able to sleep without them whispering at you, to be able to walk along a series of reflective windows without a shadow flying next to you?

"But now I'd really like to find a way out. You asked how I got in here. The way I remember it, I was standing in my bathroom, looking in a mirror. I was just beginning to think that I wasn't the only one who could see the shadows, that there were others like me in the hospital."

Our stories are so similar, a pang of compassion surrounds my heart. "Then what happened?"

"A shadow came." He grimaces. "Its black wings scraped the side of the mirror and emerged into mine. Then its hands. Strong, sinewy hands that ended in long tapered, clawed fingers. One of its hands went around my neck, the other under my chin." He scratches at his throat, as if he can still feel the claws. "Those wet sucking sounds." He grimaces, and my heart thuds in my chest. "It pulled my face towards the mirror until its mouth covered mine. Then I felt myself being sucked into its world. I could feel the cold. And where its hands were on me, it burned. It sucked out my soul and took me to the other side."

My knees tremble. "Your soul?" I never really knew what the shadows wanted. Or maybe I suspected, deep down, but whatever their purpose, I know it's not a good end for me. "Wet sucking sounds? I hear them all the time."

"Soul, consciousness, essence. Whatever you want to call it. The thing that makes me, me." Elijah shrugs. "They make those sounds when they feed."

The shadows are in the hospital. The shadows are feeding on people.

"What about your body?"

"Clever girl." Elijah wags his index finger. "My body is still on your side somewhere. It's being kept alive by someone. That's why I still exist on this side."

That's why Elijah is alone over there. That's why he survived the shadows. I'm sure others have been taken, and killed, their bodies discarded on my side made to look like accidents or victims of human misdeed. Someone on this side of the mirror must have witnessed Elijah's attack, someone is keeping his body alive.

"But where, Elijah? Where should I look?" A thick tension lands in my shoulders. The shadow at Elijah's back isn't far away now. We don't have much time left.

"Somewhere in the hospital." He staggers away a step, one eye on me and the other on the shadow. "I only ever see rooms within the hospital from my side of the mirror. I don't think I can stray too far away from it, so I assume my body is there somewhere."

"Where, Elijah? Where?" I rack my brains trying to think of where a seventeen-year-old body could be hidden within the six floors of the hospital. I come up blank. The building isn't that big that a body can be hidden, much less kept alive, for twenty years.

"Find the person who's keeping me alive. Maybe then we can find my body." He smiles apologetically, the shadow almost upon him, and tugs his hood up over his head. "But be careful who you talk to." He lowers his voice, and although he's whispering, I can hear him clearly and the note of fear that makes it tremble. "It's dangerous, Georgia. Not everyone wants to help me. Please be careful." He darts away from the mirror.

I lay a hand on my side of the mirror. It ripples again. I pull it away before I'm sucked in. I'm not ready to enter Elijah's world yet. I need to find his body. And the person who is helping him. And avoid those who aren't. And I really suck at cryptic puzzles.

LATER THAT NIGHT, AFTER DINNER, AND AFTER THE medication line during which I manage to cheek my pills successfully, I go directly to my bedroom and prepare for bed early. June is already there and she gives me a shifty look. She confirms with a series of hand gestures that we're going to wait until midnight, then we will advance on Kiara's room.

I nod my agreement and clamp down on the urge to tell her about Elijah. I can't figure out why I want to keep him a secret; it's an instinct, and I've learned to listen to my instincts.

June lays a finger on her lips as Liz stirs in her bed. She stretches, groans and rolls onto her side.

I pretend to read *Little Women*, but my thoughts are far away from the March family. Instead, I scroll through the list of staff in my mind. I've already dismissed any of the patients as the ones who are helping Elijah. The patients don't have a free reign over the facility; it'd be impossible for one of us to keep Elijah hidden and alive. It has to be a member of staff, but I have no idea who. And it isn't the sort of thing you just go and ask someone. Not without a trip to solitary and a needleful of tranq.

I can imagine Paul's reaction if during our next smoke break together, I blurt out; "By the way, Paul, I know there are strange creatures in the mirror, and I know there is a human boy stuck there on the other side. I know someone is keeping his body here, healthy, alive. It wouldn't be you by any chance, would it?"

It isn't the sort of risk I can take. Not if I want to help Elijah. I'm his one shot at getting back here and he's my one shot at proving to everyone I'm not crazy. So, it's going to take some time and some good old-fashioned detective work. Move over Nancy Drew and Veronica Mars, here comes PI Georgia Boone.

I can talk to Kiara and June about it later, sound

them out about other entities that might be in the mirror, see if they have an inkling about Elijah's existence.

I jump when an orderly knocks on the door, signalling lights out. Without glancing at June, I flick off my light and pretend to go to sleep. The taps progress down the corridor, followed by the snap of lights and the soft thuds of doors with well-oiled hinges.

Tension hangs in the air, thick and tangible. I feel June on the other side of the room, barely breathing, biding her time. Liz mutters in her sleep, rolls over again and then remains still for the next few hours.

I open my eyes to see June's face merely inches from mine. I must have fallen asleep after all.

"It's time," she whispers, poking my forehead. At least her touch is in the middle and I don't have to ask her to balance me.

I creep out of my bed, wincing when a floorboard squeaks. We tiptoe to the door together. June lays her finger over her lips and cracks the door open an inch. She sticks her nose into the gap, scanning the corridor.

"Are we good?" The tension coiled in my limbs is so tight, I want to get this over as quickly as possible. If I'm found breaking the rules so soon after the drinking incident, I'm afraid I'll end up with a worse punishment than a night in solitary.

"Wait," June says, her index finger raised.

I stick my head over hers. The corridor is brighter than it should be at this time of night. A light shines in one of the rooms further down.

"Shit," June mutters.

Willow and Marion come out of a room. Kiara's

room. Maybe the new girl is having trouble settling. Something, instinct maybe, tells me this night-time visit has nothing to do with Kim.

The nurses stand in the corridor, whispering to each other. A moment later Paul appears with a sedated Kiara in his arms. There is a gurney parked outside her room. He lays her down on it and buckles the restraints around her wrists.

"Where are they taking her?" I whisper to June.

"I don't know," she whispers back. Stuck close to her, her heart pounds fast against me. "She's not been making trouble. I don't understand this."

We watch silently as Paul follows the nurses down the corridor to the service elevator. He wheels the gurney transporting the sedated Kiara inside. With a gentle whoosh of the elevator doors, they're gone.

Kiara's bedroom door opens again. Kim stands there, her eyes wide and puffy. She looks in our direction and locks eyes with us. June lays her finger across her lips again and her gentle *shhh* travels down the corridor to Kim. The frightened girl retreats back into the room, closing the door softly behind her.

June mirrors her actions and shuts our door.

"Well, that's that then," she says. "We'll not see Kiara again."

"How do you know?" I ask. "Maybe she had a medical emergency."

June jabs a finger at my chest. "Did that look like a medical emergency?"

"I guess not." I sag against the door. "But there might be a valid explanation."

June snorts. "You really think so?"

"What's the alternative?" All sorts of scenarios play out in my head, most involving guns or restraints or shadows, and all of them violent.

"I can think of one or two." June's breath irritates the skin under my ear.

"This is the best hospital in the southeast for mental health problems. If they were doing away with their patients, wouldn't it be on the news?" I try to sort through the logic, to calm myself with rational thought. If the hospital is involved in some sort of scandal, how could they get away with it for so long? And yet girls don't return. So, where the hell do they go?

"Most people do make it out," June says. "But something else happens to the rest of them."

Ice freezes my fingers and toes as I creep to my bed and pull the covers high.

June climbs into her own bed. "Something bad."

I don't want to think that gentle Willow or kind Paul are capable of something not quite right, that they might be responsible for some suspicious goings-on. Willow has been to Hell and back, like most of us. Surely, she's an ally, a link to the side of authority that understands how the patients feel and could, therefore, be our advocate in our treatment here.

Marion, although not unkind, is practical and would belong better in the army than trying to comfort teenage girls. But that doesn't make her an evil person. There are other nurses and orderlies and doctors that I don't know as well, but it doesn't explain what Willow,

Marion, and Paul were doing. One of them has to know something.

Body snatching and selling off organs. At least that's the first idea that pops into my mind. With the external existence of the shadows proven, my mind is free to imagine any number of possible scenarios, no matter how outlandish they first appear, and consider them a real possibility. But Willow, Marion, and Paul being involved is something I can't get my head around. Something isn't making sense. And then, as the squelchy sounds start up in the walls, a new thought slams into my brain. If mental health patients have an aptitude for being aware of the shadows, and Willow was once a mental health patient, perhaps she, too, is aware of their presence.

SEVENTEEN

HOURS PASS. The heavy weight of sleep tugs at my eyelids, but I can't close my eyes. I get up and go into the bathroom. Closing the door, I lean back against the cold tiles, the coolness refreshing against my flushed skin.

I pull the cord of the light above the mirror. I stare at myself.

"Elijah," I whisper. "Are you there?"

I wait a moment.

"Elijah?"

"Here," he says, his image popping into view. He rubs his eyes as though he's just been asleep. He pulls his hoodie tighter around himself and in doing so, brushes a hand against his shoulder. The wounded one. He winces, peels back his hoodie and glances at the wound. It's still angry, and is it turning black at the edges? He recovers it quickly and goes back to rubbing the sleep out of his eyes.

"Were you sleeping?" I lean against the door. "I'm

sorry, I didn't mean to disturb you, I didn't think you did sleep."

"No one looks in the mirrors at night. The shadows aren't interested in me at night, so I rest."

"I've been thinking about what you said." I step forward and rest my hands on the sink. "I have some questions, but if you want to go back to sleep . . .?"

"S'ok." He brushes a foot of snow off a rock and sits down. The snow glints under a muted sky, appearing like shimmering crystals. "We'll have more time to talk now. The shadows will leave us alone."

"Thanks." I examine his face. Growing stubble sprouts from his chin and I wonder how he trims it over there. His skin is pale, which only emphasises the dark circles under his eyes and the haunting look in his pupils. But despite all that, his good looks come across in the shape of his nose and the angle of his jaw. I stare at his lips, soft and tender, and wonder what it would be like to kiss him.

He pulls the hood of his sweatshirt around his neck and tilts his head. "What do you want to know?"

I scan the darkened landscape behind him, thinking of a place to start. "You're the only human on your side of the mirror?"

"Yes."

"The shadows feed on people's . . . souls?" A prickly feeling of being watched erupts over my skin. I glance right and left; but I'm alone.

"Yes."

The questions rush out of me. All the things I've always wanted to know. "Why aren't there more people over there? Why don't they take more victims?"

"They do," Elijah says, his breath white and pluming. "I'm the only one who survived."

I slump back against the door, my thoughts racing, my knees heavy.

"The shadows can only take the souls of those who can see them. They suck the life right out of them. I've seen it happen. That's what they tried to do to me. But instead of me dying over there on your side, my soul went through the mirror, kicking and screaming, and I managed to escape. The others aren't so lucky. Their souls are taken, and their bodies die. Sometimes it's quick; all the life sucked right out in one breath. Other times it slow, the shadows taking their time, spending days feeding on one particular victim, rendering them to comas, or worse, before they eventually die."

"How did you do it?" I frown and raise my hands.

Elijah shoots out a bitter laugh. "They still hunt me, Georgia. My body is on your side and what you see now is my soul. They still want it. I run, and I hide, and I hope for a way out of all this."

A sudden injection of courage propels me forward and I touch the mirror. I want to lace my fingers through his. I want him to feel human contact, to know there's someone in this world who knows of his existence and is fighting for him. I know what it is to be lonely. I want him to feel all of that in my touch.

My fingers seem to melt into the mirror. Triumphant, I smile as my fingers close around the pads of Elijah's. His eyes widen and he snaps his hand away.

"No, Georgia. It's likely you'll be pulled into my side. And then what would we do?"

I take my hand away. My fingers tingle from the brief contact. His hand was icy. So frozen that my heart aches to press my body against his and offer him my heat. I want to sit with him in front of a fire, a great roaring bonfire, where I will lean against his shoulder, and we'll feel the heat of the flames on our faces. He is so pale, so cold, all of the time.

I dip my head. "Elijah, you said you've seen others taken?"

"Yes." He blows on his hands and shoves them under his armpits. "One last week sometime. I couldn't see who it is, but I saw the shadows at the mirror sucking . . ." He shudders. "The victims come from there, Georgia. They're patients at the hospital. It's the best feeding ground for miles around."

It's the same thought I've been thinking for the last few days. And it isn't really a thought per se, more the inception of one. I've been too afraid to form the words, to allow the idea to become tangible. The loose thread was floating, and I picked at it, picked and unravelled and picked some more. With Elijah's words, the entire knot untangles. I can see the connection so clearly now.

I've suffered from this plague for so long, everyone assuming it's down to me to fight my visions, my demons, my eccentricities, my OCD. But now I know the problem of the shadows is a real, concrete thing that neither I nor anyone else has an ounce of control over. Supernatural entities do exist. They mean harm, and they are hurting the patients here. They are killing them. They got Sarah, and now maybe Kiara.

"It's as if by having a mental health condition, we've tapped into an area in our brain that allows us to see the shadows," I say.

"That's the conclusion I was coming to when I was taken." Elijah climbs off his rock and walks close to his side of the mirror. "But, Georgia, the shadows feed every night. They can make one human subject last for weeks. But in order to do that they have to have access, they have to have the body restrained and repeatedly accessible."

"But no one here is just going to let the shadows feed off them. You should have seen the girls the other day when the shadows flooded the windows of the common room. No one would want that."

"Georgia," Elijah says, staring at me purposefully. "Of course they wouldn't. Someone is helping the shadows. Someone on your side."

Ever since I saw Willow, Marion, and Paul dealing with Kiara last night, it's the same conclusion I've been coming too. Deep in my mind where my denial is strongest. But I struggle to believe what's right in front of my nose. Paul? Willow? Marion? Were they trying to help her or are they all in it together? The shock rakes through me in violent shudders. No one is safe.

I squat down on my haunches for a moment, my brain fried from all this new information, trying to make sense of it, trying to put all of the pieces together, trying to figure out who in this hospital is evil.

"There's more, Georgia." Elijah's voice is softer

than the snow that surrounds him.

"More?" I ask, standing up again.

"Just like I came into this world. A shadow escaped into your world. That's who will be helping the rest of them to feed."

I reel against the information. "But I don't see any shadows walking around the corridors. They're only in the mirrors."

"It took on human form. If a human is particularly vulnerable, and a shadow is particularly strong, they can pass through the mirror and use a human body as a host."

There is a shadow walking around Brookwood Hospital. June's ghost stories cut closer to the truth than she realises.

"Just one?" I ask.

"Yes," Elijah says. "In all the time I've been here I've only seen it happen once."

Willow, Marion, and Paul. If one of them is a shadow, what were the other two doing with Kiara last night? Coercion? Some other kind of symbiosis?

Perhaps the incident with Kiara was innocent. Patients do experience medical emergencies. Or the three of them could have been up to something dubious that has nothing to do with the shadows at all.

Then I think about the patients. Elijah says the shadows can take over a particularly vulnerable human. A human with issues, mental health problems that plague her life. Liz? Sweet, reluctant Liz with the many personalities she carries. Could one of them be a shadow? And what about June? She's been here a very long time. It's possible. One of my roommates could be the embodiment of my deepest fear.

But there are many patients here and every one of them is a viable suspect.

"Someone is helping the shadows, Georgia." He looks left and right, then locks his eyes on mine. They're greyer than the rocks at his back. "Someone on your side is bringing kids like offerings."

"But why? What do they want? What are they?" I ask.

Elijah hunches his shoulders and huddles against the wind. Small icicles hang from his eyebrows and snow clings to his stubble.

"The shadows are created by humans. All of our disappointments, our fears, our nightmares, our petty jealousies, our greed, all of the selfish, hateful motivations that drive us to commit terrible acts and feel abhorrence for another person are transformed into a shadow. Every time someone looks into a mirror, all of their emotions are transferred to the other side. They are born from fear and violence. They know only fear and violence, so their existence on this side of the mirror is full of it. They know no kindness. They have no reason. They are primitive, primal beasts that only know how to feed their insatiable hunger. Brookwood Hospital is their Garden of Eden. The fear and uncertainty and shame here drive the shadows crazy with thirst. Most of the patients can see them. It's like shooting fish in a barrel."

"Will it ever stop?" My voice trembles. I grab at my throat as fear tightens my voice box. How many shadows have I created with all my self-doubt? With my longing to live another life, be another person. But I saw the shadows before any of that started. It's a chicken and egg situation. Or perhaps the answer is stored in my DNA.

"I don't know. I don't know how to stop them." Elijah's frozen hair quivers. "I don't know if they can be stopped. I haven't seen anyone manage it in the twenty years I've been here. Every single victim has been taken. And the shadows become stronger."

"Strong enough that more may come across to my side?" The words leak out of my mouth, lower than a whisper.

Elijah's cheeks tighten and his grey eyes brighten to a fearful blue. "That's what I'm afraid of."

I take a step towards the mirror, towards Elijah, and lay my hands either side of it on the cold tiles. "Elijah. I'm scared."

"I am too." His breath fogs up the mirror and he quickly wipes it away. "That's why you need to be careful."

"I will."

"We know two very important things." His solemn eyes lock on mine. "Someone in the hospital is keeping me alive, so I think we can assume that person would also be willing to help. But someone else is helping to feed the shadows. You must avoid that person at all costs."

"Ok." I swallow hard. The cold of his world leaches into my small bathroom and seeps through the tiles on both wall and floor. "Any ideas on who?"

"I'm afraid not, Georgia. I can't actually see anyone else. It's going to be up to you to figure out who we can trust." He lips curl into a worried grimace. "And who we can't."

Elijah and I spend the next hour talking about the nurses, orderlies, and patients in the hospital. I describe each one, and we discuss and dissect each personality and appearance, but we're left no closer to finding any answers. As we talk, daylight crowns the mountains behind him. It's a golden colour, so different from the brilliant white of the snow or the depthless black of the rocks I've become accustomed to while talking to Elijah. It gives me hope. But then I see the shadows creeping down the mountain too. Their red eyes glowing with a new intensity.

"I better go," Elijah says when he notices them.

"Be safe." I raise my hand in a half wave, then think better of it and blow him a kiss.

"You too." He pretends to grab my kiss and sticks it on his cheek. He smiles, a fully loaded, partners in crime, blood brothers, we're-in-this-together-at-the-end-of-the-world kind of smile. And then he's gone. A little piece of my heart goes with him.

In that moment, I stop wishing for a rescue from Bart. Even if he could get me out of here through the legal channels, I doubt he's up to the task. He's committed a crime. He's an alcoholic. He might be more troubled than me. He can't save me. I have to save myself, and Elijah, and everyone else in this hospital. And I'm not even angry. I love my brother, for his strengths and weaknesses and how he's taught me to have more faith in myself. That's what I'm going to do; be strong and face my fears, once and for all.

When I tiptoe out of the bathroom, it is dawn. Past dawn. Liz isn't in the room and June sits on her bed crossed-legged, fully dressed, studying me with two raised eyebrows and two flared nostrils. She looks like she's been waiting for me to come out of the bathroom for some time.

"It's all yours." I gesture to the open door.

June hops off her bed and shuts the bathroom door with deliberate slowness. "I don't need to use the bathroom, Georgia."

I turn my back on her, start making my bed and then fiddle with Bart's picture. I double tapping everything even though I don't really feel the need, hoping if I act busy enough, she'll stop looking at me so warily.

June clears her throat. "Are we going to talk about it?"

"About what?" I ask, still not turning around. I open the drawer on my bedside table. Shut it with my other hand. Open it again. Shut it again.

"Who you were talking to in our bathroom in the middle of the night? All night. I think you know something about the shadows. Well—" She laughs suddenly. "We all see them. But I think you know something. Something more, something big, something that can help."

I wriggle under the scrutiny of her gaze. "I told you about the boy in the mirror, remember?"

"I thought you were joking." She storms into the bathroom, snaps on the light, and inspects the mirror.

No shadows. No Elijah. She turns back to me with a what-the-hell-are-you-talking-about face.

"I'm the only one who can see him," I say.

June walks back to me and looks me up and down. "Why?"

"I have no idea."

"Who is he?"

"Elijah. He lives on the other side of the mirror with the shadows."

June's eyes water. "Rebecca . . . does he know . . . did he see . . .?"

"There's no one else there," I say, touching both her shoulders. "It's only him."

A growl rumbles in her throat and she slams a fist at the wall. "I know, I know, I was just hoping . . ." She kicks the wall, twice, three times, then crumples to her bed.

My instincts tell me June isn't behind any of the malevolent deeds concerning the shadows. My gut tells me she's just as terrified of the shadows as I am and that she's looking for a comrade to sort through the whole thing. So I tell her everything. About when I first met Elijah and what we know so far. She sits on her bed and listens to it all.

"But what are we supposed to do?" she keeps asking.

"We have to save Elijah. We have to find the shadow living in the hospital—"

"But how do we do that, Georgia?" Her voice is hollow and afraid. "I don't want to die like my sister."

I won't be able to rely on June. She may come

across as the feisty, confident chick with all the attitude, but deep down she's even more scared than me.

Elijah needs my help. I must protect him; I'm the only one who can. And June. And Liz. Crash Helmet Annie. All of them.

With an awkward smile, June leaves the room. She runs her fingers down my arm as she passes, but doesn't say anything. After she leaves, I lean back against the wall and do a breathing exercise to ease the anxiety swimming in my limbs.

I feel the hourglass of time trickling away and my heart squeezes for Elijah. I like him. As a friend, as a person and we share the bond of horror that binds souls closer together than blood. But that isn't all there is to it. The selfish corner of my soul knows if I can help Elijah out of the mirror, we can show people where he's been. We can reunite him with his family and then they'll have to believe. Him. And me. I won't be crazy anymore. I won't be the weirdo girl who sees strange things in a mirror. I won't be the one who ran away screaming from shops and windows. I won't need to drink to obliterate the world around me. I can be normal again, have friends again, have parents that look at me as though I haven't just arrived from another planet and aren't taking up all of their patience with every sentence of the unusual I utter. My OCD, I'm sure, will continue to diminish until it vanishes completely. I can be free.

Free.

It's a small word on the surface. It's so much more than a word to me. It's a sentiment, a ticket, an emotion, and a god-damn human right.

EIGHTEEN

Hɪᴅɪɴɢ in the book corner from everyone, I watch Paul and the nurses through the observation window. Paul must feel my glaring stare as he turns around and gestures for us to go outside. On the way, he produces two cigarettes and hands me one. When we reach the back door, he lets me key in the code.

Outside, the world is grey and cold. The trees have shed their leaves and are now no more than skeletons. I spot a hint of the murky, stagnant canal in the distance. We sit down on the old, wooden bench and hunch our shoulders against a bitter wind. Frozen clumps of grass crest like irregular waves and I imagine the eyeless lady stumbling across the uneven ground with her arms laden with crows.

"Still got the matches?" Paul asks as he removes a lighter from his pocket.

We dip our heads together and shelter the cigarettes from the wind. He lights them both at the same time.

"Just in case of an alien invasion where all our technology is incapacitated, and we can no longer rely on the ancient hospital boiler?"

He smiles at my joke and takes a long pull on his cigarette. "Exactly. Could happen any day now."

We sit in silence for a few moments. The questions churn in my stomach, and finally, I decide I'll never discover anything to help Elijah if I don't take a risk.

"Paul?" I look at him sideways, assessing the stubble on his jaw and the yellow tips of his fingers. His cheeks hollow as he takes another drag. "What happened to Kiara?"

He hides his reaction well, but the twitch in his jaw and the ever so slight wince gives him away. His cigarette hand trembles, which could be the cold. But I'm sure it isn't.

"What do you mean?" He stamps his feet on the ground and rubs a thigh with quick strokes.

"She wasn't in the common room this morning." I have to play this very carefully, one small nudge at a time.

"And that's concerning why?" He takes another drag.

Now is the moment. I can either dance around the subject and never get a clear response, or I can put it all out there and gauge his reaction. If he is part of Team Shadow, I'll know soon enough.

"I saw you carrying her out of her room late last night." I shift my body to face him, my own cigarette burning down between my fingers, the smoke torn away by the wind.

"You did?" He deadpans, no flicker of emotion

whatsoever. "I'm sorry you saw that. Was it upsetting for you?"

I frown down my nose at him, sneak a quick drag. That isn't the reaction I was expecting. "That depends." I try to keep the fear out of my voice. "On where you took her."

Paul sighs and the ash on the end of his cigarette swirls into the air. He throws his cigarette butt to the ground and watches it burn out. "She went to the hospital. She took too many meds and needed her stomach pumped."

"How did she get a hold of so many pills?" I ask, suspicion layering me like a wetsuit.

"She'd been cheeking them for a while, storing them up. Took them all at once. Although we do room searches every week, I think security's been a little lax." He glances at the door and I know he's thinking about the fact that I know the codes. But escape is the last thing on my mind right now. I wouldn't get two feet before my tracking bracelet sent an alarm. And I need to help Elijah. "We haven't had an incident like that for a long time. It's a shame. No one realised she was suicidal."

"She wasn't suicidal." She wasn't. We were supposed to have a covert meeting last night, and she was eager to exchange secrets. She wanted information —about the shadows, maybe how to fight them. She wouldn't have committed suicide.

"How do you figure that?" Paul looks at me for the first time, a quizzical eyebrow raised. I think he genuinely wants to know what I think. "She took the pills. It's a pretty clear sign."

I snort and cold air bites the back of my throat. "Like June slashing her wrists before she came here?"

He tucks his chin into the collar of his shirt. "Yeah, that too."

"Kiara wasn't suicidal." I dare to poke his arm. "She was afraid."

"Everyone here is afraid." He turns his cigarette pack around in his hands. "You're all here to face your deepest fears. It would be weird if she wasn't afraid."

"That's not what I mean."

"Then what do you mean?" His face is open and questioning. It seems Paul believes the overdose story. No one is that good at lying. Not even an Oscar-winning actor.

I scan the bleak landscape, the sky white and unforgiving, the ground muddy and colourless. "There are different types of fear."

Maybe Kiara decided she needed to get out, away from the hospital, away from the shadows, even before we had our conversation. Something must have frightened her so badly that she risked the overdose. A medical emergency seems about the only way out of here.

"Unfortunately, it often amounts to the same thing," he says.

I think about that for a moment. He's probably right. The end result is that Kiara ended up in the hospital needing her stomach pumped. How the pills got in her stomach to begin with or why is immaterial.

"But what actually happened, Paul?" I ask, tucking my hands into the ends of my sleeves. "Were you the first on the scene?"

A flicker of a frown crosses his forehead and he drops his gaze. He twirls the cigarette packet then clears his throat. Once, twice, three times. That's when I know he knows something. A big something or a small something, I'm not sure. But he knows *something*.

"No, Willow and Marion were there. They sent down the alert. I think they arrived just after it happened." He flicks his lighter on, off, on, off. "Tried to make her throw up, but she refused. Then the effect of the drugs took over and I took her to the ambulance. Another orderly drove her to the hospital."

I stand. "But you didn't see her take the pills?"

Paul's frown deepens. "What are you getting at, Georgia?"

It isn't safe to reveal everything I know, not to a member of staff, not to someone who has the power to lock me up or cart me away. Did she really swallow down a line of pills, or did someone force her to look in a mirror until a shadow ripped her soul away?

"I'm not sure." I toe the broken patio with the edge of my plimsol. "Will she be coming back?"

"I imagine so. When she's feeling better." Paul puts the lighter back in his pocket and looks at me. I can't read his expression. He's good at masking his emotions on his face, but his jittery actions paint a different story. "Although it's possible they might feel a more appropriate facility is better for her considering her recent actions."

The answer is too quick, too prepared, delivered with no hesitation. He moves his gaze to the frigid canal.

Indignation oozes out of my pores. "What would be a more appropriate facility than here? Isn't this supposed to be the best mental health hospital in the southeast? Where else would she go?"

"I don't know, Georgia!" Paul stands. "I'm not in charge of these things. The doc makes those decisions. He has his reasons, and I don't ask questions."

"Why not?"

He paces a few steps, swivels back towards me, then points a finger toward the door, refusing to answer.

"Are there questions that need to be asked?" I stand in front of him so he has to look at me.

He jabs his finger at the door, and I realise I'm not going to be getting anything more out of him today. Gritting my teeth, I follow him inside. He opens the door of the common room for me. "If you can refrain from asking quite so many questions, I might take you out again this afternoon."

I nod. A flicker of hope blooms. I might be able to break him down later.

He plasters a smile on his face and walks away.

So Paul doesn't ask questions. Which means there are questions that need asking. But what are they?

Paul spends some time in the office observing us through the window. I stand in the middle of the room for five minutes watching him, but he doesn't acknowledge me. Instead, he chats with Willow when she enters the room.

I turn in a slow circle, trying to decide what to do with myself, trying to figure out what Paul's cryptic responses mean. I spot June in the games corner playing chess on her own. Slipping into a chair opposite her, she doesn't bother to acknowledge my presence either. I'm beginning to think I've turned invisible.

"Was your sister bipolar too?" I ask her.

"No." June keeps her eyes on the board and moves a white pawn. "But she suffered bouts of depression and anxiety."

I draw a circle on the table with my finger. "That makes sense then."

June flicks her dark eyes at me. "What makes sense?"

"Only people with mental health conditions see the shadows," I say.

"Shhhh!" She frowns at me and glances at the office. "What, like, it's part of our DNA or something?"

I prop my elbows on the table. "I don't know, maybe."

June sags back in her chair. "And how does that help us now?"

I sigh. "I don't think it does. I guess the why isn't really important."

June starts setting up the board again. "You need to figure out what they want and how to kill them."

I fiddle with a pawn. "Me? What about you?"

Her dark eyes brim with conflicting emotions. "I'm not taking the meds. I can feel a depressive episode coming. All this talk of the shadows . . ." She runs a finger along the length of one of her tattoos. "I'm as useless as a snail without a shell when the vortex sucks me down."

"Can't you . . . stop it?"

She shakes her head.

"I'm sorry. Is there anything I can do?"

June commences a solitary game. "Just don't let the shadows get me."

I reach for her hand. "I could really use your help, June."

She sniffs and keeps her eyes on the board. "I'll do what I can."

In the bathroom, I give Elijah a brief update. My suspicion that Paul knows something about the shadows, but I haven't yet determined if it's a good something or a bad something. He tells me to keep prying. I leave the bathroom and make my way to the gym to pound out my frustrations on the cross trainer. As I pass the nurses' station, Willow smiles at me. Behind her, through the window, the sun peeks out, and it looks like this October afternoon might be more temperate.

Willow turns her attention back to paperwork on the desk. On the far wall behind her, there is a stack of cardboard boxes. Filing, I think. Until I see one with my name on it. A box I recognise. That's where all my personal effects are being stored then. If only I could get to my phone. But who would I call? Who would believe me?

Bart. He's been pretty useless at a rescue attempt, but I know he'll believe me. He's the only one who never judged. He never doubts what I say. I have to call him, or at least try to. He might be the only one who can help.

A DISAPPOINTINGLY UNEVENTFUL WEEK DRAGS BY. There are no more mass witnessing of the shadows. Kiara does not return to us, and we're told she's still receiving treatment at the general hospital. June sinks into a depression and barely manages a conversation. Anytime I mention the shadows she winces and shrinks away. Liz remains her usual quiet and subdued self. Group therapy carries on with new girl Kim bearing her soul while the rest of us sit there and try to figure out what the hell is going on in the privacy of our own heads. We go from group to art class to outside activities. The younger girls attend classes and, occasionally, I sit in on a math class, just to keep my brain ticking over. It's possible to study for A-levels or a Btech, but I don't have the concentration levels at the moment; every ounce of energy is going into figuring out how to rescue Elijah. And besides, I don't intend to be in here long enough to complete a course.

Ninety days. Well, less than that now, if I can convince everyone I'm healed.

Therapy with Dr. Zaleski is the only thing that's progressing—until the shadows launch a new visceral attack on me and scream at me from every flash of reflective surface from within his office; the window, the nameplate, even his glasses.

"Keep trying, Georgia. You've been doing so well;

I'd hate for you to lose all this progress." He leans over his desk and the shadow skitters across both lenses.

My double tapping intensifies again, and I long miserably for Bart, for home, for something safe and familiar. Paul, true to his word, continues to take me for smoke breaks. True to my word, I don't ask any more awkward questions. Not because I don't want to, but because I don't know what to ask. Not without revealing all I know, and perhaps the depth of my apparent insanity.

Elijah and I confer in my bathroom when we can. But we're no closer to any answers. Perhaps a more daring approach might be necessary. He's reluctant. But we're caught in a stalemate. The shadows are going to make a move. I want to make one before that. Team #Georgia&Elijah.

June stares blankly at me every time I came out of the bathroom. Whenever I give her an update, she just stares at me and says; "But what do we do?"

What can we do?

Knowing the shadows are real is one thing. But she's right; what do we do about it?

She doesn't even read, her stack of paperbacks collecting dust on her bedside table. The vortex of depression has stolen her from me. I need her help. Perhaps I can save her from her depression. Maybe I can penetrate that thick layer of apathy. I need her, goddammit.

One day, after lunch, I go in search of her. I haven't seen her since we all woke up in the morning and I want to try and get through to her.

Having checked everywhere else, I make my way to our bedroom. Outside the doorway, a sudden and overwhelming feeling of dread washes over me. My knees tremble, and my breath catches in my throat. I want to run away, out the front door and into the woods. The compulsion is stronger than an OCD urge. Logically, intellectually, I know I can't run forever, but right now, that's the only thing I want to do.

I don't run. With both hands evenly placed on the door, I push it slowly open.

June lays in her bed, where I left her this morning. But she isn't alone. Marion sits on a rickety wooden chair beside her bed that squeaks when she shifts. One hand strokes June's short hair, the other rests in her lap. She hasn't noticed my entrance. She whispers to June. A soft cooing. Maybe a lullaby. A thoughtful frown punctuates the middle of her forehead. Is the nurse planning on taking her away?

"She's not depressed, you know." A defensive anger masks the dread still quivering in my knees. I need to think quick if I don't want June carted off to the general hospital or some other more *appropriate* facility. She's my friend. She's the only person here who makes it bearable. "I mean, she *is* depressed. She's just not suicidal."

"I know that, Georgia," Marion says, without looking at me, continuing to stroke June's hair. Perhaps she knew I was here all along.

I step closer. "Kiara isn't depressed either. Let alone suicidal."

She sighs. "I know that too." The chair creaks as she shifts her weight.

I inch towards her. "Then why isn't she here?"

The silence stretches on so long I don't think she heard me.

"Kiara is not coming back, Georgia," she finally whispers.

That doesn't really answer my question. But it does answer the one I was going to ask next.

Marion raises her eyes to me. An intrinsic warning flashes through them. I was about to ask her where Kiara is now, or if she had help ingesting a handful of half-digested pills, but something in her eyes stops me cold. Nothing evil, per se, but something. And it brings me no closer in determining if Marion is involved in helping the shadows.

Marion pushes herself out of the chair and wipes her hands on her dress as if she's just been baking and they are coated in flour.

She lays a heavy hand on my shoulder. "It's not healthy to ask so many questions, Georgia."

I tense, half expecting her beak nose to grow larger and her fingers to taper into claws and her skin to turn as black as coal and her eyes to turn red and infected. But she remains human.

"It's best to concentrate on your own recovery, Georgia." She leaves the room, and a cold draught sweeps inside to take her place.

"June?" I whisper her name across the room. I walk over to her bed and plonk myself in the seat Marion vacated, glad to take the weight off my shaky knees. The chair is still warm.

The blanket is pulled up past June's chin, almost to her eyes. I startle when I realise she's not sleeping. Her dark eyes are open, glazed, not really seeing.

"June?" I pull the blanket down an inch. She shifts in the bed, rubs her eyes, and focuses on me. "Are you taking the meds?"

She shakes her head. He short hair is stuck up on one side.

I prop my elbows on my knees. "Are you ok?"

This time she shrugs.

I sit there for a moment, wondering what I can do to help. What will pull her out of it?

"I need your help, June." I place my hand on her bed. "I can't do this on my own."

"It's too late, Georgia," she whispers, then closes her eyes.

"It's not too late." I lean towards her and rest my hand on her bed.

She doesn't reply. I poke her. Hard. What does she mean?

"June?"

"I don't care anymore, Georgia," she says. "I don't have the strength, or the energy, or the . . . guts."

"But you're the bravest person I know!" She doesn't react. "You've survived in this place for five years. How?"

One eye opens and locks on me. "Exactly. I think my time is running out."

The dread comes back, this time as a flush that

creeps up my neck. I haven't thought of it that way. Luck running out. Like frequent flyers fearing each flight with increasing trepidation.

"Then we need to prepare," I plead with her. "We need to save Elijah, all the girls here. We need to prove the shadows' existence—"

"And what?" June laughs. A high-pitched strangled noise. "Stop it?"

"Yes." I jab a finger into her duvet. "Yes. We need to stop it."

She raises an eyebrow and shakes her head, very slowly, then rolls away from me.

But she's right. How am I, mere mortal and mentally addled, going to stop a supernatural being?

NINETEEN

EVERY TIME I speak to Elijah his voice is lined with concern and his eyebrows are permanently knitted together. I want to place my fingers on his forehead and smooth all those worried wrinkles away.

"It's dangerous."

"We're not getting anywhere." I poke the mirror, then quickly withdraw my finger when it starts to ripple.

He pokes back. "That doesn't mean you can throw caution to the wind."

I take a measuring breath. "Elijah. I think that's exactly what it does mean." It's time to upset the boat and see where the chips land, as Bart is fond of saying.

I go through what I know, trying to separate fact from assumption:

- Both Sarah and Kiara disappeared since I've been at the hospital. *Fact*
- Although the nurses offer perfectly reasonable explanations, I know from Paul's

twitchiness on the subject there's more to the story. *Assumption—but I'm sure I'm right*

- I have the distinct impression that another girl might suddenly go missing soon. *Assumption—but I can feel the truth of it in my bones*

It's coming. Something is coming. A thing, a person, or an it. I'm positive. Events are building towards some kind of crescendo like an amassing tornado on the horizon. Not that I've ever experienced a tornado, but I used to have a morbid curiosity and would spend hours watching clips on YouTube about natural disasters. So often it starts with a warm, sunny day. Then a bit of a breeze picks up. Then the sky turns green—and wham! A tornado appears on the horizon, sometimes right on top of unsuspecting or uninitiated victims.

- June refuses to get involved. *Fact*
- Marion and Willow still scare the hell out of me, and I have no idea if I can trust either one of them. *Fact*
- I'm pretty sure I can trust Paul, (*Assumption*) but I hesitate to confess to him. I can't bear for another person I care about to look at me like I'm crazy.

As I make my way to Dr. Zaleski's office, I decide to feel him out. He can be the next person to eliminate from my list. He's so bogged down with paperwork and therapy sessions it's easy to dismiss him as the suspected shadow or the Elijah abetter. He's just too busy, too distracted. Yeah, he might look at me funny, but the worst he can do is up my meds. I'm cheeking them anyway.

I knock on his door with one hand, refusing to give into the urge to knock with my left hand too.

"Come in, Georgia," he says, and gestures to the club chair in front of his desk. "How are you today?"

"Fine. Good. I guess." I pull at my sleeves, a surge of adrenaline making me twitchy.

"You've been here over three weeks now." He opens a file on his desk. "We've made progress with your therapy. Some minor setbacks, but I feel we're on the right path."

"Yes." I slink into the chair.

He holds a pen poised. "How do you feel the medication is helping?"

An unexpected laugh bursts from my throat.

An uncertain smile quivers on his lips. "Georgia?"

I look at the doctor, his grey tufts of hair are wild and messy. It's late afternoon, the sun already setting behind the trees in the distance, leaking a pink light into the dim office. Dr. Zaleski removes his glasses and rubs at the bridge of his nose.

I take the plunge. "I'm not taking the meds. I've been cheeking them."

This time Dr. Zaleski laughs. "Why does that not surprise me?" He drops his pen, sits back in his chair, and folds his hands over his stomach.

Relief rushes out of me in a shudder. "You're not mad?"

"No, Georgia, I'm not mad." His smile turns paternal, and I yearn for the father I never really knew. "You're on a placebo anyway."

"I am?"

"Yes. I don't think you really need the drugs. But I was hoping the placebo would help you open up and explain your fear of the mirrors. But it hasn't done that yet." His look turns somewhat reproachful, but there's humour in it too. "You don't quite trust me."

"I don't trust anyone." I cross my legs.

"Why not?"

I shrug. "Trusting people is what got me here."

"Is it really so bad here?" He folds his hands over his stomach. His blue pinstriped shirt doesn't hide the coffee stain above his breast pocket. "What could I do to make it better?"

Tell me who the shadow person is on this side of the mirror, how to free Elijah and oh, also how to be rid of the shadows. Permanently.

I sigh. "Nothing. I'm fine."

Dr. Zaleski gives me a once over. "There you go again. Not trusting anyone. Why don't you trust me, Georgia?"

"Because I don't believe everyone here has the patients' best interests at heart." It's the only way I can think of saying it without mentioning the shadows.

"You don't think I want you to get better?" He leans forwards and places his hands on the desk.

It's my turn to relent. "You. Yes, I do believe you want me to get better."

"Is there someone specific you're thinking of? Has

something happened, Georgia? We take incidents very seriously—"

"Nothing's happened," I say. "And no one specific."

"Then what, Georgia? What's holding you back?"

I search for the words. How do I explain this without sounding crazy? It's impossible. "I can't explain it. I'm sorry," I add when I see the doctor's disappointed look.

He rubs at the bridge of his nose again. "So like your father."

I sit up straight in the chair. My heart stutters in my chest. "You knew my father?"

He raises a hand. "No. No, I didn't know him. But I've read his file. I requested it when I knew you were coming here."

I perch on the edge of my chair. My fingers dig into the leather arm rests. "He had a file? What kind of file?" The horses in my chest keep right on galloping.

Dr. Zaleski pauses again and steeples his fingers over his stomach. "A psychiatric one. It's not much of one, because his problems weren't really addressed until he reached adulthood and he pretty much refused any kind of treatment."

"What . . .? How . . .? What was wrong with him?" I glance around the office, reading the titles of the journals on the shelves, but not really taking them in. Instead, wondering, thinking . . .

"Some kind of severe paranoia. Might have been schizophrenia."

Schizophrenia, my ass. My dad saw the shadows too. I'm certain of it. Relief floods my body, pulsing through my limbs, right to the tips of my fingers. A shuddering relief. I'm just like my dad. And not in the stubborn, obstinate way my stepfather refers to, but in the way that makes us see supernatural entities.

I've never wished so profusely for him to be alive than I do right now. I want to know what he knew. I want to talk to him. I want his knowledge, and his love.

"And of course, there's always your brother's alcoholism." Dr. Zaleski pours water into a glass from a bottle on his desk.

How does he know about Bart?

He raises the glass but doesn't take a sip. "These things do tend to run in families, and it seems that you and your brother both got a dose of it."

Alcoholism? My mother and stepfather are very careful not to mention that particular word. But that is telling in itself.

I peer out of the darkening window. Night is almost upon us. I stand, close the blind without asking the doctor and go back to my seat. He doesn't comment.

Bart drinks a lot. My father never touched the stuff. Claimed it dulled his senses too much, apparently. Bart said our dad always wanted his wits about him. But Bart does drink. I drink. But that's because it helps block the shadows from my mind.

Bart almost killed a lady while drunk driving. I thought he drank to obliterate the memories. But now, on reflection, I realised his drinking started long before, when he was a teenager. Connecting dots form a nice neat line. Why didn't I see it before? Does Bart drink to block the shadows too?

If only I could talk to him, but I still have another

few days before I gain telephone privileges. I have a feeling it will be too late by then. Maybe I can break into the nurses' station and retrieve my phone. But it's manned twenty-four-seven. Impossible. Unless I find someone to help. But who?

"Bart's had some troubles," I say.

Dr. Zaleski slips his glasses back on. His eyes are magnified. He leans over the desk and props his chin on a hand. "We're not here to solve Bart's problems."

"No, we're not." I force myself to relax into the chair.

"What do I have to do to make you trust me?"

I look around the room and again find the lack of familial evidence strange. "Tell me about your son."

His bushy eyebrows shoot up and his face drains of colour. "What do you know about my son?" He takes a sip of water.

My fingers dance over the armrests. "He was here. And then he wasn't."

Dr. Zaleski picks up the pen and taps it against his finger. "He's dead, Georgia. He died a long time ago. He committed suicide. He wasn't well."

"I see."

His gaze roams to the window. Rain spots the glass. "There's not much else to the story."

"Why don't you keep a picture of him?" I wave a hand around the office.

"It was too painful, to start with." His head dips. "And then, well, so much time passed, I didn't see the point. I don't need a daily reminder that I failed him." He slips his glasses off again and chucks them across the desk. "Is that all, Georgia? Have I answered enough questions now?"

My heart rate reduces to the slugging beat of guilt. Dr. Zaleski is just trying to help those like his son, and I've brought up his loss all over again. Not cool. But at least, in my mind, it rules him out as being in league with the shadows. (*Assumption—but a good one*) I'm pretty sure he's clueless as to the evil machinations that run his hospital. But also, I'm no closer to finding anyone to help.

"Yes," I sigh. "That's all."

I leave Dr. Zaleski's office shortly thereafter and go to the downstairs bathroom. Devoid of other patients, Elijah is already there, waiting for me.

"Short of asking people straight out what they know about the shadows and gauging their reaction, I don't know what else to do. June's depressed, Liz is, well, not Liz half the time. I don't know any of the other girls that well. I'm on my own in this here, Elijah, and I really don't know what to do." I stand in the middle of the room, feet planted wide, fists curled into my sleeves.

Elijah cocks his head, watching me, and offers a sympathetic smile.

"I'm sorry." I uncurl my fist and push the tension away. "This isn't about me. It's about rescuing you. And I'm failing you."

"You're not failing me, Georgia." He pushes off his hood and his watery blue eyes find mine. "Even if I'm stuck here for the rest of my life, at least I get to talk to you. I have that."

And I will always have him too. But he should have

more, much, much more. He should be held and kissed and loved at the very least.

I stare at Elijah and his snowy world, shifting my weight from one foot to the other, wondering if I should express my last idea. I know he'll be worried, but the thought nags at the back of my mind, and I'm not going to be satisfied until I explore every avenue of inquiry.

"What is it?" he asks, squinting at me suspiciously.

"The top floor," I say. "It's locked and a forbidden area for patients. I didn't really think much of it, assumed they used it for filing, but now I'm beginning to wonder."

Elijah smiles. A huge, genuine smile of unabashed hope. And he doesn't tell me to be careful. Not right now, anyway. "Check it out, Georgia. Maybe that's where my body is."

I run my teeth across my bottom lip. "Or the headquarters of the nefarious goings on of the shadows."

Now, he frowns. "Have you seen anyone go up there? Who told you it was forbidden?"

"Willow," I say, trying to place her on a team. Team good or team bad? If she suffers from mental health problems, she might be one of the shadows—or she might be the one helping us. "When she gave me the tour of the place. But I've seen other nurses and orderlies on the stairs leading up there."

Another vague thought pushes to the forefront of my mind. Didn't June ask me about Sarah, when she was taken, whether they took her up or down the stairs? Does she know what's up there?

"Ok, start keeping an account of who." Elijah ticks

points off on his fingers. "That will help narrow it down. And check it out, Georgia, see if you can get up there."

"Ok." I grin back. We're moving forward now, doing something concrete. We're going to make some progress. I can feel it.

He points a stern finger at me. "But be careful."

"I will," I reply, as Crash Helmet Annie is escorted into the room by Marion.

Marion stops at the threshold and looks me up and down. Twice.

"Felling a bit panicky today." I offer her a weak smile. "Trying to talk myself out of it." I gesture to the mirror and my reflection, which is currently obscured by a worried Elijah. He takes the hint and disappears.

"I see." Marion gives the mirror a once over and then ushers Annie further into the room, pointing her into the stall. "You know it you're finding things hard to handle we can always up your meds."

Why does she suggest that? Surely she's privy to the information that my medication is a placebo?

We stare at each other for a moment. Me, trying to look into her grey eyes to determine if the essence of a shadow is filling out her human husk. Her, well, I don't know what she's trying to glean from my impassive face, but she stares hard. Hard enough to make my insides turn to mush.

"I'm trying to handle as much as I can on my own," I mutter, backing towards the door. "I don't want to take pills forever."

"Good for you," she says, voice neutral, attention

being drawn away by a banging noise in the stall that Annie occupies. She sighs, pushes open the stall door and turns Annie around.

I use the opportunity to creep away. Running up the stairs to my room, I glance briefly overhead when I reach the landing, wondering when I might get the opportunity to explore higher up.

I burst through the door of my room, panting, knees gone to jelly, feeling decidedly out of sorts.

The toilet flushes behind the closed bathroom door.

"June, I really need your help," I say. "I'm really scared." I sit on my bed, double tap Bart's picture and wrap my arms around my knees.

The door opens, but it isn't June who comes out of the bathroom. It's Liz. At least I hope it's Liz.

TWENTY

"WHAT ARE YOU AFRAID OF?" Liz moves around my bed and sits next to me. A waft of strawberry shampoo floats around her, and her hazel eyes look almost as pale as her skin.

My hands tremble so I grip them harder around my knees. "I don't know who I can trust." I daren't look at her. Not in the eyes.

"Yes." She plucks one of my hands away and holds it in hers. "You do have to be careful. Has something happened with the shadows?"

I blanche. "How much do you know?"

"We're all victims, Georgia." Gone is the timid girl I first met, replaced with a maternal tone that sends a flush of homesickness through me.

And then I look at her. Right in her shining eyes and see the truth. So I tell her everything: the first time I saw the shadows, how they've accosted me my entire life, but more importantly, the predicament Elijah finds himself in, and how I feel duty bound to help him.

"I just don't know who I can trust," I say again, glancing at the closed bedroom door.

"I know who the shadow person is," Liz says. She glances from side to side, towards the window, back to me.

I go with my gut instinct. "Marion?"

"No," Liz says.

"No?" My insides go all mushy again. Please don't let it be Paul.

"Willow."

My mind reels as this new information filters through and I rebel against it. "How do you know? I thought she'd been through mental health problems herself? I thought she was sympathetic to the patients here?"

"She is." Liz nods, pressing a finger against her lips. "Before she was possessed. I saw it happen. And then she never shared her life experiences with us again."

"But she lets us cheek the meds." I half stand, trying to make sense of it all.

"She does," Liz says, her hand dropping from mine. "Because she's looking for the right person to be her companion."

"Huh?" I sag against the wall. I never expected Liz to be the one to hold all of the answers. I hope I can keep her talking before one of her other personalities cycles through.

She tilts her head and pats the bed, but I remain standing. I'm too edgy to sit right now.

"A shadow can only possess a person if they're clean. In other words, not taking any medication.

Willow would like to have another shadow cross over from the mirror and join her here. To what end, I'm not sure. Maybe she's lonely, maybe she wants to take over the world, but that's why she passively encourages an anti-med rebellion."

I slip down the wall until I'm sitting on the floor. "Is that why you take the meds?"

"Yes," Liz says. "I've taken myself out of circulation as an appropriate candidate. The downside, however, is if you take the meds it means you're more docile for the shadows to feed on. You're more likely to become shadow food. Like Sarah."

I rake my fingers through the roots of my hair. "Isn't that worse?"

"Not to me." Liz shakes her head. "I don't ever want one of those things inside me. I saw how it took over Willow." She shudders.

"And that's also why June refuses to take the meds," I think aloud. I stand up and pace towards the bathroom door, then back towards the bedroom door. Back and forth, back and forth.

"Yes." Liz leans back on the bed, her arms straight. "She would rather be possessed than food. Or at least she'd like the opportunity to fight possession."

"And Kiara." I stop suddenly and throw my hands out. "She was taken. I think. But she wasn't taking the meds." My brain hurts from trying to figure out what the hell is going on.

"A candidate for shadow possession." Liz watches me pace again. "Perhaps she was being tested."

"But where is she now?" I ask.

"I don't know, Georgia." A quiver of fear in her voice and the Liz I know is back.

I still don't know if Kiara was removed from the facility for benign purposes or other more untoward experiments. Despite the explanation Paul gave me, I don't know whether Kiara might still be in the building. Tied down. Forced to look at a mirror until a shadow takes over her soul. And if Willow is responsible and she took Kiara, then how are Paul and Marion involved? Could they be under some sort of mind-control? But no, Paul was decidedly uncomfortable when I quizzed him. Surely, if his mind is controlled by another, he wouldn't have allowed a facade of impassivity to slip so easily. So it has to be something else. Something that Willow has over them. I remember the way Willow ran one long, sharp nail down Paul's bicep. The tentative smile on his lips that I read as sexual attraction. Perhaps it wasn't sexual attraction, perhaps it was fear.

"Can she be saved? Willow, I mean?" She didn't start off bad. She started out just like me. Like so many others here; with anxiety, depression, OCD, an extreme phobia, or any number of other mental health conditions. She didn't start out a shadow, she was taken by one. Maybe she can be un-taken.

"I don't know." Liz shrugs. "She might be too far gone."

I sit down next to her and take her hand again. "Then how do we help Elijah?"

"I don't know the answer to that either." Liz squeezes my hand back. "But at least now you know

Willow is the bad guy, it will be much easier to find the person who is keeping his body alive."

We sit there for a few minutes, each with our own thoughts, me now seeing everything with fresh eyes, but still not having any tangible way to help Elijah.

"Liz? Will you help me?"

She shakes her head, her brown hair tumbling over her shoulders.

"No?"

"I'm not Liz," she says, with a surprisingly masculine voice that sends chills racing down my spine.

I let go of her hand, suddenly feeling the contact inappropriate.

"I'm going to take a nap now," Not-Liz says.

I back away from the bed and watch her approach her own, pull back the covers, and settle in.

I creep around to her bed and whisper in her ear. "Do you know anything about the shadows?"

"Don't go upstairs," Not-Liz whispers. "For all our sakes, don't go upstairs."

But that's exactly what I need to do.

Loneliness winds its way over my shoulders and through my chest. Settling in. A tear rolls down my cheek, which I wipe away. I can't give up now.

June has shut down, Elijah is stuck in the mirror, Bart is in London and ignorant to my plight, my mother unreachable—not that I would try and contact her for help; she never believed my stories to begin with. Paul is a potential option, but I know he is either friendly with Willow or under her power somehow. Does he know what she really is? And Liz, is well, Liz. As helpful as Liz's information is, she isn't a useful ally in this coming war against evil.

I grab Bart's picture from my bedside table and tiptoe into the bathroom. I'm half tempted to call Elijah, but I don't want him to see me like this, all red-eyed and blotchy and desperate. Instead, I slink down the closed door and hold Bart's picture tight against my chest, wishing I could speak to him, and my father.

A shadow floats across the mirror. The biggest one I've ever seen. It flies from one corner to the next, filling it up, magnifying, until the mirror fills with black and two, huge red eyes fix me to the wood at my back.

It opens its massive beak of a mouth, slowly, wider and wider until the mirror becomes nothing but mouth and needle-like teeth. I cling to Bart's picture like a life-line, wishing his natural confidence would seep out of the picture and into me. But then the shadow's mouth protrudes into the room. That's when I almost lose it. But passing out from fear isn't going to stop me being taken.

"No!" I scream.

The shadow stops, beak fully projected into the small bathroom, and lets out the loudest, most primal scream I've ever heard. Its breath rushes towards me on a freight train wind, pushing my hair back from my face, making my eyes water from the impact and forcing me to hold my breath. It smells of death and fear and despair and rotting corpses.

I turn my head to the side, to better avoid the noxious fumes, and keep one eye trained on its progress. But it doesn't emerge any further out of the mirror. The scream continues, shaking the glass in their window panes, rattling the shelves and toppling creams and moisturizers to the floor. The toilet lid flaps open, then closed, then open again, a gaping mouth, adding to the chaos of noisy assaults. Grout from in between the wall tiles crumbles, the screws holding the mirror to the wall begin to unwind. My hair is blown back in a continuous stream, and I can barely keep my eyes open against the force. They water, stinging. When I suck a breath into my mouth, the air is hot and reminds me of the desert and violent sandstorms that can change their landscape irrevocably. And suddenly the scream stops, the cessation of noise almost violent in itself, and the shadow opens its beak and speaks.

"You will not take him from us. That is the deal."

The voice is deep and guttural, as if speech is not its natural method of communication. It's the first time I've heard a shadow speak anything other than my name. It stares at me, and I stare at it, and then it disappears.

I'm left clutching Bart's picture, quivering on the floor, wondering if what I just saw really happened.

Crawling to the toilet, I throw up lunch into the bowl. I wipe my mouth with the back of my hand and crawl out of the bathroom. Climbing into my own bed, my entire body trembles. I watch Liz, or Not-Liz, or whoever she might be right now, sleep, wondering if the shadow is referring to Elijah. Knowing it is.

I spend the afternoon in bed, shivering, from cold or fear I'm not sure. The why doesn't seem to make much difference. When Marion comes to check on me, I tell her I don't feel well, and she gives me some painkillers.

When the sun fades, I edge away from the room and head to the cafeteria. The dinner hour is almost over, the large room practically empty. But I spot June in a corner on her own, playing hide a tomato under a lettuce leaf. I grab a roll and some cheese and go to sit beside her.

"What do your tattoos mean, June?" I ask as I slide onto the bench opposite her.

She gives her wrists a cursory look and pulls her sleeves down to her knuckles.

"Fortitudo means strength. Virtute means courage," she says.

I nod. We could all use a little of that. "Does it help?"

June shrugs. "It used to." She looks down at her plate, nudges the tomato out of hiding with her fork. "Not so much lately." She raises her eyes to me. Her usual spark is missing. In fact, they look downright watery, as if she's about to cry.

"I'm sorry I can't help you," she whispers.

I pick the crust off the roll. "Why not?"

She looks away for a moment and covers her mouth with a hand. Her hand shakes. She looks down at her plate again. "I'm sorry, Georgia, I just can't. I'm scared."

"I'm scared too," I whisper back. I don't want to be on my own in this, and I never thought that feisty, rebellious June would back away from the fight.

She breaks up the tomato with the side of her fork. "Some of us have more to lose."

"Do we?" I take a bite out of my roll, even though I'm not really hungry, but I should keep up my strength.

This time she doesn't reply, just continues to pulverise her food. I sigh, loudly, hoping to stir an element of guilt in her.

"I want to help. I really do." Now she does look at me. "I just don't want to face off against a shadow. That's a fight I'm afraid I'll lose."

"Will you at least talk to me about it?" I smack my roll against the table, causing crumbs to skitter across the surface. "The shadows? Will you help me figure some stuff out?"

She wipes her eyes with her sleeves. "I think I can manage that."

"Ok, good." I take a breath, then plunge right in. "Willow is a shadow person inhabiting a human body. She is responsible for all the disappearances, feeding patients to the shadows and she's taking more kids, more often...I think she's planning something big and it's going to go down soon and we . . . I . . . have to stop her—"

"Whoa!" June holds up a hand. "Slow down. Willow is a shadow person?"

I tell her all about my conversation with Liz and that Not-Liz told me not to go upstairs.

"Then that's exactly where you need to go." June smiles wickedly, some of her spark reigniting.

"My thoughts exactly," I say.

She pushes her plate to the side and folds her hands on the table. "Maybe that's where Elijah is being kept."

"Oh, so you were listening to me." I throw a piece of the roll at her.

"Or." She frowns. "Or something else."

"Yes," I say. "It could be something else entirely."

She flicks a few of the crumbs off the table. "We need to go look."

"Yes, we do."

"Not me." June shakes her finger at me. "I meant you."

"I know." I re-tie my ponytail, pulling all the loose strands into the tight elastic. "I'm going tonight."

June glances left and right, then leans in close. "And then we need to figure out a way to kill a shadow."

TWENTY-ONE

EVEN THOUGH THE idea of killing a shadow has occupied my mind for years, and even though I want nothing more than for them to suffer miserable, drawn-out and excruciating deaths, when June puts the idea out there in the spoken word, it sends a shiver through me. Not to mention fear. But the biggest question of all is the how I'm going to kill one on my own.

An idea niggles. Every time I see a shadow in the mirror, and through every conversation I've had with Elijah, their world has been covered in ice and snow. It's very, very cold over there. It stands to reason that the shadows don't like heat. Perhaps it also follows that they're afraid of fire.

I consider the other nagging sensation I've had during my conversations with Paul—all of those ridiculous situations we spoke of when a book of matches would come in handy. Not that Paul has ever confirmed his knowledge of the existence of the shadows, but it seems pretty obvious he knows something. As Willow has been identified as the bad guy, it stands to reason that Paul might be the good guy, and that thrusting that little book of matches on me and insisting I carry it everywhere I go, is his way of protecting me. I smile at the thought. Maybe he even knows where Elijah is.

And then, I realise as I walk the upper corridor of beady-eyed ancient oil portraits, even if I know fire is the weapon to use in the fight against the shadows, it will be too dangerous to wield until I've located Elijah's body. I sigh as I enter my room. It will all depend on what I find up the forbidden staircase later tonight.

As I push open the door, June is already preparing for sleep. Liz, or Not-Liz as I now think of her, is no longer in her bed. Perhaps she's still down at the medication line. Or maybe she needed a walk around after spending most of the day in bed.

June and I snuggle under our respective blankets. I try to settle on *Little Women*, but my thoughts are a couple of floors above my head picturing a plethora of disturbing scenarios. When an orderly taps on the door at ten o'clock and Liz still isn't back, June and I exchange a worried look.

Instead of turning my lamp off, I steal out of bed and stick my head around the door. Willow loiters in the corridor. I almost fall back into my room. But no, she doesn't know that I know what she is. And so, with my heart pounding through my chest and throat, threatening to escape out of my body all together, I call to her.

"Nurse Willow?"

Her head snaps in my direction with the reflexes of a prowling predator.

"Yes, sweetheart?" She retraces her footsteps towards me.

Sweetheart.

"Where's Liz?"

She hesitates, only briefly, but I catch the misstep as she comes down the corridor.

"She's not going to be coming back tonight," she says, fixing me with her blue eyes. She reaches my doorway and stands there towering above me.

I look unflinchingly into those icy blue eyes, wondering how this frail, nervous person could possibly be the manifestation of my darkest nightmare. Maybe part of the real Willow is still in there somewhere.

"But where is she?" I try to make my voice confident and strong to show I'm not one to be messed with.

Willow taps long fingernails on the wall beside my door. "One of her more confident personalities got the best of her. We thought it best she wait out the cycle in solitary. One of the nurses is with her. She'll be fine."

It has the ring of truth to it. It's a plausible explanation. But Willow waits, watching me, perhaps to see if I accept her statement.

I keep my face neutral, nod demurely, and retreat into my room. What more can I do? If Liz was taken to the shadows, there's nothing I can currently do. Drilling Willow any further will only alert her to the fact that I know she is not who she claims to be. And that, in turn, could spiral a series of events I'm not quite ready to encounter.

"What are you doing, Georgia? Why are you trying to engage her like that?" June hisses at me.

"I don't know, June, I'm just trying to make sense of this whole thing."

"Well, would you mind doing it when I'm not around?" June plumps her pillow and then sags into it. I'm not interested in being shadow food."

The door creaks open. Willow sticks her head around the opening and peers at us. "Everything ok in here?"

I freeze, with my back turned to her. June's eyes go wide and she nods her head, very slowly.

"Everything's fine." I push the words out, cursing the tremor in my voice.

Even though she's at least four feet away, Willow's breath smacks against my neck.

"Very well," she says. "And please don't worry about Liz. She'll be back before you know it."

Liar!

Then she shuts the door and leaves.

My heart beats double time. Did she hear our whispered conversation? If she suspects anything, I don't have much time.

I crawl into my bed, but instead of even trying to sleep, I sit up with my knees hugged to my chest and wait for the world outside my room to fall quiet. Even though I know it's too dangerous to talk with June any further, I can't imagine she's sleeping either. But after a few minutes, her soft snores drift towards me, and the wet, squelchy noises wriggle up the wall.

Close to midnight, I slip out of bed on shaking knees. I inch towards the door and crack it open. The corridor is deserted. The only noises I hear are the groaning of the ancient boiler and the sluggishly moving water in the pipes, and my own irregular heartbeat.

I edge my way down the corridor, feeling invisible eyes gauge my progress, waiting for a cry of alarm to go up in the form of an ancient gong, pointing fingers and wilding uncontrollably shrieking that the enemy is among us. I try to laugh off the image, but the seriousness of the situation smacks my teeth together instead.

I reach the end of the corridor just as the grandfather clock down in the large foyer chimes the twelve beats signalling the witching hour is now upon us. Glancing out the window before the stairwell, I catch a glimpse of a bright full moon. The wind blows wildly and a small branch thuds against the window before another gust carries it away.

The grandfather clock stops chiming, and I'm left in a silence so complete that I feel as though the hospital building itself is exhaling expectant breaths. June's stories of the patients who lived here in the decades past fills my mind. How they died here and are buried in the cemetery within the grounds. Ghosts were born, just like the eyeless mother, and it's easy to believe they walk the corridors at midnight, invisible to the naked eye, but lamenting their past lives, unable to move on or recover from a life of pain. Their presence is heavy at night, in the eyes of the oil paintings, as if they borrowed the painted people's eyes to look in upon the world. Once or twice I've heard a cry, or a mournful weeping. But that could easily be one of the current occupants of the hospital.

I place my hand on the cold metal of the stairwell

door and a chill ripples through my spine. Steeling one more glance back down the darkened corridor, I confirm I'm still alone.

I press the handle down and push the door open, half expecting a loud groaning to accompany my illicit movements. But it's mercifully quiet and, with bare feet, I step onto the cold concrete of the stairwell. I close the door softly behind me and let out a sigh of relief. Another portentous gust of wind bangs against the window. I can't see through the veil of falling raindrops what might have knocked on the glass.

My feet are cold and goosebumps line my shaking legs. I wrap my arms around my thin nightgown and shiver there in the light of the moon shining through the window. Stealing a calming breath, I close my eyes and ready myself.

"Georgia!" My name is hissed. At first, I think a shadow has appeared in the reflective window. I keep my eyes closed for a moment longer, delaying the moment, realising at the same time the voice is more reprimand than threat.

I snap my eyes open to see Paul climbing silently up the stairs.

"You shouldn't be here," he says.

"I . . ." I've not prepared an adequate story in case I'm discovered. "I couldn't sleep."

Paul climbs the last few remaining stairs until he is on my level.

He rests an elbow on the banister. "It's late."

"I know." I chuck him an *aw, shucks* look. "I thought walking around a bit might help."

He leaves a couple of seconds pause before saying; "You know that's not allowed."

I manage to pull off a one-sided shrug. "I'm not causing any harm."

He sighs as if he's been holding his breath for an eon and has finally decided to let it all go. He stares down the dark stairwell, then glances over our heads at the next flight. Two cigarettes emerge from his pocket, and he offers me one. He opens the window that's slatted with bars and a gust of cold air rushes in.

"Thanks." I take it, eyeing the stairs, wondering if I still might be able to go exploring tonight. It's getting more difficult for Elijah on the other side and his hidden presence weighs on me. June says girls are disappearing faster and faster. Kiara, Sarah, and Liz in quick succession. I need to act. I shift my feet restlessly, smoking the cigarette with Paul by the open window, listening to the wind howl, my thoughts on Elijah and the snow and burning the shadows. And then thinking of Elijah's sweet, sweet smile.

"Where were you going, Georgia?" Paul asks as a gust of wind blows his exhaled smoke back into his face. Raindrops dot his cheeks. I have the urge to wipe them away.

"Nowhere really, just walking around." I take the last drag of my cigarette and throw the butt out the window.

Paul closes it with a bang and then runs a hand through his damp hair.

"You really can't be walking around here late at

night, Georgia. I don't want to find you out of bed again. Got it?"

He's never used that kind of tone on me before and an embarrassed flush heats my cheeks. I nod, but I don't mean it, and my cheeks burn hotter. Perhaps that's the worst of it. Lying to the one person in this facility who I actually trust.

As Paul walks me back to my room, a tense silence hangs over us. The portrait eyes watch our progress and a ghostly draught sweeps through the long corridor. I half expect to see the eyeless mother, with shadows instead of crows perched on her outstretched arms, floating down the corridor.

"Where's Liz?" I ask as we approach my room. We stand outside the door. I search Paul's face for the truth, but he won't meet my eyes.

"She's resting," he replies, stealing a quick glance over his shoulder. There is a bang from downstairs somewhere, like the slamming of a door.

A twitch of anger curls my lips. If he knows of the shadows, then how can he let the abuse continue? Girl after girl, taken, killed. I don't want to think about all those who might have fallen victim to the shadows before I arrived. I won't let another girl be taken. And he's been here for two years. How could he?

I turn to my door, so he won't see my tears.

"I know you know something," I say, with my back still turned. "About Liz and Kiara and Sarah. I know you know something, something that could help us."

There is a long, tense pause. Neither of us breathes. My hand rests on the doorknob, and I wait.

I sense him reaching for me. I know he wants to comfort me. I can almost picture his hand hovering in the space between us, so close to my back, or arm, that my skin prickles. But there's no gentle touch. He must change his mind.

"G'night, Georgia." He turns and walks away, his guilty footstep fading on the plush carpet.

I stand there for a moment, wishing him back, wishing he would help. Finally, when the door at the end of the corridor slams, I go inside my room. June sleeps with her face pressed close to the wall. Paul roams the corridors and Elijah lays upstairs somewhere. I'll just have to try again. And soon.

Huddling in my bed, I remove the book of matches from my bra. I hold them tight in one hand and mumble a pray under my breath. Wishing for strength and courage.

TWENTY-TWO

DESPITE MY FAILED covert operation and the lack of sleep, I wake early. One glance out of the window reveals a grey day as miserable as the night before. The wind pounds the trees outside mercilessly, snatching green leaves from their anchoring branches prematurely. The outside landscape appears as bleak as my hope.

I roll myself out of bed and dress. In the bathroom, neither Elijah nor the shadows visit me.

June begs off breakfast and stays cocooned in her blanket. I wind my way downstairs, avoiding the beady dark eyes of the portraits and sliding my hand along the polished banister. In the cafeteria, there are only a couple faces I recognise. I slide into a seat next to Kim and nibble on a couple pieces of buttered toast. Kim doesn't look up and pushes dissolving Shreddies' squares around her bowl.

Paul enters the cafeteria, walking right past my table, his tie brushing ever so faintly against my back.

But he says nothing and won't meet my eyes, even when I drill holes into his skull.

I sip at tepid tea and nibble on my toast, not really hungry. Willow waltzes into the cafeteria with her head held high and her shoulders thrust back. She pauses just inside the doors and surveys the girls present. Finally, her eyes settle on me. As she marches towards me, my stomach flip flops. Is it my time to be taken? But would she make such a public display? Surely she knows I'll fight?

Instead, she smiles sweetly at the girls eyeing her progress, kneels down gracefully beside me, lays an assumingly gentle hand on my shoulder. As she whispers in my ear, her fingernails dig into my skin.

"I know you were up last night when you weren't supposed to be. There are rules, sweetheart. Make sure you follow them, or there will be consequences." The fingernails dig deeper and I wince.

I sit still as she looms over me, her breath heating my ear, her nails close to drawing blood.

She waits for me to say something. A square of toast sticks to the roof of my mouth. I wiggle my tongue around to free it. My cheeks heat. First with fear. Then anger.

A faint blonde eyebrow arches high. Her blue eyes communicate a dangerous threat. "Do we understand each other?"

I nod.

"Good." She rises to her feet and smooths out her dress, all pretence at nervousness and comradery gone. She leaves the cafeteria with a clack of heels and a flick of her long hair, which suddenly seems more vibrant than usual.

My stomach quivers. I clutch at the solid table for support. Kim is still face down in her Shreddies. When I look across the cafeteria, Paul locks eyes with me. There is no sign of last night's reprimand on his face. In fact, he seems to communicate an apology in his curled lips.

But I've been warned. My time will come. Soon. If I put a foot out of line. I'll have to be much, much more careful.

Nauseous, I leave the rest of the toast and go to the bathroom. I retch into the sink, once, twice, but nothing more than bile comes out. Turning on the cold tap, I splash my face with water, then dab at the back of my neck with a wet paper towel. I turn the tap off and lean my hands on the counter top, staring into the sink as if it's an ancient cauldron of the supernatural and can provide me with answers or magical powers. Either one will do.

"Georgia." My whispered name sounds softer than silk, softer than the caressing wind that carries dandelion seeds in summer. Elijah.

I look up, my smile prepared, glad to see him, my comrade in this war against evil. But he gesticulates wildly, and shoots words faster than I can follow.

"It's June! It's June! You need to hurry! Now, Georgia!" He flashes out of view and I'm left staring at my own flummoxed expression.

I turn, mount the forbidden front stairs two at a time, run down the corridor to my room, and burst through the door. I suck in air to seizing lungs and clasp my hands to my beating chest.

June is lying in her bed, a Mona Lisa smile curling the ends of her lips. I sag with relief against the door. She isn't in the middle of an attack by the shadows. Willow isn't dragging her off by her punk hair. But then I notice her blue blanket isn't blue anymore. It's red and darkening. It's covered in blood.

"June?" I take a hesitant step forward.

She looks up, her eyes registering my presence.

Her left wrist is bleeding. She holds a jagged piece of glass in her right. A quick glance at Bart's picture confirms the glass came from his frame.

"I'm sorry, Georgia," she says, swapping the glass to the other hand.

"Oh, June!" I rush to her side. "What have you done?" I take hold of the wrist holding the glass. It doesn't look like she's cut an artery, but the blood flow is alarming. June drops the shank without a fight. I grab her blanket and wrap her wrist as tightly as I can manage, screaming for help at the same time.

"I can't do it anymore," June says, flopping back on her pillow. "I don't want to be afraid anymore."

"So you try and kill yourself?!" I tug the blanket, making it tight. June winces, but I don't stop.

"I'm not trying to kill myself." Her eyes close for a moment. "I cut horizontally, not vertically."

"You don't look so good to me," I snap, still calling for help around my admonishments.

June opens her eyes. "I'm sorry, Georgia. I'm not strong." She glances at her tattoo. "I'm not brave. Not like you. I need out. I'll be taken to a general hospital."

I sigh, holding tight to her wrist, ignoring her grimaces. "You are strong and brave. We all are. And we're weak too. We've been fighting all of our lives, and we're all so tired."

Her eyes flicker. "You understand."

"I do." I sit down on the bed next to her. "But there are shadows out there too you know."

"I know," June says, turning her head away. "But not as many."

"Please don't give up on me, please don't leave me here." Unexpected tears sting my eyes.

She turns her head back. "I'm sorry, Georgia." Then her lips sag and she closes her eyes again.

Marion charges into the room with Paul. They approach June, wrap her wrist in bandages and place her on a gurney. As they wheel her out of the room, the siren of the hospital ambulance wails into life. June is going to hospital. A real hospital. She is going to be ok.

She is going to be ok.

But I may not be.

Now the only occupant of the room, I slump down on my bed. June's mattress contains a dark red patch and I realise my hands and sweatshirt are bloody. I pull off my sweatshirt and tracksuit bottoms and look for a clean pair. In the bathroom, I wash my hands, biting back a plethora of emotions. I raise my eyes to the mirror, expecting Elijah's face to flood my view, a look of relief on his face, glad that I saved the day. But it isn't Elijah staring back at me. It's a shadow, still and glaring and threatening without having to utter a single sound or move a single muscle.

I back away from the mirror and slam the door on its ugly face. I stare at the empty room, the blood on June's bed, it's sweet smell cloying and coppery. There's nowhere to go. Crawling into my bed, I pull the blanket over my head and inhale the heated air. Underneath the covers, I squeeze my eyes shut and mumble desperate prayers.

Dragging footsteps sound in the corridor. Willow. I know it's her. I can feel her insidious presence. Perhaps she's arrived for her reckoning. And right now, I don't care. Let her try and take me. Perhaps I'll fight, perhaps I'll go easily. I'm not entirely sure.

The footsteps pause outside my door and the handle squeaks as it turns. A shaft of light reaches me through the blanket, and nails—or maybe talons—click on the door frame. I clench the cotton in my fists. Maybe I can tangle her in the blanket and run. To where? Upstairs of course. And then what?

But she doesn't approach me. Material rustles as she gathers June's blankets and my blood-soaked clothes. The clink of a bucket. The swish of a mop. An ominous hum under her breath. Tension fills the space between us. My muscles coil tightly, ready to spring up, ready to run, ready to fight. I feign sleep and the occasionally mournful groan. I'm sure she knows it's all an act. I'm sure she can hear my pounding heart and shallow breathing.

Her footsteps move back to the door, the bundle of bloody sheets in her arms, I imagine.

"You have therapy with Dr. Zaleski in half an hour, Georgia, don't be late." The door shuts softly. I'm not sure if she's left or if she's hovering in the room.

I think I hold my breath for a full five minutes, terrified she'll return and utter a warning far more menacing. Twenty minutes later, I crawl out of bed. I look for Bart's picture, but the photo from the damaged frame is nowhere to be found. I bypass the bathroom, sensing the shadow is still in there, and make for the bedroom door. With fear and compulsion strong in my chest, I double tap everything I come into contact with. Admonishing myself for giving in to the OCD now, I tuck my hands in my sleeves. I pat the side of my bra, reassuring myself the book of matches is still there—a new compulsion, but one I know can save me. Maybe. I tiptoe down the hallway, avoiding the watchful portraits, staring at my feet as they sink into the carpet. Creeping down the forbidden front stairs, I halt halfway down and catch sight of the bird statue. Its eyes are bleeding. I blink and rub at my own eyes, but the ominous red colour still fills the stone bird's eye sockets.

I hurry down the rest of the stairs, intending to run past the stone creature and make for the safety of the doc's office. I'm almost past the towering statue when I stop and turn around—possessed by an unknown will—and march up to the stationary threat.

Looking up into its red, bleeding eyes, I dare it to act, to attack, to fight, to gobble me whole or whatever it is that shadows do. But the statue, while its presence is ominously coincidental, is that of a crow, not a shadow—despite the similarities between the two.

I reach up to touch one of its red eyes and my finger does not come away covered in blood. Looking around the room, I spot a red vase of cut glass crystal on the foyer table. The sun has briefly come out from behind the thick rain clouds and shines on the red glass, causing a reflection, the source of the portentous effect of the bird's eyes.

Feeling ridiculously triumphant, I laugh out loud. I faced my fear, and even though it's a small success, I take confidence from the fact that this dented creature no longer has any power over me. I'll need to draw on that confidence much more in the coming days, when I feel like it least.

I hurry away from the statue and along the corridor to Dr. Zaleski's office. Not bothering to knock on the door, I march straight in to find Dr. Zaleski and Paul deep in conversation. Paul sits perched on the edge of the doc's desk, tapping a cigarette against his thigh, some of the tobacco coming loose and falling to the floor. They both look up and stare at me.

"Sorry." With my heart stepping up a beat, I back towards the door.

"Is it that time already?" Dr. Zaleski says, gesturing to one of the club chairs.

Paul stands. He rests a hand on my shoulder and gives it a gentle squeeze. But I don't meet his eyes. I'm afraid of what I might see there. Pity. Fear. Either will undo me. He leaves the room without a backward glance.

I face the doc. He doesn't get up, just watches me as I take my seat.

I tuck my feet up on the chair and wrap my arms around my knees. "More mirrors?" I ask, breaking a prolonged silence.

"Not today." Dr. Zaleski takes off his glasses and places them on his desk. He rubs at the bridge of his nose—a habit of his—wipes his lenses on the hem of his shirt, but doesn't place them back on his face.

"You're doing well, Georgia," Dr. Zaleski says.

I can't remember the last time someone told me I'd done well. And the pride that flashes through me is both ridiculous and untimely. Doing well will do nothing to help the shadow situation. I smile back at him, none-theless.

"I thought we could forget the exposure therapy for today," he says, crossing one leg over the other.

I cock a quizzical eyebrow at him.

He fiddles with a gold cuff link. "I'm worried about you. I thought you might be able to get out of here sooner than your ninety days, but I'm worried what the effect of June's decision may have had on you."

"June?"

He pulls at his tie for a moment, as if contemplating loosening it. "It can't have been easy to see her like that."

"I'm not worried about June," I say. Yeah, there was a lot of blood and yeah, cutting your wrists is a terrible thing to do, even worse is to feel like it's your only option. I know that kind of pain and have fantasised about my own death. Not because I'm depressed, not because I don't want to live, but because I don't know how else to get away from the shadows. Living a life in fear is not living at all. Sometimes death seems preferable. I don't begrudge June her choice. I understand why she did it. But I'm angry she left me alone here.

Dr. Zaleski takes out his cookies and this time I take one. "I've heard from the hospital. She's going to be fine."

"I know."

Dr. Zaleski slips his glasses back on and appraises me with his magnified eyes. "I thought you would be more upset."

I take a bite of the cookie. "I'm more worried about Liz."

"Liz?" Now it's the doc's turn to look quizzical.

I don't reply.

"She's in solitary." He rolls up the empty cookie package and throws it in the bin. "One of her rarer personalities has decided to stay as dominant for longer than we were expecting. Willow assures me she's doing fine."

"Willow?" Just the right amount of challenge in my voice and steel in my eyes. "Willow said that, did she?" And then the sarcasm floods in.

Dr. Zaleski frowns and taps his pen against his desk.

"Yes, Nurse Willow." He keeps his eyes on his desk. Pen tap-tapping away. Foot twitching on his knee. The slightest of tremors in his hand. He fears Willow. He fears her too. But if he knows of her true face, what on earth does she have over him to make him acquiesce to her demands and ignore her murderous deeds?

"There's a storm coming," he says, glancing at the window.

Dark rain clouds swallow the sun. But then it always seems permanently night around here. Or perhaps that's just my mood. Rain drills against the windows and wind rages around the four corners of the building "I have a property on the coast. I'll be leaving shortly to check on it. The windows need to be boarded. I'll be gone for the weekend, but when I get back on Monday, I think we should talk some more, about June."

"I'd rather talk about Liz."

He slams his hand on his desk and I jump in my seat. "Dammit," he mutters under his breath.

He's never made such a sudden movement before. He's never expressed a flicker of anger before. His eyes remain on the window. I follow his gaze and watch the storm build. The wild grass is blown flat, the trees look ready to take flight into the world of Oz and great swirls of leaves and dirt slam against the windows. That's all I can make out through the obscurity of the rain and dark.

"We'll talk on Monday, Georgia, about June." He stands and waits for me to get to my feet. "If you need anything in the meantime, the nurses will help. I'd suggest a sedative tonight."

"Ok." I rise slowly, my legs suddenly shaky, my thoughts scattered and uncertain. I leave his office, knowing by the time he gets back, the hospital will be a very different place. It's all going to happen over the weekend, whatever evil is coming, back-dropped perfectly by the storm and the absence of the good doc. And when he returns, I'll either be shadow food, or I won't.

"Bye Doc," I add, as I double tap my way through the door.

"Georgia?" He calls after me.

I pop my head back into the office, waiting for a kind word, hoping for a lifeline, fantasising that he might take me with him to his unprotected house on the coast. I can picture it, a little two-bedroom cottage with pictures of ships hung askew. Perhaps a ship in a bottle on a windowsill and a bottle of whiskey in a kitchen cabinet that squeaks. The small fridge will contain a lump of forgotten, mouldering cheese. The freezer, a half-empty carton of ice cream left over from the summer. The bedroom upstairs will comprise of a single bed, unmade, with a throw carpet on the wooden floor beneath. The house will face the beach, and through a window, you can watch the waves roll in, and the fisherman sail out. I wish for it so hard, storm or no storm, I can almost feel a salt water breeze on my face.

"Paul will be here, over the weekend, if you need him." He taps his pen again.

I rap the door with the flat of my fist in acknowledgement, then leave him alone, wondering how much he knows, if he really knows anything at all, or if the hidden warnings in his haunted eyes aren't warnings at all, but grief for his lost son.

I stand in the foyer, my back to the bird statue, hesitating. I could go back to the doc, confess all, reveal I know the truth about Willow, beg for his help to find Elijah. I shift my weight to my other foot, intending to move any moment now, knowing I need help, someone, anyone. But I don't take a step. I remain rooted, transfixed by some presentiment I can't begin to describe or understand, and listen to the side door bang closed.

I catch sight of the doc running to his car in the rain, his balding head covered by a newspaper. Before he jumps in his seat, he looks up once at the building, taking in all of the windows and the expanse of concrete. Then he climbs in, slams the door and drives away. I don't move, knowing it's too late. Any help I might have received from the doc has slipped through my fingers. Would he believe me anyway? Or, is there anything he can actually do?

TWENTY-THREE

I SPEND LUNCH WITH KIM, shovelling congealed spaghetti bolognaise into my mouth, the fatty mince refusing to disintegrate without serious effort. For the first time since solitary, I long for a glass of wine, or a bottle, or a beer, whatever I can get my hands on. An image of my mother pops into my head. I've been trying to ignore the hollow area in my chest that misses her dreadfully because when I think of her, my next thought is always of my stepfather and how I'm convinced that it was his idea I come here. And then, following that chain, there's my father. My real father, who is more image than reality to me, who apparently suffered from his own mental health problems, who I'm certain also spent a lifetime battling the shadows. Perhaps his death, in a desert country in the Middle East, wasn't as benign as it appeared, but was caused by the claws of the shadows sucking his soul from his body.

I only have to last through the weekend before I gain telephone privileges, before I can hear my mother's voice again. I've been here almost four weeks, and so much has happened, so much has changed that those four weeks feel like a lifetime. But I know even if I could speak to my mother now, there's nothing I would tell her of my current plight. Even if she believed me, she wouldn't be able to help. She doesn't have a mental illness, so she can't see the shadows. You can't fight what you can't see.

Swallowing the last mouthful of spaghetti around the lump in my throat, I wash it all down with some lukewarm water. I attempt small talk with Kim, but I'm not in the mood for that much, and she isn't providing much distraction. Maybe I should involve her in the war against the shadows. But she's so young, so thin and so afraid-looking, startling at her own shadow, leaking tears around every corner, not yet settled into hospital life. I can't ask her to help with this. Before she gets any worse, I need to stop the shadows.

I leave Kim at the table with some of the other girls and make my way into the common room. I spend the afternoon pretending to thumb through a dusty paperback whilst really checking on the reflective properties of the windows through the slatted blinds. Occasionally I think I see a flutter of wings or hear a muted, primal shriek of an unearthly beast. But then the thunder and lightning, which started just before the lunch hour, don't help matters either.

The day crawls arthritically by while the rain pours and the thunder booms and the girls watch TV and ignore the shadows at their backs.

After dinner, I sweep through the medication line

and throw the pills between gum and cheek. By the time I make it back to my lonely room, one of the sedatives has mostly dissolved. I reason that when the will is strong, and my adrenaline has kicked in, the sedative won't make any difference to the coming night.

In my room, June's mattress has been removed, and there's no sign of the earlier violence, save the missing picture frame of Bart. I crawl into bed. Even though I finished it long ago, I prop *Little Women* on my lap. Patting the matches in my bra, I remove my compact mirror from my bedside drawer. I flip it around my fingers, not opening it, just thinking, and wait for night to claim the day. Then I'll go upstairs. Tonight is the night when it's all going to go down. I can't wait any longer; I can't bear the anticipation and want to take the offensive if at all possible.

I sit with the book on my lap as the storm-dimmed daylight fades to night and the lightning streaks flash into the room with increasing vehemence. I wait and I wait. I wait until the lights-out knocks progress down the corridor and the hush of night falls over the hospital. And then, with eyelids drooping, I wait some more.

It turns out that the offensive is not mine after all and the attack begins in my sleep.

I dream of Elijah. I don't find him in the snowy landscape of the shadow world as I might have expected. Instead, we walk along a deserted beach together, the sun setting at our backs and warming our shoulders with the last of the day's heat. We leave foot-prints in the untouched sand and follow the curving beach adjacent to a thick forest of palm trees and other jungle vegetation. The flames of a vast bonfire leap to the sky and native children add palm leaves to its growing girth. With no particular destination in mind, we walk together, just enjoying being with each other and feeling safe. Safe. He holds my hand. A gentle touch, but firm, letting me know he's there and always will be. The lightness of happiness swells my chest. If only I could exist in this moment forever.

Elijah gestures to some hammocks strung up between some large palms. We veer away from our course and climb into a double hammock. It sways gently with our movement and the serenity of the moment lulls me to sleep.

"Georgia," Elijah whispers, still holding my hand.

I close my eyes and smile.

"Georgia."

"Shhh," I reply sleepily.

"Georgia!" Elijah calls.

His voice isn't coming from next to me in the hammock, but somewhere farther off.

"Georgia! Wake up!" This time it's a scream, and it catapults me from my bed before I'm truly awake. *Little Women* topples to the floor and I fall out of bed after it. I land on my hands and knees, and the compact mirror clatters down next to me. The foggy surrounds of the dream shroud me in unreality. Elijah calls my name again. It comes from my compact mirror. Footsteps sound in the corridor outside. I roll under my bed, all military style, before the door opens and a crack of light widens into the room.

"Nothing to worry about, Georgia, just a little late-night therapy session," Willow says, as she creeps towards my bed.

I hold my breath and finger the matches in my bra.

She throws back the covers of my bed and gasps. "Well, well, out gallivanting again I see," she mutters and retraces her footsteps towards the door. "I wonder where you've gotten to."

She doesn't close the door behind her. I wait under the bed for my breathing to normalise. I inhale deeply. In and out, in and out. Just like I was taught in my relaxation classes.

I stay under the bed for a full fifteen minutes before I'm brave enough to act. Can I make it up the stairs undetected? I cock my head at the sound of shuffling of feet and footsteps leading away from my room, accompanied by an exclamation of annoyance. She was waiting out there this whole time, just to see if I would reveal myself. Even though I'm not standing, my legs start trembling, and I have to start the breathing exercises all over again. This time I wait half an hour until I'm sure she has truly left.

Elijah whispers at me from inside my compact mirror. Retrieving it from the floor, I flip it open, but it's too small to make much out of him. Instead, I listen.

"Something's happening. The shadows are gathering. More than I've ever seen. You need to find my body now."

I step over the threshold into the corridor just as thunder claps. Wincing against the cacophonous noise, I imagine people of ages past believing the heavens were at war, or that pagan gods were signalling their wrath.

Another clap. Much closer and louder. Jumping, I almost scream at my jerking shadow. I snap my head to the far window as something from outside slams into it. I expect a spiderweb of shattering glass. But nothing happens. Maybe it's just the wind. The lightning flashes. My own frightened reflection stares back at me from the storm-assaulted window. That, and flapping wings.

"Georgia," Elijah whispers from the mirror in my hand.

Instead of heading towards the staircase, which I've been so desperate to ascend, I head to the other end of the corridor, down the forbidden entrance steps, catching glimpses of Elijah in the polished wood of the banister as I run. The bird statue gives me no pause nor offers any form of resistance as I fly towards the nurse's office. At this hour of the night, it's deserted.

Elijah appears in the glass half of the door, his face contorted in desperation. His frown deepening each time the lightning flashes in the world outside.

Kneeling in front of the door, I examine the key code. I have every intention of heading upstairs to find Elijah's body, but first, I need to contact the outside world. I have a feeling I won't be able to fight all the shadows on my own. And there's only one person I trust to come to my aid.

Punching in the four-digit code, I pray it's the same as all the other doors. I close my eyes and wait. *Click.* The door releases. As I push it open, Elijah urges me to hurry from every reflective surface available, his image growing exponentially in the mostly glass room.

During the next flash of lightning, I survey the small

room and locate the boxes on the shelves behind the desk. Mine is on the top shelf just out of reach. I stand on tiptoes but can only reach the bottom corner. Jumping at it, I manage to pull it a little farther off the shelf. Another jump, and this time the box tumbles forward, pulling two others with it.

Crash!

I throw my arms over my head and wait for the mess to settle on the floor. Dropping to my knees, I glance at the open door, but the hallway beyond remains empty.

I rummage through my scattered belongings until my fingers close around my mobile. I turn it on, the wait agonisingly slow while it boots up, then thumb in my access code. Five percent battery. I find my brother's number and hit the call button.

Call failed.

The message flashes at me mockingly. There isn't a single bar of reception.

"Arrgghhhh!" I almost throw the phone across the room.

The next boom of thunder has me scrambling to my feet and holding out my phone and mirror like a sword and shield. As if they could do anything against a shadow.

Sneaking out of the nurses' station, I poke my head into the deserted common room. With the coast clear, I hurry to the far stairwell. The one that will take me up and up and hopefully to Elijah's body.

With every step, my pace slows as the fear that I might bump in to Willow intensifies. Her claws out. Pretence gone. It will all be over so fast. My soul sucked away. Urging myself to carry on, my progress is painfully slow as I hide behind pot plants and pause behind corners, waiting for the courage to dash into plain view.

Constantly jabbing at the redial button on my phone, I make it past the floor of my bedroom. And then up into the part of the stairwell I've never been before. I climb and I climb, cursing at my useless phone. Eventually, I arrive at the top and stand in the dusty eaves before a wooden door. Gathering my courage, I recognise the area from the day I arrived, the floor where the windows aren't curtained.

The door, much stronger and thicker than any others in the hospital, also has a key code. I punch in the four-digit code and I'm again rewarded with the lock releasing. Even though the sound is small against the backdrop of the storm, I hear it clearly and worry it marks my presence as visibly as a homing beacon. I glance at my wrist, tugging at my tracking bracelet, wondering if Willow is downstairs somewhere, huddling over a computer, watching my progress on a monitor.

The door opens a couple of inches. Darkness crouches in the space beyond. Complete darkness. The very space that I've been longing to discover, and yet I hesitate. Even Elijah has gone quiet from within my mirror.

I suck in a breath. Remembering June's tattoos, I pray for the kind of bravery she thinks I have. Before I can contemplate what might be waiting for me in the darkness, I pitch myself through the door. A door slams at the bottom of the stairwell. I need to move. Fast.

I leap into the darkness and shut the door softly behind me. The lock engages. Turning, I rest my back against the door. The attic is pitch black. I smell dust and mildew mingled with the fainter stench of my own body odour. A flash of lightning streaks outside, revealing many boxes and shapes and draped sheets, but no more. The one-second illumination wasn't long enough.

Rain lashes against the roof as if trying to pound the building into submission. I slip down the back of the door until my butt reaches the floor. Thumbing my access code into my darkened mobile, it reveals a single bar of reception. I hope it's enough. The red battery icon hovers at four percent.

I click on Bart's picture and press the phone to my ear. It rings. There's static, but it's ringing. I stand up, wanting to get as high as possible to ensure the best signal. I edge towards the nearest window with each flash of lightning.

The phone rings and rings and goes to voicemail.

"Dammit, Bart!"

The phone rings again.

"Hello?"

Thank God!

"Bart?" There is discordant noise in the background, music and laughter. It sounds like a party, or a bar. And my side isn't much better with the rain drilling into the roof and the wind howling just beyond my head.

"Georgia? Is that you?"

"Bart? It's me! It's me!" I quash the urge to jump up and down.

"Where . . . you? Is every . . . ok?" I can only hear every other word against the noisy music and storm.

"I need your help!" I scream into the phone. "I need you to come get me!"

"Georgia? I can't hear you."

Dammit, Bart, you're at a party and you're drinking! Why did I think he would be able to help?

I snatch a breath, and with all of the strength I can muster, I scream into the phone. "Bart, the shadows are coming, and I need your help!"

The line goes quiet. Or rather, Bart does. At first, I think we've been disconnected, but the blaring music of his side of the phone call is still transmitting through my phone.

"Georgia? Stay away from the mirrors. I'm on my way." This time the line really does die.

Bart is coming. Bart is going to help me. Bart sees the shadows too.

TWENTY-FOUR

WET, squelchy scratches sound above my head, under my feet, in all of the surrounding walls. Louder than I've ever heard them before. And so many, as though an army of bats and octopi are up here. Something is up here with me.

My hands trembles as I glance at my phone. One percent battery. I have no one left I need to call, so I flip on the torch app. I'll use it as a flashlight until it runs out. The small light only illuminates the immediate area in front of me, and thankfully no monsters. I have the impression of a vast space. Perhaps this attic room runs the length of the entire building. As the sucking sounds quieten, I climb over boxes and gingerly make my way across the room. A shriek freezes me at the halfway mark. The light quivers with my trembling fingers. I stand, listening, wondering if the noise came from inside or out. Perhaps a bird caught in the open storm. Perhaps a shadow sucking away a patient's soul.

I shine the light in a circle, stretching my arm to

probe further into the darkness. Shinning it at the ceiling, the sight that meets my eyes snatches the breath from my lungs. The ceiling consists only of mirrors. Mirrors from door to far window. And within those dark mirrors are hundreds of red, glowing eyes. Feathery wings begin to flap and the sucking sounds come back. It's them. It was them all along.

The shadows are here, more than any I've ever seen before. An army of them.

I shrink away from the mirrors, cowering under the open flap of a cardboard box. My torch light hits something else on the other side of the room. The gleam of a metal handrail. A hospital bed. And there's a body on it. Dead or alive? A sheet is pulled up to a neck and I can just make out a large black helmet. Crash Helmet Annie. How long has she been missing? How could I have missed the absence of her head-banging routine? But here she is now, her wrists in restraints, her body inert apart from the shallow flutter of an unsteady breath.

I hurry to her side, my phone battering dying on the way, the torch winking out. Chucking it on the floor, I stumble as I reach the bed. In the dark, I feel for the restraints. But they are buckled tight and the flapping sound intensifies over my head. If I delay much longer, they'll be upon me. I grab her helmet and yank it from her head. It takes everything I have not to unleash a terrified scream.

It's Annie who lays there, but her face is altered, withered, aged as if the life has been sucked right out of her. But then I suppose that's what the shadows do to you. Her cheeks are hollow and sunken, her skin lined and cracked, her hair brittle and straw-like. The sucking sounds come right above her head, and her cheeks sink deeper as a thread of golden light begins to rise from her mouth to the mirror above my head. They are sucking her soul.

THEY'RE SUCKING HER SOUL RIGHT NOW.

I pass a hand in the light, but its journey to the mirror doesn't falter. I want to scream, cry, collapse on top of her and ignore the shadows at my back. They call my name, a curse on their lips, eager to come for me.

I lift my head from Annie's stomach and spot several other beds. Other patients, other girls. There is Kiara and Sarah and Liz, poor sweet Liz. Golden lights rise from all their mouths, illuminating the sucking beaks in the mirrors. It's too late for them, the shadows are feeding off them, and they are as good as dead.

"Georgia!" I hear my name called on the other side of the attic door. It's Willow. She's found me.

I back away from the beds. Hunching down, I crab-crawl away from the shadows overhead. A wingtip grazes my cheek and a claw slices down my back and face. The warmth of blood spills over my cheek. The shadows stretch out of their mirrors, wings and claws and beaks, whispering my name, louder and louder, reaching for me. Launching their attack.

I scramble faster, not knowing where to go, not knowing what I can do. Fire. I need a fire. Holding my compact in one hand, I wrestle the book of matches from my bra. It's time to use them. But where is Elijah? I was so sure he would be here. I jump back as another wingtip slices in my direction.

As the noise of a thousand wings deafens me, I stumble backwards. I trip over a box and fall to my butt. My momentum keeps me moving, performing a haphazard backwards roll. I smash through some kind of weak plyboard, scraping up my ankle and releasing a new line of warmth the length of my shin. And then I'm falling. And I don't stop falling.

I grasp out for a handhold to slow my quickening descent. Going head first, my hands squeak over a metal surface, causing friction burns to sting my palms. I fall, faster and faster, like Alice in her rabbit hole. And Willow is the Queen of Hearts. My nails scrape along the tunnel and the book of matches and compact skitters down in front of my nose. Darkness surrounds me and Elijah calls to me through my small mirror.

And then it's over. I land in a heap on the floor, my knee banging painfully against concrete, my thigh scraped raw. I lost three fingernails in the descent.

I grab the matches and the compact and pop to my feet, despite the pain, looking for the next ambush, trying to make sense out of where I am.

The storm is quieter down here, the windows high above my head and those awful sucking sounds muted. The next flash of lightning reveals a large, empty basement. But no, not empty; there's a dim light on the other side of the vast room and I make my way tremulously towards it.

I turn my back on a stack of boxes towered up to the windows and side-step towards the light, keeping one eye on the darkened hole from which I emerged, and the other peeled to the darkness all around. As I near the light and no shadows emerge from the hole, I let out a shaky breath.

The light reveals another body on another bed. A quick glance upwards shows there are no mirrors in this basement. I inch closer, absently rubbing at my injured thigh and shin, hoping against hope.

I stand in the midnight shadows, closing my eyes against the tension, not ready to discover if my hope is about to be rewarded.

I glance towards the soft light. It is a bedside table lamp, a dim bulb, the kind you expect in a serene bedroom. The only other object on the small table is a framed picture. I recognize Elijah immediately; he looks exactly the same as he does in the mirror. I recognise the other person in the picture, too, and it makes my heart pound and my brain whirr with confusion.

Another streak of lightning has me moving away from the table and closer to the bed. The body is breathing, the chest rising and falling. Then I lift my eyes to the face. It is Elijah, sleeping like Snow White in her glass coffin. Perhaps love's kiss is enough to rouse him.

There's an IV line attached to a vein in his arm. Fluids and nutrients provided by whoever is keeping him alive. I step closer and place my hand in his unmoving one, so glad I am finally able to touch him. His skin is soft and warm, and my heart surges for this young, kidnapped boy. For the both of us, together. We are now together in our plight against the shadows.

Reaching towards his face, I let my fingers hover over his skin and marvel at how well he looks. His hair is long, and he wears the same clothes as he appeared to me in the mirror. His grey hoodie is torn here, too, and I can make out his shoulder wound, red and black and angry and not healing properly. Whatever happened to him on the other side of the mirror, happened to him here too. But it's been treated. Bandages and antibiotic cream spill out of a first aid box laid at his feet.

I lean over him and gently place my lips on his, hoping it will be the antidote to this strange stasis. Now that I've found him, I have no idea what else to do. There is no change in him, no absent stirring. I straighten as all my hope drains away, replaced by a profound foolishness.

"Georgia." Elijah's voice from within my mirror. "Show me the mirror."

Bringing it close to my face, I hope he didn't feel the touch of my lips where he is now.

"Georgia!" Not Elijah this time, but Willow's voice echoing down the chute I fell through, coming after me.

"Quickly!" Elijah urges.

I move the small mirror towards his body and hold my breath.

More shouts and other inhuman noises echo from the chute, raising the hairs on the nape of my neck and sending adrenaline through my legs.

"Elijah!" I beg, desperate for him to do whatever it is he needs to do and help me in this imminent battle.

A golden light flows out of the mirror and towards Elijah's body. It's a stream of golden goodness, filled with brighter, cosmic shapes. I wave a hand through the strange occurrence, but I'm unable to deter it from its course. The steam flows gently, as if meandering through a viscous liquid, not hurried or affected by time or space or my increasing fear. The volume of the screams and shrieks at my back notch upwards. We don't have much time.

"Elijah!"

The stream of gold stops. I snap the mirror closed, lest anything follow it out of the shadow world, and drop it on the bed.

Elijah, the Elijah in the bed in front of me, seems unchanged. But then his breathing falters and he sucks in a great big breath as though he's been underwater for hours. Then his eyelids flicker and he pushes himself into a sitting position.

"Georgia!" He smiles at me. "Georgia!" He doesn't need to say anything more, his gratitude is communicated with that one call of my name and the expression on his face, in his eyes, in his very beautiful blue eyes that are now so alive with the presence of his soul.

"Elijah!" I wrap my arms around him and breathe in his very human smell. His frozen eyelids tickle my cheek and his warm breath brushes against my neck. How amazing it is to touch him. Finally. To feel that he is real.

His arms go around me, and for a moment we stay like that, each of us drinking in the other. I don't want to let go.

He pushes me gently away and looks me up and down, then touches his lips, as though he can still feel my kiss.

"We have to hurry, Georgia." He swings his legs over the side of the bed. "Help me."

I disconnect his IV line and throw some sterile gauze under the shoulder of his hoodie. He winces but doesn't protest. He pulls the needle from his arm and chucks it behind him, then grabs my compact from his bed. I hold his arm and help him down from the bed. His knees give way, and he stumbles against me, arms around me.

"It's been such a long time since I've used real legs," he says.

"You can do it," I say, offering him my shoulder. He wraps his arm around me and laces his fingers through mine. He stares at me, and I wonder if he's about to kiss me, but then an almighty crash thunders in the chute, followed by a terrifying scuttling sound.

"It's Willow," I say. "And the shadows. They're trying to escape the mirrors. We have to move."

Elijah nods and allows me to help him half hobble and half run to the other side of the basement. Towards the windows.

"Do you have the matches?" Elijah asks.

Whatever is coming down the chute sounds like it is almost here. Lighting flashes again. Thunder claps. Rain lashes against the single-glazed windows, threatening to shatter them.

I pull the matches from my bra. He takes them and lights one in a single fluid movement. He opens my compact mirror and somehow passes the match over to the other side. Despite the snow and the ice and the cold, the other side ignites immediately, and all I see is yellow as he snaps the compact shut. Then he lights a second match. We turn just as Willow exits the chute.

"Georgia!" she bellows. Her eyes go wide when she catches sight of Elijah.

"No!" She skitters towards us on morphing legs. I stumble away from her. She is enormous, no longer the Willow I met on my first day. With her dress splitting, she towers a couple of feet above us. Clumps of hair fall from her head, revealing great bald patches of scalp. Claws grow from her finger and toes. I am unable to move.

She reaches for me and digs her clawed hand into my shoulder.

"You don't have to do this!" I say.

"I am merely fulfilling my destiny!" she roars.

Wincing, I crumple to one knee. Elijah flicks the match towards her. It lands on a box between her and us. We all stare at it for a moment. Us, in desperate hope, her, perhaps in hesitation. Then, with a sudden whoosh and a high-flying spark, the box takes, and the whole thing erupts in flames. Then the box next to it and the one next to that. In seconds, there is a wall of fire between Willow and us. Raising her wide mouth-beak to the ceiling, she howls and removes her grip on my arm. The fire dances high, licking at her grasping fingers. She backs away a step, then another. She narrows red, inhuman eyes at us.

"No you don't!" she yells.

Not wasting a second, I stack the few remaining boxes not on fire against the wall to reach the windows above our heads. Elijah scurries to help me while chucking quick glances over his shoulder. Willow dances at the edge of the fire, trying to figure a way through. Her skin turns black and feathery, barely human.

"Can you manage it?" I ask, gesturing to the boxes.

Elijah nods and climbs to the window above our heads. I scramble after him. When we reach the top, balanced precariously on mouldy, damp boxes, Elijah bangs at the window lock. It doesn't move. Not even an inch. I glance at the fire behind. Willow edges around one section of the flames and advances on us. Elijah bangs again. A box to her side catches fire and the flames streak along discarded plywood and broken palettes with a thirsty vigour.

"No!" she yells again.

Shrieks and feathers tumble out of the chute. Shadows. Many of them burning. The squeal as they flap their wings.

"Watch out!" Elijah hammers at the window pane.

I cover my face with my hands as glass explodes around us. Elijah knocks out the remaining shards, grabs my hand, and urges me towards the window.

We climb out into the rain, immediately soaked. Willow scuttles after us on legs that have turned black with backwards knees and clawed feet. Bird legs. The screams of the dying shadows behind her deafen me.

"What about the others?" Elijah asks, pulling his hood over his head.

I shake my head. "It's too late for them."

Elijah ducks back through the broken window, strikes another match, and throws it directly into Willow's furious face.

We don't wait to see if it takes. Instead, I pull Elijah

to his feet, and we run through the sodden ground, slipping in puddles of mud, saturated by the rain, only seeing which direction we are running in when the lightning chooses to flash. Thunder booms again. We dash around to the front of the building, heading for the main drive. But when we reach the imposing entrance, I look up at the attic windows. Girls bang at the imprisoning glass. Liz, Sarah, Kiara, Annie, and others. Hammering at the windows, their only way out, or down the chute to the fire below.

"Look!" Elijah points. "They're ok!"

"We have to go back," I say. "We have to help them."

We run to the front door and I key in the now-familiar code. Elijah and I burst into the foyer. The bird statue stands there, and I laugh at it, nervous energy bubbling out of me. But Paul is there, a fire axe in his hands.

"Georgia, there you are." He looks at Elijah. "Elijah? Are you Elijah?"

Elijah nods. "How did you—?"

"No time to explain," I say, pulling Elijah towards the stairs.

A smoke alarm wails and we have to shout to make ourselves heard.

"Willow, she's . . . she's . . ."

"I know, Georgia," Paul says, resting the axe over his shoulder and following us to the stairs.

"I know you know," I say. "We have to help the others. They're stuck in the attic."

The three of us mount the stairs two at a time and

run down the corridor towards my room. Girls spill out of doorways, and Paul urges them to run downstairs and out the open front doors. Marion appears and ushers them away. The sprinklers come on, and while that is good for the girls in the attic—if there *are* sprinklers in the attic—it isn't so good for our fight against Willow.

We reach the far stairwell and climb up and up, towards the attic. I key in the code and an opaque cloud of smoke tunnels out, along with a line of coughing girls, somehow returned to their normal selves, no longer the desiccated version of themselves they appeared to be when I first entered the attic.

"You need to get out of here, Georgia," Paul says over the sirens and the screaming girls and the thunder and lightning. "Willow is looking for you. She wants you. And the boy."

We lock eyes. Is it too much to hope that Willow is already dead? He reaches towards me, grabs my wrist, and swipes his thumb against my tracking bracelet. It unlocks, and he throws the bracelet into the dark attic. I nod my thanks and rub at my freed wrist.

"I used the matches," I say.

"I know," Paul replies.

"Because it really is the end of the world," I say.

Paul looks briefly into the attic and offers a hand to Liz, who is just climbing out. "It sure seems that way."

"We need to go, Georgia," Elijah says, dancing from one foot to the other.

I step forwards, towards Paul and throw my arms around his neck. "Thank you."

He wraps his arms around my waist and squeezes

me back. Then he pushes me away, a serious look in his eyes. "You need to leave now. I can't protect you for much longer. Willow is too strong. I only ever stayed to try to help, in any small way I could. But now you need to run. I'll get everyone else to safety."

"You saved us!" Liz says, coughing and pulling her sweatshirt up over her nose.

"Hurry now!" Elijah takes Liz's hand and ushers her towards the stairs.

Hesitating, I wish Paul would come with us. But he has to stay behind to help. I want to hug him again and thank him for all that he's done for me, but there isn't the time. I have a terrible feeling I'm never going to see him again.

"We need to go, Georgia. Now." Elijah yanks me to the stairs.

We fly down the stairs, half running, half jumping, half falling, until we reach the bottom. We run outside again. With the apocalyptic weather hammering us from all sides, it really is like the end of the world. Hopefully it will be us who wins.

Elijah and I run past the central fountain towards the woods. But visibility is next to zero and we are forced to slow to a walk. Headlights appear through the trees.

"We can do this," Elijah says, searching for my hand again.

I squeeze his fingers, glad for the warmth in his touch.

A shriek above my head snaps my eyes towards the storming sky. Willow emerges out of one of the high windows of the hospital, screaming my name into the wind.

"Georgia! Georgia!" Her beaked mouth sucks out my name.

No more sweetheart for me.

With her uniform long forgotten, and her head now entirely bald, large, feathery wings flank her sides. All signs of her humanness vanish. Her transformation is complete. Her body is as dark as midnight and her eyes as red as blood. She stretches out her powerful black wings, jumps from the window and glides through the air, searching with her red eyes. Her primal calls send terror rippling through me.

"It's her!" Elijah says, pushing me behind him and backing away.

The windows of the attics pop out of their frames. The fire has crept up the chute and now blazes brightly, destroying anything and everything in its path. I think I can hear wails of pain inside and hope it's the shadows dying slow and miserable deaths.

Paul appears on the drive with a group of thirty girls. And Marion, whose only concern is the fire as she pats embers out of girls' hair and offers comforting arms. She shakes her head in bewilderment as the girls cower under Willow's wings.

The headlights arrive at the drive. With the light of the fire, I spot Bart behind the wheel. He throws the door open and screams my name.

"Go, Georgia, I'll hold off Willow," Paul grips the axe in two hands.

I look from Paul to my brother to the circling demon

overhead. Finally, still holding Elijah's hand, I tug him towards the car. Willow descends from her swooping circle. Beak open. Claws reaching. Red eyes glowing unnaturally. Elijah and I dive into the back seat of the car in a tangle of limbs and pull the door shut behind us. Bart hits the accelerator. The car skids and spins. Bart shoots out a few curse words and pounds the steering wheel.

Willow lurches like an arrow towards the car. With her wings tucked tight against her muscled body, her inhuman face reveals malicious glee. Before she collides with the car, Paul jumps, placing one foot on the bumper, the next on the boot, and leaps into the air, swinging the axe. Does he see her, or is he guessing her location? Then the car gains traction on the gravel and speeds away from the hospital, vomiting mud in every direction.

I turn in my seat to look out the rear window at the scene we're leaving behind. Willow and Paul hover in the air, their fight almost graceful in their balletic movements. The axe glances off her shoulder. Then Willow's large, clawed hands grip Paul around his head and she snaps his neck with no more than a flick of her wrist.

"No!" I grip the headrest.

I wince as he falls to the ground, landing in a shallow puddle. Willow perches on his dead body for a moment, crowing over her victory, and then her red eyes turn towards me. After a second's pause, she takes to the air and barrels after us.

TWENTY-FIVE

"FASTER, BART! FASTER!" I scream. Keeping an eye on the advancing Willow, I fumble with my seatbelt.

Elijah buckles his own belt and reaches for me. Bart floors the accelerator and the car bumps over dips and potholes. Willow flies through the woods after us, her red eyes like lasers pinpointing her target. I feel one right above my heart.

She streaks through the night, faster and faster, and then opens her enormous beak and reveals needle-like teeth. She screams, louder than the wind and the thunder and the lightning. And in that scream, I hear my name, and Elijah's.

"Faster!" Elijah calls.

"I'm going as fast as I can!" Bart yells.

The car swerves dramatically around a pothole. Elijah is thrown against me and I thud against the window. I rub my head at the impact point.

Flashing lights appear in the distance, at the beginning of the drive, and the noise of the sirens follow shortly after that. Fire engines and police cars. Lots of them, making their way up the dark road. Perhaps we'll be rescued from Willow's pursuit after all. But they won't be able to see her, now that she's in her shadow form.

Bart risks a glance over his shoulder as we half bump and half speed along the rough road. His eyes widen, and that's when I know for sure he can see the shadows too.

Elijah undoes his seatbelt and winds down the window. He balances the book of matches in his hand and tries to strike a match. Nothing happens. The rain soaked it through before a spark could be produced. When he almost tumbles off the seat, I hold on to his hips to keep him from falling. The sirens wail. The lights flash, casting the woods and road in an eerie blue glow. Willow howls and dodges around trees as she zooms after us, closing on my window. She stretches out her arms, readying herself to pounce.

I grab the matches from Elijah and yank my window down. After five strikes of a second match, it finally takes, and I look at the shrieking Willow with a triumphant smile. I throw the match towards her. She's right at the window, her beak wide and I shove the match in her mouth. She ignites immediately and a new kind of shriek erupts from her flaming throat.

"Look out!" I point ahead. A man stands in the middle of the drive. Bart swerves just in time. And then everything speeds up.

The charging fire engine spots the man at the same time and swerves in the opposite direction. Willow, perhaps also seeing the man or maybe she's distracted by the flames creeping up and down her torso and onto her wings, alters her course of direction. To avoid the man, or chase after us, or to find a muddy puddle to douse the flames, I'm not sure, but the end result of her dramatic swerve sets her on a collision course with the fire engine. Bart's indelicate change of direction sends us crashing through ferns and bushes.

Elijah twists in his seat. "Dad!" The car thuds into a ditch.

My head bounces off the window and my knees slam into Bart's seat. The car shudders to a halt. A new kind of agony rips through my skull. And then suddenly the pain is gone, and I'm watching the scene from above. I can see my body in the car, I can see the fire engine pull off to the other side of the track. The firemen jump down from the vehicle and douse a fire under their wheels. But it's not just any fire: one of Willow's large wings protrudes from beneath a wheel, blackened and charred. It's much smaller now, a mere suggestion of what it used to be.

A dizzy spell tips me sideways, and I'm back in my body. Everything hurts, and then everything goes numb. I lean my head back against the headrest. There's a little bit of blackness in the dark night, darker than the night itself, despite the flames and the lightning, and it engulfs my vision until it takes over completely, and I no longer see or hear or feel anything. Apart from the rain. For some reason, I can still hear the rain and feel its wetness on my face.

I blink my eyes a couple of times. I'm not entirely

sure where I am. Then I remember the car. Bart is in the driver's seat, slumped against the steering wheel, a ribbon of blood dripping from a cut on his temple. The horn blares. The windscreen is shattered. The engine steams. And someone calls my name. *Elijah!*

But it's not Elijah. When I swivel my head to the open window, which sends a stab of pain up my neck and into the base of my skull, Dr. Zaleski stands there looking at me.

"Georgia, are you ok?"

Through the pouring rain, I take in his concerned face. He wears a rain jacket, but his bald head drips streams of water into the car and rain splatters on his glasses. I shiver. I'm wet and cold.

"Where's Elijah?" I ask.

He frowns. "Elijah?"

"He was right here," I say, attempting to sit up. I pat the seat around me, searching. He can't have gone far. He was right next to me.

The front seat emits a groan. Bart lifts his head from the steering wheel and leans back. His hand floats to the cut at his temple.

Dr. Zaleski shakes my shoulder. "Elijah is here?" His tone is total disbelief.

I nod, but even that small movement causes fireworks of pain.

"Right beside me." I try to open my door, but it's stuck. I crawl towards the other side, where Elijah was sitting, where Dr. Zaleski now stands. Elijah wasn't wearing his seat belt. His last action before we swerved was keeping me steady as I threw the match at Willow.

We killed her together. She is burned and squished under the wheels of a twelve-tonne fire engine. How appropriate.

When I reach the other side of the car, Dr. Zaleski holds out a hand and pulls me out. Bart staggers out of his seat too. The three of us huddle together, but Dr. Zaleski snaps his head frantically in all directions, calling Elijah under his breath, and then louder and louder. Bart and I join in the search until we heard a faint; "Here!"

I run towards the voice, ignoring each throbbing step, and collapse at his side. He is a good twenty feet clear of the impact site.

"Are you ok?" I roam his body for injuries.

"I'm ok." Elijah tries to sit up. "Just a little dazed."

Dr. Zaleski stands a couple of feet away, staring at Elijah.

Elijah looks up at the looming figure, puts a hand to brow and squints into the rain. "Dad?"

"Elijah?"

Elijah nods, and the doc crumples to his knees and engulfs his son in a bear hug. Elijah winces, his hand going to his side, maybe a fractured rib, and the doc pulls back, apologising. Then they stare at each other for a minute and then they grin.

"Does someone want to tell me what the hell is going on?" Bart asks, leaning against a tree.

"It's a very, very long story," I say. "Perhaps we should get somewhere dry."

"And safe," Elijah says.

"She's dead," I say. "The match killed her. And then the truck."

Elijah sighs and sags against me.

A fireman approaches and asks us to follow him, if we're able, to a triage unit. We walk past the parked fire engine. Other trucks and firemen pass and are busy putting the fire at the hospital out.

"This way," the fireman says.

We follow him to the side of the road. He leads us past the parked truck, but I stop and inspect under the wheels. Bart and Elijah hover at my side. A crumpled black wing pokes out from underneath the truck. A lower limb is severed in two. Willow's black inhuman face stares up at us. The red eyes blink and her beak moves.

"She's not dead," Elijah whispers.

I march forward and stamp my head into her skull. Her bird head crumples instantly and the red eyes dim.

"She is now," I say.

The fireman comes back. "I was hoping you wouldn't see that."

We all look at him, then back at the dead shadow. Still black. Still feathery. Still dead.

"It was a horrible accident." The fireman shudders. "She ran out of nowhere. All naked and no one saw her until it was too late. We assume she was a patient."

What does he see when he looks at the corpse? For Elijah, Bart and I, it's a dead monster. For the fireman, perhaps something else.

Elijah squeezes my hand.

"Jesus H," Bart mutters.

The four of us follow the fireman towards the main entrance, this time obeying him when he warns us not to look in varying places. A mobile triage offers shelter away from the still towering inferno, and we're ushered inside and out of the rain. I have a concussion, Elijah two fractured ribs plus the older shoulder wound, Bart also a concussion and a sprained wrist. The doc is fine. We are lucky, so the paramedic tells us. If only he knew the half of it.

"Where's Paul?" I ask the paramedic's back. He swabs at the cut on Bart's temple, about to apply butterfly stitches. His gloved hands hesitate, hovering in the air for a fraction of a second.

"Paul?" he asks, not turning towards me, keeping his eyes on Bart's head.

"He was a doctor here," I say, my voice automatically low, already using the past tense, knowing in my heart that he's dead. He gave his life buying me a fraction of time.

"We haven't come across a doctor," the paramedic replies. "Anyone male actually, apart from you," he says to my brother, Elijah and the doc. "All the girls are in the other unit. Most have been checked out. A little smoke inhalation, nothing serious."

"And the casualties?" I ask.

"You'll have to talk to the police about that." He turns, finally meeting my eyes, giving me the knowledge I already possess in my heart. "They're taking statements. I think they'll be along soon."

I look out one of the plastic windows. Someone zips up a body bag. Paul. I recognize his nose and a swatch of visible hair and a corner of his pin-striped shirt. Paul is dead. His neck broken savagely. Saving me. A strange strangled, gargling sound burbles from the back of my throat. A swell of emotion washes over me. It's so intense it's almost physical, a great pressure on top of my head, sitting on my chest, making my stomach nauseous, almost felling me to my knees. Bart limps towards me and closes the window flap. He pulls me back into the room and wraps his arms around me, one hand stroking my head, shushing me. I melt into his touch, into arms that love me, into strong, safe, protective arms. Bart is here now. Bart saved me too.

I lock eyes with the doc. Tears brim in his eyes. He sags in a chair and takes off his glasses.

Once we're bandaged, I sit by Elijah to wait for the police. Now that he's here, on my side of the mirror, actually flesh and bones, I can't bear to be apart from him. I take his hand in mine and he squeezes it affectionately. The doc stares at us, muttering things about how Elijah hasn't changed one bit. Bart stares at us, too, and at the doc and the girls and the hospital.

A little while later a paramedic comes in with a change of clothes for us all. The fit isn't great, but at least the clothes are dry. I change behind a curtain, glad to be out of mud-encrusted, saturated clothes.

"The police are going to be a while. They want to wait until the fire is out and it looks like a tough one. The firemen are calling for backup," a paramedic informs us.

"Let it burn," Dr. Zaleski says.

The paramedic pauses before he leaves the portacabin, raises an eyebrow in the doc's direction. "Looks like that's what's going to happen. It's an old building, they go up like a book of matches."

I allow myself a small smile at that comment, thinking of what else goes up as easily as matches. Black, shadowy things with needle-sharp teeth.

Dr. Zaleski hands me a cell phone and I see it's connected to St. Peter's Hospital. I put the phone to my ear and say; "Hello?"

"Georgia?"

"June? Is that you? Are you ok?"

A loud sniff comes down the phone. "I'm fine. More importantly, how are you?"

"I'm fine, too!" I cry into the phone. "I got Elijah out, and the shadows are dead. Everyone is ok. Liz, Kiara, Annie . . . everyone."

"I knew you could do it."

"Thank you, June," I hold the phone to my ear, the shock of what I've just been through finally seeping in. "I'm going to come and visit you as soon as I can."

"I'd like that."

I hand the phone back to the doc and blow my nose.

"Let's get out of here," Bart says. "I could use a drink."

We stare at each other for a moment.

"My car is at the beginning of the drive," Dr. Zaleski says. "I had to abandon it. It wouldn't make it up the drive. If you're all ok to walk?"

One by one, we sneak out of the mobile triage unit and slip into the woods. Dawn is a mere suggestion in the sky. A dulling of the stars. As we walk through the woods together, I realise it's stopped raining. Despite the storm, the hospital burns intensely, is still burning, almost like it's meant to.

We reach the beginning of the drive, and I smile with relief when we approach a very comfortable and very safe Volvo Estate. The four of us get into the car. The doc performs a slow circle and then we speed away from Brookwood Hospital. It isn't until we reach the motorway that I let out a breath.

"I could use a drink," my brother repeats.

"We need to tell mum," I say to my brother.

"Not yet." Bart shakes his head. "I'm not ready for that yet."

Elijah stares out the window, marvelling at all the lights and cars and how much the world has changed. We drive on the M3, on the slow lane, the doc too shaken to drive fast. The speeding cars passing us and the headlights coming at us from the other direction brings a slice of normality to my very bizarre world. I start to laugh, hysterically. And then we all laugh like we've heard the funniest joke ever and then I remember to avert my gaze from the windows. Although dawn is approaching, I can still see my reflection and I don't want to see anything else. I want to believe the shadows are all dead. I'm not ready to face the alternative.

The doc signals at a services and parks in front of the building in a disabled bay. The four of us trudge towards the bright fluorescents. Bart buys a bottle of whiskey from the off-licence and adds a shot to four steaming black coffees. No one protests. The first sip scalds my tongue but sends a comforting warmth into my belly.

"It's so warm," Elijah says, cradling his cup. "I forgot what warmth feels like."

"I'm going to repeat," Bart cuts into the silence. "Does someone want to tell me what the hell is going on?"

"The shadows, which we both see in the mirrors, are real." I turn to my brother. "People with mental health conditions can see them."

"Or people that can see them develop a mental health condition," Dr. Zaleski says. He touches his son's shoulder, gently, as if still not sure he's real.

"And in turn," I continue. "The shadows feed off us. Willow was a shadow and made it across to this side of the mirror. Elijah was trapped on the other side. Willow wanted to bring the other shadows here, and she used the patients at the hospital to feed the shadows and make them strong." Elijah nods along with my words. Bart's shoulders slump lower. "The doc here is Elijah's father and has been keeping his body alive, waiting for the day when Elijah might return. Does that about size it up?" I ask of the other three stricken faces.

The doc nods.

Bart's eyes almost goggle out of his head. "I'm going to need some time to compute this." He takes a large swig of his whiskey-laden coffee.

"Thank you." Elijah slings an arm around me. "Thank you for rescuing me."

I tilt my cup towards his. "To daring rescue missions."

"Why was Elijah not killed long ago?" Bart asks. He shrugs out of a crumpled suit jacket and slings it over the back of the booth.

The doc clears his throat nervously. "Willow allowed me to keep him alive as long as I turned a blind eye to the patients she was taking to feed the shadows." He hangs his head. "But I wasn't going to give up. I wanted to get Elijah back here and I knew that a patient would be the key. A very special patient. Someone strong." He looks up. "You, Georgia."

I feel a massive metaphorical pat on the back. But I'm too tired for praise and too much has happened to feel good about it.

"I asked Paul to look out for you." The doc pulls at the tufts of grey above his ears. "He's the only other one that knew. He couldn't see the shadows, but he had reason to believe in them. And then he couldn't turn away."

"And Nurse Marion?" I ask.

"Oblivious. Willow is very clever at creating her stories and transfers to 'more appropriate facilities,'" the doc replies. "Marion isn't the suspicious type. But I guess she might have a few questions now."

I tilt my head. "Or not."

"Or not," the doc agrees and takes a sip of his steaming coffee. "If only you would have trusted me."

I circle the cup in my hands, just one direction, not compelled to reverse. "You can understand why I couldn't."

"We got there in the end," Elijah says, his fingers playing with the ends of my hair. We still haven't gotten over the shock of being able to touch each other.

Bart stirs whiskey into a second cup of coffee. "And the shadows?"

"Willow is dead," I say firmly. "We saw her shadow body under the fire truck."

"I saw her human body," Dr. Zaleski says.

Elijah shakes his head. "I saw her shadow body."

"And me." Bart swigs straight from the bottle.

"They're all dead," I say, more as a prayer.

My right hand rests on the table, my left in Elijah's. Unbalanced. But I don't have a single urge to make things even. I don't need to anymore. Nothing worse could happen now. It's all over. The shadows came for me, and I won, for now, at least. Double tapping a cup or a table or a picture of Bart will do nothing to change that.

"Maybe we should check," Elijah says, rising to his feet.

"I'll stay here," Dr. Zaleski says. "I don't see them."

Elijah, Bart and I make our way to the toilets. We bypass the women's and the men's and head for the large disabled stall. Bart opens the door for us and the light flickers on. The fluorescent hums into existence and I instinctively reach for one of my brother's hands and one of Elijah's. Together we face the large, rectangular mirror and stare.

The first thing I see is my reflection. Or, what passes for my reflection. My blonde hair is caked in mud and not so blonde anymore. Dirt covers my face and my eyes are red-rimmed and sore. Elijah doesn't fare much better. Bart is beaten and bruised. We look like a motley crew. We look as though we've been to Hell and back. We *have* been to Hell and back. We stand there together, holding hands, staring at the mirror, staring at our bewildered faces, waiting. Waiting and staring, staring and waiting. We stand there for so long that the doc knocks on the door, worried we've been taken in a new attack.

"I'll go tell the doc the good news," Bart says, and leaves Elijah and me alone.

"Willow is dead." I repeat the statement five times, each utterance growing in confidence.

"The shadows are gone." I manage a smile at my bedraggled appearance.

"For now." Elijah raises our clasped hands.

I turn towards him. "For now?"

"Remember I told you the shadows are a product of human violence and greed?"

I nod, my smile turning to a frown.

He squeezes my hand. "There will always be human violence and greed. The shadow world will be rebuilt."

No. *No.* "But you burnt it down."

"I did. And it will stay burnt for a long time, but eventually, the shadows will reappear." He pulls me in front of him, both of us facing into the mirror, and rests his chin on top of my head.

"So it was all for nothing?" I say, my shoulders slumping.

He smooths my dirty hair away from my face. "Not for nothing. They're gone for now. We can live without fear."

I can barely stand. Weariness pushes on my shoulders and winds through my limbs. "For how long?"

"Long enough, Georgia, long enough." And then he turns me towards him and does what I've been wanting him to do since the moment I first laid eyes on him. He kisses me.

ACKNOWLEDGMENTS

WP, my most supportive writing friends. And not just writing friends. We've been through it all together and I couldn't have done it without them: Stuart White, Ellie Lock, Caroline Murphy, Anne Boyere, Anna Orridge, Lydia Massiah, Sally Doherty, Jeanna Skinner, Emma Finlayson-Palmer, Emma Dykes and Lorna Riley.

My Curtis Brown Creative Group who have been a bottomless well of support, especially: Lydia Massiah, Mellissa Welliver, Julie Marney Leigh, Sharon Hopwood, Lindsay Sharman, Tasha Harrison and Ralph Browning. And obviously tutor Catherine Johnson.

Nicole Tone, my fabulous editor at Magnolia Press for believing in me and my book and helping it fly out into the world. Also Dionne for the fabulous cover art and Laynie for all her marketing help.

The rest of my Magnolia author family! I truly feel part of something special.

My husband, Neil Blagden, for all his cheerleading as I wrote draft after draft.

My parents; Larry & Rita Woelk, who read everything I write and have encouraged me every step of the way.

All my early supporters, friends who've encouraged me along the way: Sasha Newell, Michelle Oliver, Nikki & Adrian Kane, Rhia Mitchell, Kathryn Richards, Mary Bryant.

The amazing writing community on Twitter. There is so much support and help and I couldn't have done it without your encouragement. Special thanks to: Anna Britton, Lorretta Chefchaouni, Charles Femia, David Neuner, Clare Harlow, Amy McCaw, Hannah Kates, Tammy Oja, Debbie Roxburgh, Amanda McLachlan, Sarah Dresser, Kate Foster.

My debut 2019/20 group who are too numerous to name but navigating the waters with you has been a fabulous experience.

Everyone at #WritersWise, especially; Noelle Kelly, Sharon Writes, Viv Conrad and Liam Farrell

My career coach, Kate Brauning – so much good advice and helping me to stay focused.

Sarah Lewis and Jo Gatford at Writers' HQ – who without them I would never have learned to plot properly, let alone edit!

My A-level English teacher, Michael Fox, who taught me to first think for myself and then to defend my ideas.

Last not but least – all of my readers. Without you this wouldn't be possible and I hope you stick around to discover some of my other books

ABOUT THE AUTHOR

Marisa Noelle is the writer of middle grade & young adult novels in the genres of science-fiction, fantasy & mental health. *The Shadow Keepers* is her first novel. *The Unadjusteds* is due out in November 2019.

When she's not writing or reading or watching movies, she enjoys swimming. In the pool she likes to imagine she could be a mermaid and become part of some of her make-believe words. Despite being an avid bookworm from the time she could hold a book, being an author came as a bit of a surprise to her as she was a bit of a science geek at school.

She lives in Woking, UK with her husband and three children

Lightning Source UK Ltd.
Milton Keynes UK
UKHW012159161019
351716UK00003B/741/P